FISH STORIES

Fish Stories

All Rights Reserved © 2002 by Kathleen H. Nelson

No part of this book may be reproduced or transmitted in any form or by any means, graphic, electronic, or mechanical, including photocopying, recording, taping, or by any information storage retrieval system, without the permission in writing from the publisher.

Writers Club Press
an imprint of iUniverse, Inc.

For information address:
iUniverse, Inc.
5220 S. 16th St., Suite 200
Lincoln, NE 68512
www.iuniverse.com

Any resemblance to actual people and events is purely coincidental.
This is a work of fiction.

ISBN: 0-595-23145-4

Printed in the United States of America

FISH STORIES

Kathleen H. Nelson

Writers Club Press
San Jose New York Lincoln Shanghai

This book is dedicated to: Miss Christine Pirog, Mr. Greg Bell, Ms. Evian Simkovich, Mr. Bruce Barmak, Mrs. Sandra Brassard, Mrs. Elizabeth Mullen, Dr. Tim Allen, and Dr. William H. Stone—educators who inspired, encouraged, and/or challenged me to push the boundaries of my own potential. A belated, heartfelt thanks to them, and to all of the teachers who gave of themselves to shape my life.

And; as always, to my beloved husband, Les. You and me, scuba-boy—how 'bout it?

Acknowledgments

I would like to thank Patricia Hall, RN, for making her medical expertise available to me; Sergeant Fred Hall of the Enfield, CT Police Department for allowing me to ride with him and observe police procedure; Ms. Joan Canty, a writing instructor at Columbia College, CA, for her constructive criticisms and those late-night heart-to-hearts about writing; and everyone else who has gone out of their way to support and promote my work. I thank God daily for all of you.

CHAPTER 1

The last leg of a twenty-five hour plane ride is finally coming to an end. I know this before the pilot announces our final approach to the Hartford-Springfield area; before the order to stow all dinner trays and return all seats to the upright position crackles over the PA; before the fasten-seatbelt signs light up overhead with a ping. I know because I can feel the change in altitude in my guts. It's a subtle, fluttery sensation—gravity fishing for a fingerhold. I don't want to think about what might happen if it ever got its hooks in me.

A flight attendant strolls down the aisle, collecting trash. She looks a bit footsore now; her perky facade has wilted. I hand her the plastic wine glass that nobody offered to take after dinner, then shift toward my window to watch our descent into Tobacco Valley. At first, there's nothing to see except fog and the wingtip's strobing white light. Then the jet drops below the cloud-cover and the Connecticut River sprawls into view, glimmering in the dark like a fat, serpentine brushstroke. Back in the '70's, that river was so polluted, you could often see wads of toilet paper floating along on its murky brown surface. River lilies, my best friend and I used to call them. We joked about the low-tide stench as well. My brother tells me that those lilies are long-gone, and that the water is now clean enough to attract weekend boaters and fisherfolk. The catch, he says, is mostly crappies. Which just goes to show you that nature has a sense of humor, too.

The plane passes over stubbled cornfields and large, wooded lots; a constellation of small dairy farms; and a couple of wannabe swamps. Connecticut is supposed to be a densely populated state, but you can't tell from where I'm sitting. There's plenty of open space between the houses, and only a smattering of headlights on the black-ribbon roads. I could be flying into Belize or New Guinea or Bimini. Well, OK, maybe not Bimini—the runway there is all packed red dirt. But the backwater feeling is the same.

I hear a protracted whir, then a clunk: the plane's wheels locking into place. The captain urges the crew to prepare for landing. As they hurry off to their seats, a different, more manic sort of fluttering breaks out in my bowels. This is my past stirring within me. This only happens when I come home.

※   ※   ※

The woman at the rental car check-in counter is a young, full-busted, gum-snapper who's way too pale to be wearing so much blue eyeshadow. When I hand her my driver's license, she does a triple-take in an effort to reconcile the long-haired, ex-swim-team geek in the photograph with the short-cropped, sun-bleached adventurer that I've become.

"Amazing what a few years can do, isn't it?" I say.

"No kidding," she agrees, in a tone that is both awed and off-hand. Then, as she enters my license number into her computer, she asks, "Where ya coming from?"

"'Stralia," I tell her, saying it like the Aussies do. "The Great Southern Bite, to be exact."

"Lucky you. I'd love to get away from this dump for a few days." She strikes a key with unnecessary force, then asks, "Would you rather buy your last tank of gas from us, or bring the car back full?"

"I'll bring it back full."

"OK." As she types my preference into her computer, she says, "My boyfriend and I were supposed to spend Thanksgiving in Florida with my momma this year, but his boss offered him the chance to work OT at the last moment, so there went our vacation. You want liability insurance?"

"No, thanks. Why didn't you go by yourself?"

She dismisses the suggestion with a shrug and a scowl. "It wouldn't have been any fun without Tim."

"Oh. Well—" I'm tempted to make a smart remark, something like, *you'll never get anywhere with that attitude.* But what the hell, it's Christmas. If she'd rather spend her life waiting for someone else to take her away-away, who am I to call her a bonehead? "Maybe next time, hey?"

"I hope so. A change of scenery would be *so* nice."

She presents me with my contract. As I sign on the dot-matrix line, she says, "Your car's in Row 5, slot 7. If you need a map, the guy at the gate will give you one, no charge. Have a nice Christmas, OK?"

"Thanks. You, too."

I turn up the collar of my oilskin raincoat, then collect my luggage-cart and go in search of my appointed slot. It's warmer outside than I thought it would be—thirty-five degrees, maybe even forty. Everything looks like it's shivering, but that's just the wind. Happily, there's no snow on the ground.

My car is big and blue. The interior smells strongly of lemon air-freshener. I load my camera-case and two Samsonite suitcases filled with Christmas presents into the trunk, then sling the clothing-stuffed duffel into the back seat. Except for the few sundries that I store at Mom's house, and the dive gear that's on its way to Aruba, this is the sum total of my belongings. I definitely live lighter than I travel.

That really bugs my brother.

But that's Jay's problem, not mine. I'm happy this way.

I haven't driven on this side of the road since the last time I was home—when was that, three years ago already? Funny, it didn't feel that long. So I start off slow, steady as she goes: left at the guard shack, two white-knuckled blocks to the stop-light, then a more relaxed left onto Route 75. I don't know about the rest of the valley, but this area sure as hell hasn't changed much in my absence. Sleep-cheap motels, fast-food roulette, and the eternal Bradley Bowl still occupy one side of the road; miles of razor-wire-topped fences and blue-lit runways still dominate the other. My dad once told me that he used to bring my mom here when they were dating. He said he'd park his Rambler in one of the fields that bordered a runway, and they'd sit there for hours and watch as planes took off over their heads. My dad was an engineer; my mom, a farmer's daughter. I can see how such an outing might have appealed to him, but I have yet to figure out what she got out of it. Which is par for the course. There are millions of things about Robin Middlefield that I can't figure out.

First chance I get, I trade the highway for more scenic backroads. These take me past a patch of shade-tobacco land and into the woodsy river valley hills. It's very pretty up here, the New England of postcards and poetry, and the locals have decked their halls to suit the season. I love it all—Christmas trees and fresh fir swags, big-bowed wreaths, colored lights, and the occasional cheesy figurine. I was in Australia last year at this time, and on Palau the year before, and while celebrating the birth of Christ on a beach with a mob of party-hardy sailors had its charms, this—the icicle lights, the smoking chimneys, even the wood-scented cold—this is how Christmas is supposed to be.

O Tannenbaum, O Tannenbaum, la-la-la-la la la-la!

The river valley hills are homey little toes compared to the Berkshire Mountains that range northwest of here, but they turn the road I'm on into a two-lane roller-coaster track just the same. I'm not stressed, though, because these are my old stomping grounds. Here's Devil's Bend, the hairpin curve that killed handsome Eddie Bartenello on his way home from Class Night back in '79. And over there, we have Hell's Last Acre. Back in my day, this was an out-of-the-way pasture where high-schoolers and other creatures of the night converged to drink beer, smoke dope, and make out. Now, it's a ritzy residential development full of two-story, four-bedroom frights.ABby says she can get me into one of the high-end models for a hundred-kay including closing costs, but she's talking to the wrong girl. I don't need that much roof over my head. And even if I did, I wouldn't live around here. No way. No how. I have moved on. Thank God.

Speaking of Abby, that's her parents' driveway over there on the left. You can't see their house from the road, but it's big and old and imposing. Two hundred years ago, it was a tobacco baron's country estate. Now it's registered with The Connecticut State Historical Society. Abby and I spent the summer of '71 digging up the grounds in search of a horse thief's bones. Supposedly, he'd been hanged right there on the property. We thought we found his coffin, but it turned out to be a rather thin-skinned septic tank. Mrs. Cox wouldn't let us near a shovel after that.

Oh, Holy Night! The stars are brightly shining….

I'm at a crossroads now. If I go right, I'll be home in a twinkling. Left will take me to Jay's place. But while I'm mostly looking forward to seeing my family again, I'm not ready to take that plunge just yet. I need a little more downtime first—time to relax and adjust and be with myself. I need a pack of cigarettes, too. So I go straight past the stop sign and head for Hobson's Corner. There's a convenience store at the far end of town. I'll stop there first and then double back to Mom's. She won't be happy about the smokes, and I can't say that I blame her, but there's just something about being home that makes me crave tobacco. The only other times I want it these days is when I'm pissed off or drunk. Maybe it's the insecure teenager in me, trying to look tough. Or maybe it's just me at thirty-five, out to show the world that I'll do as I damn well please, no matter where I am. Whatever. I'm sure my lungs won't appreciate the distinction.

Ah, and here's Hobson's Corner now. It's grown a little since the last time I was here. That McDonald's at the corner of Delaware and Main is new. So is that squat brick bank on Sharpe. But these developments haven't changed H-C in any significant sense of the word. My hometown is still a parochial drive-through village, possessed of one grimy old gas station, three bars, and a post office that doubles as a video store. If it weren't for the KOA campground down the road, the town probably wouldn't even be on the map.

I drive past The Sudsy-Duds Laundromat and Dandy Don's Diner, then pull into the parking lot that beards Green's Market. A frosty breeze raises the hair on my nape as I emerge from the car. I heave a sigh, expelling the last wisps of sultry Australia from my body, then hunker down in my oilskin and head for warmer spaces.

Green's is a sprawling clapboard shack with "Shiners For Sale" and the going price for Bud scrawled across its front window. The smell of ammonia assaults my nose as I enter the store. The stink is part of the walls, a permanent tang, the price old Greenie has paid for selling beer and bait to the KOA crowd since the world's first dawn. If this place ever went up, it would smell more like a Friday night fish fry than a two-alarm fire. I don't mind the odor, though; I get it all the time in my line of work. Besides, it reminds me of those long-ago summer days when Abby and I stopped here on the way back from our 'secret' swimming hole. We'd hang out on the shaded front step with our RC-Colas in hand and pretend that we were too cool for the rest of the world. Back then, we never imagined that the rest of the world would eventually return the favor.

I glance toward the cash register, half-expecting to see Mr. Green smirking away at me like he used to, but he's not there. The handwritten note on the counter says: Ring Bell For Help. That's new. Back in the old days, that sharp-eyed old shyster would've closed up shop before leaving the till unattended. And he certainly wouldn't have left his overpriced goods alone with the likes of the two teenaged boys who are huddled in front of the magazine rack. They're both Hobsons—I can tell by their wheat-blonde hair and grungy, backwoods garb. And if they're anything like the Hobson I used to know, they have quick hands, few scruples, and a damnable way with women. You'd think that the descendants of the man who founded H-C and the valley's richest tobacco barony would be upper crust all the way, but the fact is, they've been slowly going bad ever since The Great Depression. Even the best from that clan seem to develop rotten spots. Like Kyle, the Hobson I went to school with. Ab says he got busted for grand theft auto a few years back. The big jerk. I can't believe I actually voted him 'Most Likely To Suc—

"Well, I'll be damned!" a voice booms from the back of the store. The Hobson boys start guiltily. So do I. "If it isn't Raven Middlefield!"

I recognize the voice. It belongs to Junior Mayhew. He and Jay played varsity football together. Junior wasn't the most aggressive kid on the team, but he was without a doubt the biggest. Coach Macky called him 'The Wall'. Now, as he comes lumbering toward me, I see that the nickname still fits. He's at least three hundred and sixty pounds now, and probably closer to four. He makes the automotive aisle look like the narrowest of straits. With every step he takes, his belly sways and quakes beneath his holiday jersey like a monstrous water balloon. I wonder what so much flesh in motion feels like. At the same time, I hope I never find out.

"Long time, no see, Rave," he says, when we're finally face to face. "Where you been keeping yourself?"

"As far away from here as possible," I say.

He snorts as if I've just cracked wise, then proceeds to give me the ol' once-over. Afterward, he nods approvingly. "You're looking good," he tells me. "Although I think I like your hair better long."

"Long hair gets to be a pain in the ass when you spend as much time in the water as I do."

"Oh, yeah. That's right," he says, snapping his meaty fingers as if to mimic the sound of a synapse firing. "Now that you mention it, I remember Jay saying something about you working underwater." He snaps his fingers again. "You take pictures of fish, right?"

Leave it to someone from Hobson's Corner, USA, to distill my life's passion into a spoonful of cod-liver oil. Leave it to the past to make my present ambitions seem small. I feel compelled to set Junior straight. I feel an awful need to brag. So I open my mouth, meaning to say that taking photographs of fish is just a hobby of mine, and that what I do mostly is work for a company that makes underwater documentaries, and that it isn't just a job, it's a bitchin', all-expenses-paid adventure. But before I can get a word of that out, Junior's twice-broken nose crinkles like a riled dog's, and he jabs a finger at the Hobsons.

"If I catch either of you delinquents trying to walk out of here with something that doesn't belong to you," he barks, "I'll knock you both clear into next Tuesday."

"Take a chill, Junior," the taller of the two boys says, sounding more annoyed than intimidated. "We're just browsing here."

"Yeah," the other chimes in. "Lighten up."

With that, they return to their huddle. Junior hitches up his Big 'N' Tall Levis with a scornful sniff, then shakes his head and says, "You can't trust kids these days."

"You sound just like Greenie," I say, only half-teasing.

"I guess I do," he says, a grudging admission. "I guess it comes with the territory. Speaking of which, I'd better get back to my post. You know how the old man is about leaving the register unmanned."

I'm standing between him and the place he wants to be, and since there's no way he can go around me without bringing a section of the aisle down, I head for the register, too. There, he settles down on the padded stool that's on the employees-only side of the counter and then produces a box of Russell Stover chocolates from a hidden stash. With a small flourish, he slides the box toward me. All I had for dinner was a turkey sandwich and a mostly empty bag of chips, and that was several hours ago, so even though it looks like Junior has already culled all of my favorites, I go hunting for a piece that will tide me over until I get to my mother's house. As I'm considering my choices, he says, "So while you're in town, how 'bout we get together for a few drinks and reminisce about the good old days?"

I freeze over the chocolate box and think: *no fucking way*. Because I know damn well he's talking about high school; and what might have been good for him back in those days had only been old for me—old and awkward and awful. Despite my intense desire not to, I remember myself as I was in my sophomore year: too-tall and shy, a swim-team geek and budding shutterbug who was content, almost grateful, to move unnoticed among the student body. Then the fattest kid in Tri-Town High history developed a very public crush on me. Junior taped notes to my locker and left wilted wildflowers on my desk. He picked me for his partner in science lab and PE, and for the homecoming rally, he painted a heart-encased 'JM + RM' on his broad, hairless canvas of a belly and swanned around like that. I hated him—not because he was fat, but because he was fat and relentless, and because he called too much of the wrong kind of attention down upon me. *Oh, look, Dee, two untouchables; think they'll make Prom King And Queen, tee-hee?*

"I don't know, Junior," I say, deciding to give the chocolate a miss after all. "I'm only home for a few days. As soon as the holidays are history, I'm off to Aruba."

A mild scowl ridges his brow. "Where's that?"

"It's an island off the coast of Venezuela," I tell him. "The company I work for is starting an all-inclusive documentary on the Caribbean."

"No kidding." His tone is expansive but ambiguous—he could be impressed, he could just be stringing me along in the hope that I'll reconsider that drink. "Think you'll see any sharks?"

Just about everybody who knows that I'm an underwater photographer has asked that question at one time or another. Sometimes it gets old because there's so much more to the world's oceans than sharks, but tonight it's OK because I'm fresh off the boat from an absolutely mind-blowing experience. And—he's given me the opening I need to do some serious bragging.

"Oh, I see sharks all the time," I say, casually, as if we're discussing the weather or lawn clippings. "As a matter of fact, I spent the better part of the last six weeks in the water with a bunch of great whites."

He gabbles—a most pleasing reaction. I love the way I look in his eyes right now. "No way. Really?" At my nod, he shudders. "Christ, Raven, you gotta be out of your mind."

"I was in a steel cage most of the time," I say. "But it was the grandmother of all rushes just the same. Imagine, Junior: a fish the size of a Cadillac swimming right at you. It's got a grill full of double-edged teeth and a two-ton chassis made of solid muscle. And there you are, suspended in mid-ocean, a bento-box lunch if something goes wrong."

He shudders again. There's a moderate chop to his dark blue eyes. "That's one helluva crazy way to make a living."

"Yeah, well—" I flash a grin, all derring-do and pride. "—it's not for everyone." Then, while he's still boggled, I decide to make my break. "Speaking of things that aren't for everybody, lemme have a pack of Marlboro Lights. Hard-cover, please."

He heaves himself onto his tiptoes to inspect the upper reaches of the overhead cigarette dispenser. As he does so, I hear the door creak open behind me. An instant later, one of the Hobson boys squawks, "Holy shit! He's got a gun!"

Before I can turn around to see what they're yammering about, a forearm encased in scratchy blue denim snakes itself around my throat and chokes off my breath.

"You two get your asses over here!" a voice barks in my ear. "Now!" Over the patter of teenaged feet, that same voice says, "And you, Fat Boy—no bullshit or I'll blow this bitch's head off."

Something hard and cold and circular digs into my right temple. My vision blanks for a moment, whitewashed by a mind-numbing wave of fear, then hazes back into focus. Junior has his hands over his head now. There are big, wet crescents under his armpits. His face is pale like chalk, all except his cheeks, which have turned rash-red.

"Whatever you want is yours, mister," he says. "Just don't hurt her."

"Shut up." The gunman's breath stinks of cigarettes and beer. His jacket-sleeve smells even worse. "Give me all the money in the till and a carton of Camels. And you," he adds, talking to one or both of the boys. "Go and get me a case of beer. I don't care what kind. Grab a loaf of bread and some meat, too."

Two sets of feet go racing toward the back of the store. I don't dare to turn my head to see them off, though—the dull, cookie-cutter-like pressure at my temple forbids it. All I can do is stare straight ahead at Junior. He shovels the evening's takings into a paper bag, then eases it toward the gunman like a sack of pissed-off cobras. As the loot slides across the counter, it knocks my pack of Marlboro Lights to the floor. A thought pops into my head then. It's so absurd, and so fucking ironic, I can't help myself—I start to laugh out loud. In response, the gunman jams his gun even closer to my skull. It feels like he's trying to drill for brains without a bullet.

"What's so goddam funny?" he asks.

"I'm sorry," I gabble, as I try to haul myself back from the brink of hysteria. "It's just that—my mother always said—cigarettes would be the death—of me."

"Oh, Jesus," Junior groans. He's perspiring big-time now. His hair is soaked. So is his collar. "Oh, Christ."

"Shut up," the gunman says. "Both of you."

The Hobson boys come straggling back into the picture. The younger one appears first with a loaf of Wonder Bread in one hand and a bubble-pack of Oscar Mayer bologna in the other. The older is a half-dozen steps behind with the beer.

"Put everything on the counter," the gunman orders them, "then lie face-down on the floor." As the Hobsons do as his bidding, he flicks the gun toward Junior. "You, too, fat-ass."

Now, I have run out of air with a hundred and twenty feet of water over my head. I've also been trapped in a wrecked car that was leaking gasoline. But I have never been afraid the way I am right now. Because I know what's coming: four shots, one apiece to the back of the head. Later, some poor chump on an ice-cream run for his pregnant wife will mosey in and find us sprawled in our own blood: me and the Hobson boys by the bait case, and Junior behind the counter, looking like a harpooned pilot whale in stone-washed jeans. The indignity of such an end fills me with a kamikaze's fatalistic rage. If I have to die tonight, so be it. But I am *not* going quietly—no fuckin' way!

So before my would-be assassin can jam his gun back into my temple, I drive an elbow into his midsection with all of my terrified, ship-conditioned might.

The gunman grunts. The gun goes off. My world becomes a high-speed blur.

CHAPTER 2

The first thing I see when my vision phases back into focus is the handwritten sign on the counter: Ring Bell For Help. I'm breathing hard and shaking like a sail in high wind, but even so, a laugh tears free of me like a rifle report. I cannot say what's so funny.

The Hobson boys come slinking into the open like a pair of wary ferrets. Their eyes are riveted on the gunman, who's sprawled on his back on the floor. His eyes are shut. His mouth is slack. There's no blood in sight.

"Holy fucking shit," the older boy says, wide-eyed with adolescent wonder, "you really pasted him." He sneaks up on the gunman's unmoving body like a skittish cat, then nudges it with a booted toe and jumps back. The gunman does not react. "He's out like a goddam light."

"Yeah," his cousin echoes, but from a safer distance.

"Get away from him," Junior booms. The boys jump. So do I. Junior hangs up the telephone receiver that he's been gripping like a grenade, and in a less explosive tone, says, "The police are on their way, and they want to talk to everyone. So why don't you guys grab a candy bar and take a seat in the office until they get here?"

The boys are so stunned, they do as they're told without trying to take advantage.

Junior snags a handy spool of fishing line and lumbers over to the gunman only to decide that the bastard really is KO'ed and doesn't need tying up. He stuffs the spool under one dark-ringed armpit, then goes after the gun, which is, curiously enough, way over by the door. It's an old six-shooter, a cowboy's prop. Junior picks it up by the trigger-guard like a sitcom cop. His eyes bulge in their sockets as he flips the cylinder open.

"Fuck," he murmurs to himself. "A full load." Then he looks over at me. "You really are crazy."

I stare at the gun. Even now, I can feel its hard, cold nose digging into my skull. I don't understand how it wound up on the floor. All I remember is a deafening bang.

"Raven." Junior's tone is more emphatic now, like a shake of the shoulders or a cooler of ice-melt over the head. "Are you all right?"

"I'm fine."

But I'm not. There's a sour, coppery taste in my mouth; and my blood sugar levels are in free-fall. An experienced inner voice predicts a whopping hypoglycemic headache. I can't go home with that, not the way Mom is; I'd have a migraine before morning. I need to eat something *now*. I look around for Junior's chocolates, but spot the bologna first. The next thing I know, the pack is open and I am going to town. The first few slices disappear in a heartbeat, without the benefit of bread. I slap the next four or five more on a single slab of Wonder and bolt that down, too. It's only afterward, as I'm trying to dislodge a glob of half-masticated sandwich from the roof of my mouth, that I realize that Junior is staring at me like I'm some sideshow freak.

"Sorry," I say, waxing self-conscious as I glance from him to the counter carnage and back again. "I'll pay for it."

"No, that's OK," he replies, in the same tiptoe tone that he took with the gunman. "Whatever you want is on the house."

I shrug. As I do so, my eye happens upon the pack of Marlboros that fell to the floor a lifetime ago. The sight instigates a craving. I pick up the pack and go outside. The ground here is crunchy from the front window's blown-out remains. *Very weird.* I don't remember that happening.

Shattered: that's a slang word for falling-down drunk in some parts of Australia. I sort of feel like that at the moment—I can't think straight, and I'm an odds-on favorite to blow chow if somebody so much as looks at me the wrong way. *Shatter, shatter.* I kick a shard of glass out of my way, then circle around to the rental's rear bumper. Despite the annoying tremor in my hands, I manage to dig a cigarette out of the pack and light up. I concentrate on drawing the smoke in and out of my lungs so I won't have to think about anything else. The first draught of nicotine and cold air dries my mouth out. The second numbs my lips. I'm hoping that I'll be numb through and through by the time I get down to the filter.

But it doesn't happen.

Halfway through my second cigarette, two police cruisers come yowling into view with an ambulance on their tail. Moments later, Green's lot fills up with strobing lights and sirens. The commotion aggravates the headache that bread and bologna couldn't quite quash. Two cops come streaming out of the lights. One goes into the store. The other approaches me. I know him for a state policeman by the slate-gray Mountie's hat that overshadows his face. He's tall like most Staties are, with decent shoulders and no noticeable paunch. And although I can't say what it is exactly, something about him strikes me as oddly familiar.

"Where's Junior?" he asks. "He called in an armed robbery attempt."

"He's inside," I reply, then take a last drag from my cigarette and grind it into the asphalt with the heel of my boot.

"What about the suspect? Did you see where he went?"

"He's in there, too. Last I saw, he was taking a nap on the floor."

"How convenient."

Two paramedics come jogging toward us with a gurney between them. The Statie waves them toward the door. "Go on in," he says. "Our perp's the man down. Tell Mac I've got this witness covered." The ETs nod, then hustle into the store. The cop reclaims my attention with a sexy, lopsided smile. "So. How about a statement, Ms. Middlefield."

It's that rapscallion smile more than the sound of my name that jars the marbles of my memory, and they go clickety-clicking into place all at once.

"Kyle," I blurt. I can't believe it's really him; or that it took me more than an instant to recognize the man whom I'd both worshipped and despised throughout high school. "Kyle Hobson."

The gleam in his eyes turns sly. "Ah, so there's nothing wrong with your memory after all."

Six or seven years ago, Abby and I wandered into a sleazy, Enfield watering-hole on a whim. Kyle was in the back room, drinking shots and shooting pool with a crowd of local bottom-feeders, so we pretended not to know him when he waved. That's what's up with that remark about my memory. But now I'm wondering if maybe there *is* something wrong with it, because I distinctly remember Abby telling me that Kyle had gotten busted for trying to boost a Porsche from a Hartford parking lot. I remember because I had been house-sitting for a friend of a friend at the time, and I spilled my Bloody Mary all over his Persian rug when she broke the news. The damn glass had just slid right out of my hand. But—cons can't be cops. Or at least, that's what Mr. Straub told us in civics class. And Kyle is obviously a cop.

My head is throbbing now, a telegraph of confusion. I won't admit that to Kyle, though. He'd find a way to use it to his advantage. Besides, I'm not sure how any of it would come out anyway.

"I'm sorry," I say instead, "but I'm not entirely with it at the moment. What did you just say?"

He shakes his head—a slow, knowing, same-old-Raven. "Never mind, it wasn't important. Just tell me what happened here."

The thing is, I really don't a clue as to what went down. One moment, some sonuvabitch is holding a pistola to my head; the next, I'm standing in a parking lot on an increasingly cold night taking in a goddam miniature class reunion. Everything else is Whited-Out. I'm prepared to share *that* with Kyle, but before I get the chance, a door bangs open. I jump, but it's only the ETs. They have the gunman strapped to their gurney.

"Here's your perp, Kyle," one of them says. "He's got a nasty concussion, maybe more. The big guy in there told Mac that this one—" He jerks his thumb in my direction. "—took him out all by herself."

"Is that right, Raven?" Kyle asks.

I don't answer him—I'm too busy staring at the man who would've shot me dead. He's got a lean, haggard face, and a faded chicken-pox scar above his right eyebrow. His stringy brown hair and scratchy, four-day-old beard are flecked with gray. I commit these unlovely features and more to memory—just in case they need me to pick the bastard out of a line-up later.

"Anyway," ET One says, "we're taking him to St. Francis. If you wouldn't mind, we could use a hand getting him into the wagon. Hal's back is acting up again."

"Sure," Kyle replies, and then turns to me with a pretty-please in his pretty blue eyes. "Do you mind waiting? It'll only take a minute."

"Whatever."

I watch, dully entranced, as they wheel the gurney away and load it into the back of the ambulance. A moment later, a siren's urgent wail swells to life in my ears. I begin to shiver. I don't know if it's from the cold or what.

"Christ," Kyle says, when he gets back and sees how it is with me. "I should've had those guys check you out before they left. You're probably in shock."

"I'm OK," I tell him. "A little tired maybe. I've been traveling for the last two days."

"Hell." He drapes his body-warmed police jacket over my shoulders. I do not object. "Some homecoming, huh."

"Yeah."

"Look," he says, "I have to go to St. Fran's to make sure our boy doesn't get lost in the shuffle. Why don't you come along—you know, just so we both know that you're all right. You can give me a statement on the way."

"OK." I agree because I'm not quite ready to give him back his jacket yet; and, more absurdly, because I would've given my left tit to go for a ride with him at one time. "To be honest, though, I really don't remember much of what happened."

"That's not unusual," he says, as he herds me toward his cruiser. "Shock does strange things to a body. Fortunately, it usually wears off."

"I hope so," I murmur. But privately, I'm not so sure I want that particular chunk of memory back.

When we get to the cruiser, he opens the front passenger door and then holds it for me as I climb in. For one surreal moment, I feel like a sweet-smelling Cinderella on her way to the policeman's ball. Then I comb my fingers through my hair and recall that I'm wearing an oilskin coat, baggy jeans and scuffed-up, no-nonsense shit-kickers. Oh, well. I'm not trying to impress anyone here anyway.

A moment after Kyle gets into the cruiser, we're on our way—through Hobson's Corner, past the KOA, and then northbound on I-91 at speeds that would land a civilian the fine of his or her life. He looks at home behind the wheel of this big V-8. I remember he's always had a thing for fast cars. I recall that other thing again, too; and because it's a curiosity and I'm still a little punchy, I blurt it out.

"I thought people with police records weren't allowed to be cops."

He casts me a shrewd, sideways glance. "You heard about that, did you?"

"Yeah."

"Stupidest thing I ever did," he says then, shaking his head at the memory. "And you're right, you can't be a cop if you have a record. But that's where I lucked out. My public defender talked the judge into sending me to rehab instead of jail. When I got out, the state wiped my slate clean."

"So it's official," I say, feeling free to pick on him because this isn't the first time that he's had his meat-pie and eaten it, too. "You're a man of no convictions."

"On paper, anyway." His tone is droll; his half-smile, a deflection. I never was able to make a dent in him. "And now that we've satisfied your curiosity, why don't we work on mine? Tell me what happened at Green's. Don't worry if you can't remember everything. We can fill in the blanks later."

The feel of cold metal pressed to a very thin bone in my forehead returns to creep my skin. The rancid smell of beer, unwashed flesh, and cigarettes haunts my nose. All at once, I'm shivering again, half-capsized in high seas. I don't want to talk about this. It's too fresh, too personal. But I can't say that to Kyle. That would be the same as admitting weakness, and I can't bring myself to let him see that in me. So I turn the cruiser's heater up as far as it will go. Then, over the fan's gusty roar, I fill him in on what I remember. I start out slow and steady, determined to stay in control, but when I get to the part where the gunman orders Junior to hit the floor, my tone goes wobbly at the knees.

"He was going to kill us all," I say. "There was no doubt in my mind about that. And call me crazy—" An impression of Junior saying that to me comes to mind. I have to stop and focus extra hard to make sure I've still got my story straight. "Call me crazy, but I didn't want to spend my last minutes on earth with my face smashed against a floor that reeked of baitfish. So I jammed my elbow into the guy's breadbasket while he was waving his pistol around. The gun went off, once, I think. And—this is where I start drawing a blank. I guess I must've grabbed his wrist or something, you know, before he could get off another shot. Then somebody must've knocked him down."

"From what I hear, that somebody was you," Kyle says. "Have you ever studied a martial art?"

"Not unless you count late night 'fu flicks," I reply. "I am pretty strong, though. And like I said, he reeked of beer, so maybe he was drunk and fell down all by himself. All I know is, he wound up on the ground."

"And what about the gun? What happened to that?"

"I don't know!" I snap, annoyed with him for pushing me. "He must've dropped it when he took his header. Ask Junior about it. Ask your cousins. They were in a better position to take notes than I was."

"Yes, I'm sure they were," he agrees in a soothing tone. "And I'm sure they're being questioned, too." He pauses for a moment, giving me a chance to equalize, and then asks, "So how are you feeling now anyway?"

"Jittery," I admit. "Like I drank a whole pot of double-strength espresso all at once." At the thought, my bladder seizes up. "I'm going to have to hit a restroom pretty soon, too."

"No problem," he tells me. "We're almost there."

He steps on the gas. A block later, he flashes his lights so he can roll through a quiet intersection without stopping for the red light. The next thing I know, we're pulling into the driveway that leads to St. Francis's emergency room. I've taken this turn three times in the past: once when I was nine years old and my appendix was near to bursting; again when I was thirteen-and-a-half to get my right leg casted after my first and only try at snow-skiing; and once more at the age of fifteen when my dad was dying. But I don't want to think about *that* horrible night. I don't want to think about anything at all.

Kyle cruises all the way up to the entrance, then parks his car in a spot reserved for Security and hustles me into the building. The smells of disinfectant and electric heat envelop us as we clear the automatic doors. The combination makes me gag. Without a word to Kyle, I fast-break for the nearest restroom. An instant after I hit the stall, I blow my ballast into the bowl: bread, bologna, and bile. It feels like I am losing much more.

"Are you all right?" the woman in the next stall asks.

"I'm fine," I croak. "Just fine."

Some minutes later, I emerge from the head, relieved but not refreshed. Before I have a chance to look for Kyle, a lanky Jamaican nurse in pink scrubs whisks me off to a examining room. She takes my blood pressure, which tricks out on the low but normal side, and my pulse, which is still riding slightly high.

"How you feeling, babygirl?" she asks.

"I'm tired," I reply flatly, "and I've got a headache. Other than that, I think I'm OK."

She forks over a half-dozen Motrin sample-packs, then tells me to go home and get some sleep. I tell her no problem and break out a capsule, then hunt down a drinking fountain. The water that comes out of it is so cold, it makes my teeth ache. Even so, I drink until the cotton in my mouth is gone. Afterward, I go in search of Kyle. I find him at the Admissions Desk, chatting up a pretty, chocolate-haired nurse. As I approach, she bids him a throaty, long-lashed farewell. He responds with one of his killer smiles. I roll my eyes—same old Kyle. The thought makes my teeth hurt, too, perhaps because I find myself grinding them.

"What's the verdict?" he asks me.

Guilty, I'd like to say, but I'd be talking about him, not me, and I'm sure we both have better things to do. So instead, I flash my Motrin stash and reply, "I'm supposed to get some rest."

"I'll drive you home just as soon as Security sends somebody over to sit on our boy," he promises. "He's still unconscious, but I wouldn't want him to wake up later on and be able to walk right out of here. His name's Clifton J. Dupree, by the way; and his driver's license says he's from Williamton, West Virginia. That's all we know for sure at this point, but I have a sneaking suspicion that this isn't his first hold-up."

"Oh." What else can I say?

A bull-necked black guy in a dark blue uniform shows up then. He and Kyle huddle up for a few minutes; I lean against a wall and try not to fall down. I'm tired, so tired. Motrin, jet-lag-squared and post-traumatic shock are all dragging me toward the edge of a deep, dark hole. I imagine myself telling my mom to let me sleep for a week. I imagine myself getting that sleep before I see her.

Ooh. I like that idea. I like it a lot. So as Kyle and I are heading back to the cruiser, I tug on his sleeve like a little girl with a favor to ask and say, "Kyle, if it's not too much bother, could you drop me off at Fred's Motor Inn instead of my mom's house?"

"Sure," he says, but then arches a fatherly eyebrow at me. "Won't she be worried, though?"

"I talked the airline into letting me on an earlier flight out of LA," I say, "so Mom doesn't know I'm in the state yet. And what she doesn't know won't ruin her sleep." Or mine. "When I get up tomorrow, I'll fetch my rental from Greenie's lot, then go home and pretend that I'm just getting in. No one will be the wiser."

"You think?"

We get back into the cruiser and take off. The heater's on; the passenger seat is cozy. I shut my eyes and tell myself that it's only for a moment—just until the ache in my brainpan goes away. The next thing I know, Kyle's shaking my shoulder and telling me that we're at the Motor Inn.

"If you want," he says, as I struggle to regain consciousness, "I can go and get your luggage while you're checking in."

My mind is mush; it won't hold a thought for more than a microsecond. I string a sleepy slur of words together, but I'm not sure I say them out loud. "S'OK, I don' need it."

"I'll swing by sometime tomorrow so I can take an official statement from you. Do you have a preference as to when I show up?"

"Not early, OK? Jus' not early."

I ooze my way out of the cruiser and into the office. Kyle doesn't take off like I thought he would, though. He waits at the curb, V-8 idling quietly, as I register, and then follows behind as I go shambling off to my room. I'm in number six, the second-to-last door on the right side of the building. He waits until I'm inside before he speeds off. I'm relieved to hear him go, and vaguely disappointed—and entirely too tired to figure out what my problem is. I flop face-first onto the squeaky double bed. A moment later, I, too, am out like a goddam light.

CHAPTER 3

I'm adrift in a choppy green sea with no air left in my tank. The sky is glowering, the current's running hard, and there's not another soul in sight. I decide to try and swim for a speck of land that has just cropped up in the distance. As I do so, something wraps itself around my legs and drags me down.

I kick—

I fight—

I come awake with a drowning man's gasp. The tentacles that clutch at my legs are a sheet and a quilt. There's a sweaty pillow over my head. Even as these facts register in my befogged mind, the dream's details fade beyond recall, and I'm left with vague memories of unease. I roll onto my side, then loose a groan because it feels like someone pounded me with a Louisville Slugger while I was asleep. A moment later, I catch sight of the old clock radio on the nightstand and groan again. Nine-o-four? That's much too early! But while I'd love nothing better than to flop back over and cop another load of zees, my idiot body doesn't work that way, and so after a few slow-mo moments of wishful thinking, I get up and stagger off to the head.

Fred's is a frowzy, mom-and-pop hold-over from the 1950's. The floor in my room has a noticeable warp, the window curtain is made of a scary type of vinyl, and the Paul Bunyan wallpaper is starting to curl away from the upper reaches. But my shower is large and gloriously functional, and that makes up for any number of deficiencies as far as I'm concerned. Crikes, how I love the feel of hot water needling me from scalp to toe! I could spend a week just standing here in the steam and the spray. You can't do that on a working boat that's out to sea. Hot water is rationed: five minutes a day per cabin. And there's usually at least one beachmaster aboard who'll poach your allotment in a heartbeat if he thinks he can get away with it. A camera-jockey by the name of Hans did that to me shortly after I signed on with SeaDoc. I know it was him because I recognized the froufrou smell of his soap in my stall. So, two days later, I snaked *his* allotment and left a big crap in his toilet to boot. That sounds crude, I know, but when you're dealing with a boatload of rough-and-tumble sailors, you have to play low-brow games or else give up all hope of earning their respect. And that's exactly I did with that shitty warning shot across Hans' bow. No one ever tried to pinch my water again. And I became plain old Raven instead of 'Sweetheart' or 'Babe'.

As I'm reveling in the prickly sweetness of shower-steam and small victories, the telephone rings. I scowl, wondering who in hell could be calling me here and what in hell they could possibly want, then snag a semi-threadbare towel from the rack. The phone is in the middle of its fifth ring when I finally pick it up.

"What is it?" I ask.

"This is the front desk, Ms. Middlefield," an unfamiliar voice says, in a tone as meek as mine was mean. I'm not inclined to apologize. The room is chilly. I'm dripping and steaming at the same time—*not* a felicitous combination. "Your bag is here. Would you like us to deliver it to your room?"

That precipitates a fresh flurry of who-what-and-whys, but before I can fire them at the clerk, I come up with an answer on my own: Kyle. He's the only one who knows I'm here. And he's always been good with locks.

"Oh my God," the clerk is babbling now. "I woke you up, didn't I? I'm sorry, I didn't mean to, I just thought—"

"Don't sweat it," I tell him, still brusque but not quite so hostile now. "You didn't wake me up. And since you're offering—yes, please bring my bag."

I hang up on another string of apologies, then hoist my oilskin up from the floor where it fell last night and put it on over my towel. A minute or two later, there's a knock at the door. I crack it open partway to see my duffel parked on the stoop. The delivery dude is nowhere to be seen. I'm not totally surprised that he didn't stick around for a tip. I know I wouldn't have, in his shoes.

Oh, well.

Now that my duffel's here, though, I'm pleased to have it, because yesterday's clothes are a medium-fragrant heap of shapeless wrinkles. I stuff them into the bag along with the oilskin, then dig out my blow-dryer and turn it on my hair. The end result is a bit flat in back, but the front looks good, so I'm a happy diver. A shot of Superhold, a dab of face cream, and two strokes of deodorant later, I'm ready to get dressed. I go with black jeans; a white, V-necked sweater that shows off my tan; low-heeled boots; and lastly, my dad's old bomber jacket. I love its heft, and the smell of aging leather.

I pose for the mirror on the far wall. Although I'm two or three inches too tall, and big in the shoulders and thighs from all of the swimming I do, I'm not a total skank. My eyes are nice—wide-set and hazel. I have straight, white teeth; a nose that's never been broken; and four small gold rings riding high on each ear. I look sharp and savvy and cool, like I never did in high school. I smile: a toothy fuck-you for all the DeeDee Harcourts of the world. *Who's the geek now, you losers?*

My stomach grumbles, a churlish demand for brekkie. I give it a pat, promising to refuel at length and leisure just as soon as I get home, then zip up my duffel and head out. On the short walk to the office, a commotion in the parking lot snares my attention. Two energetic sprats dressed in mismatched hand-me-downs are chanting "San-ta, San-ta!" as a man whom I guess to be their father tries to wrestle a Christmas tree out of the back of a recycled service van. A woman is watching the kids from the sidelines. She's young, but not youthful-looking. Her mouth is puckered; her cheeks, gaunt. She has the aspect of a woman who's being sucked dry from the inside. I wonder if she's pregnant.

The guy gets the spindly-looking tree out of the van OK, but carrying it across the parking lot proves to be no easy task for him. Every other step or so, he has to stop and adjust his grip. And every time he stops, his kids grow louder and shriller. The higher their voices go, the deeper his scowl becomes.

The way I see it, anybody who has to spend Christmas in a motel already has as much aggravation as he deserves. So I set my duffel down and head over, meaning to lend the guy a hand. As I approach, his kids clam up and take shy refuge in his shadow. His wife closes ranks, too. She's dressed in sweat-clothes and an old army coat, but still looks cold.

"Hello," I say, and smile as the guy gives me a suspicious once-over. The heavy flannel shirt he's wearing is shiny at the elbows. His short, salt-and-pepper hair is flecked with dry pine needles. "Want some help with that?"

"Thanks," he says gruffly, "but I can manage."

"Just thought I'd ask," I tell him, with a no-big-deal shrug.

The little boy grabs his father's sleeve then and starts pulling like he needs to pee real bad. "Dad! Dad!" he exclaims. "I know her!"

"Dammit, Ken," the man growls in reply. "Quit hanging on me. You know I hate that." As he tugs free of his son's grip, I notice that he's missing three fingers on his right hand. The knobby ridge between his thumb and little finger is a sore shade of red. "And don't be saying you know people when you don't. That's lying."

"But I do know her, Dad!" Ken insists. "Honest. Her name is Raven. Raven Middle-Something. I saw her picture in the paper this morning when I went to the office to fetch that extra pillow for Mom."

A trapdoor snaps open in my mind, and a single breathless thought—*Oh my God*—goes falling through it. For one moment afterward, I'm so paralyzed by disbelief, all I can do is gape at the kid. Then his dad steps in front of him. I can read the guy's thoughts from his narrowed eyes. He's wondering if I'm an escapee from some women's prison, or worse, a loony-bin. I don't blame him, either, because it sure as hell feels like I'm losing it right now. I bid the family a hasty Merry Christmas and then—blam! I'm off for the office like a cannon shot. Along the way, I pray to God: *pleasepleaseplease let Jay's paperboy be sick this morning.*

There's no one at the front desk when I get there, but I hardly notice. All I can see is the copy of today's *Tri-Town Crier* that's sitting on the counter. I pick it up, then flip it open. As I do so, the sinking feeling in my gut hits a new all-time low, because there I am, front and center, just like the kid said. The headline above the photograph reads:

Local Woman Thwarts Robbery

The accompanying article goes on to tell inquiring minds who I am, where I live, and what went down at Green's Market last night. When I get to that part, I stop reading and skip back to the picture. It's a Gawd-awful shot: a pale-skinned me with defiant eyes and no smile, death's-head earrings, and long, dark hair parted straight down the middle. Somebody lifted it from my high-school yearbook. I don't know how the kid recognized me from it.

"You made *The Courant*, too." I jump back like a startled cat to see Fred himself behind the counter. He's a big, blocky guy with thinning blonde hair and old-fashioned, wire-rim glasses. He knows me through my brother, who worked for him one summer. "Front page, lower right-hand corner. No picture, though. I have a copy in back if you'd like to see it."

"No. Thanks," I add numbly. All I can think of is the king-sized cow my family must be having right about now. "If you don't mind, I'd like to check out."

"Of course." He takes the room-key from me, but when I try to pass him my plastic, he refuses it with a big, blocky smile. "Sorry," he says, "but your money's no good here. Just knowing that there are people like you in the world is payment enough for me."

Now I'm embarrassed as well as unnerved. My first impulse is to make light of the situation by scuffing at the floor and saying something like, *Aw, shucks*. But hokey or not, I know Fred's being sincere, so I curb that flippant urge and thank him with as much dignity as I can muster. Then I shoulder my duffel and hightail it out of there.

Green's is a short hike down the road, quarter of a mile max. Walking there helps to clear the shocked cobwebs from my brain. I'm still worried about my mother and Jay, though. I can see Mom in the kitchen, washing the breakfast dishes over and over again as she waits for further word of me. Jay will be at work, tap-tap-tapping a pen against the lip of his desk. Every now and again, he'll glance at his newspaper and mutter something about my reckless ways. I'm so busy fantasizing about my family's state of mind, I don't notice the Channel 4 Mobile News Unit that's parked smack-dab in the middle of Green's parking lot until I'm almost on top of it. I loose a string of curse words, then do an abrupt about-face only to discover a state police cruiser pulling onto the shoulder behind me. I swear again, unsure if I am saved or damned, but go jogging over to the driver's window just the same.

"So," Kyle says, grinning like a big salt-water croc as he glances from me to the news unit and back again. "Still think you can go home and pretend nothing happened?"

"I'll settle for one out of two at this point," I say. "And since you seem to be going my way, how 'bout giving me a lift? There's no way I'm going to be able to get my rental out of that lot without being mobbed."

"OK," he says, "go ahead and get in." As I do so, he adds, "But just this once. And just because I have some papers for you to sign anyway."

"Whatever."

He takes off with a big V-8 thrust that presses me back into my seat. As we go speeding by the market, I see a blonde woman reporter in a standard-issue trenchcoat strike a pose in front of the shot-out window. Junior Mayhew is standing next to her. I roll my eyes, then hide behind my duffel. Kyle arches an eyebrow at me.

"If you don't mind my asking," he says, "how come you're so anxious to avoid your fifteen minutes of fame? You're not wanted for something somewhere, are you?"

"No-o," I reply, stretching the denial into two get-real syllables. "I just don't want the publicity. Been there, done that. Remember what the press did to my mom?"

It all started when Mom won the Connecticut State lottery: ten-point-six million dollars. At the time, it was the largest jackpot to have ever been hit by one person. She needed the money, too, because her husband, Martin Middlefield, had died precisely ten months, eleven days and three hours earlier, stranding her with two teenagers, a run-down farm, and little else. The press made a big deal about that—you know, Widow's Fortunes Take Turn For The Fantastic—which was a little intrusive but OK. Then, being her usual peculiar, flaky self, Mom happened to mention—to a reporter, of course—that an angel had given her the winning numbers. She went from plucky widow to lucky nut overnight. The media couldn't get enough of her. I was a not-so-sweet sixteen-year-old at the time. At that age, the only thing worse than having a nut-bar for a mother is having the whole world know about it. I can still hear DeeDee yucking it up with her pack of bovine sycophants in the cafeteria: *I wonder if her kids are going to start hearing voices, too, like Elvis, tee-hee, or maybe Papa Middlefield.* Argh! I swear—if that money had been mine, I would've moved to Ecuador and started a whole new life under a new name. As it was, all I could do was armor myself with an air of indifference and a durable new undercoat of grudges.

"Oh yeah," Kyle says. "I forgot about that. Still, you did good, Rave. People are going to want to hear about it."

"That's their problem."

"Wanna bet?" He glances at me. He has nice eyes, even if they aren't cutting me any slack at the moment. "Clifton Dupree has a sheet as long as the Connecticut River; and though we won't know for sure until the ballistics report on his gun comes back, we believe he could be responsible for a whole string of armed robberies from here to West Virginia. Like it or not, that's big news. And like it or not, so are you."

We're cruising down Froghollow Lane now, and closing in on my mother's home. Angelhaven, it's called—Mom's idea, not mine or Jay's. I can see the farmhouse through the roadside fringe of bare, frostbitten trees now. It's a scruffy-looking place: two stories worth of dirty white clapboard and black-trimmed windows, all in desperate need of fresh paint. The driveway is unpaved; the yard could use a good raking. You'd never guess by looking at it that a multimillionaire lives there. And that's the way Mom wants it.

"I'll get out here," I say, as Kyle slows down to make the turn into the driveway. In response to the curious eyebrow that he arches at me, I say, "I don't want my mom to see me coming home in a police car. She's probably stressed enough as it is."

He gives me a suit-yourself shrug, then pulls the car onto the shoulder. As I shift toward the door, though, he gently hooks me by the elbow and says, "Not until you sign your statement. Remember? That was the deal."

I roll my eyes at him, only half-feigning exasperation. "All right then, let's have it. Anything to keep the rubber-hose and handcuffs at bay."

He deflects my sarcasm with a professional smile, then hands me a blue Bic pen and a form with lots of choppy typing on it. "If you want to add anything," he says, "go ahead and jot it down in the margins."

But nothing new springs to mind—the White-Out is still holding firm. So I sign off on a top contender for the worst ten minutes of my life, and hope I never see its like again.

"Thanks," Kyle says, as I hand both the form and the pen back to him. "Maybe next time, we'll meet under better circumstances."

"That's practically guaranteed," I say, thinking that no circumstances could be any worse than these were. "And if I don't see you before then," I add, as I get out of the car, "have a nice Christmas."

"You, too," he says. Then, as I turn to walk away, he says, "Oh, just one more thing, just so you know: Dupree's having surgery this morning. His doctors think he may have some internal bleeding."

Now, I can truthfully say that I've never caused lasting physical damage to another human being, and that I usually find the mere thought repugnant. But I have to admit, I'm not the least bit sorry that I hurt the man who held a loaded weapon to my head last night. The memory of his fetid chokehold competing with the hot, waxy smell of Junior's fear is still too intense. When the son of a bitch finally comes to and finds himself handcuffed to his hospital bed, I hope someone takes the trouble to tell him that Raven Middlefield put him there. Just so he knows.

"Thanks for the heads-up," I say. "And the ride."

I toss him a wave, then take off.

The dirt driveway is frost-hard beneath my feet, and dust-free like it never is in the summer. There's only one vehicle parked in the circle at the end: Jay's big, forest-green Explorer. On the one hand, I'm pleased to see that because it means I don't have to deal with roving reporters right off the bat. On the other—well, there's my brother, here at the farm when he should be at work. Don't think I won't get an earful about that! I walk past the front door, which is the entrance to the upstairs apartment, then head over to a low-slung kitchen window and peek in. Big bro' is standing by the fridge with a jar of grape jelly in his hand. I take a deep breath, then rap at the pane. The next thing I know, the back door's banging shut, and I'm being hauled into a surprisingly fierce embrace.

"Rave!" he exclaims, as he tries to squeeze the stuffing out of me. "Thank God you're all right." Then he steps back and gives me a critical once-over. "You are OK, aren't you?"

"I'm fine," I assure him, smiling into his hazel eyes. "A little jet-lagged maybe, but that'll pass. You're looking good."

He is, too. His middle is a little soft these days, and his hair is starting to go gray, but you can still see the all-star wide-receiver that he used to be. Actually, we look a lot alike with our broad shoulders and wide-set eyes and the height we got from Dad. I used to hate these similarities in my teenage years because I didn't want to be anything like my overachieving, anything-for-approval big brother; but now they're sort of comforting, a connection I can't cast off.

"I'm sorry you had to take today off," I say.

"Don't worry about it," he says, with a shrug. "I had some comp-time coming anyway. Are you hungry? There's some chicken in the fridge."

Don't worry? Want some chicken? I can't believe what I'm hearing. Where's the lecture? The finger-wagging? The notorious Jay Middlefield knuckle-brow scowl? Just when I think I know this man better than he knows himself, he goes and turns over a new leaf. I'm surprised; relieved; and just a little suspicious. But I'm not about to tell him so.

"Where's Mom?" I ask instead.

"She and Mattie took a ride into town this morning," he says. "They should be back any time now."

"Does she know about the—" I lower my voice, as if to keep the house itself from hearing. "—the robbery attempt?"

"Oh, yeah. She knows. The phone's been ringing off the hook all morning." He swallows hard, trying to hold something back, but it gets away from him. "But she says the angels told her last night."

His tone is dry, and slightly bent out of shape. It always gets that way when those heavenly headaches come up in conversation. There's a very good chance that he'll start in on them in earnest if I don't change the subject fast, but at the moment, I'm busy teeing off on a gripe of my own. I mean, here I am, home at last after three years abroad and a friggin' shoot-out to boot, and the woman who gave birth to me is out shopping like it's just another day. That's cold, even for a big-chill champion like Robin.

As I'm wallowing in the icy melt of my disappointment, a big, white sedan comes roaring up the driveway. It's hard to be sure who's behind the wheel at first, for all I can see is a green knit cap and a pair of oversized sunglasses, but then I see my mom on the passenger side and know that the driver must be my mom's best friend, Mattie. She toots the horn as she coasts by; Mom tosses me a Queen Elizabeth wave. I scuttle my wounded feelings like a good girl should, then go trudging off to say hello.

"I'll stow your bag in your room," Jay says.

"Thanks," I reply.

The sedan disappears into the drafty old shed that used to house my grandfather's tractor. A moment later, Mom comes striding out. There is much about her that reminds me of an Easter Island stone. She's a tiny woman, maybe five-one in her moccasins, but virtually unmovable when movement doesn't suit her. Her aging farmer's-daughter face can fall still for days, and her dark, deep-set eyes are often focused on things that no one else can see. She can withdraw from everyday life so effortlessly, and so thoroughly, that I sometimes want to give her a good, hard pinch just to make sure she's still alive. Even when she's smiling, as she is now, it's hard to tell if it's for you or what.

"There you are," she says, as we converge. "I was beginning to wonder."

"Hello, Mom," I reply. "It's good to see you."

We embrace—a full-frontal press that's as awkward as it is brief. As we draw apart again, she brushes my ear with her lips and says, "It's good to see you, too, Raven. I'm glad you're all right."

That's something, anyway.

As Mom withdraws, Mattie scampers in to take her place. Her smile is dazzling, a bright white crescent in her cocoa brown face. Her eyes are as lively as sparks. She gives my waist a joyous wringing. I can feel her affection radiating into me through my navel.

"Praise Jesus! Our Raven's home now, safe and sound!" she declares, and then shifts so we can stand arm-in-arm. She's two inches shorter than Mom is, and wiry as a bottle-brush. I feel like a well-fed giant. "We were so worried." She lobs a conspiring smile in Mom's direction. "Right, Rob?"

It's a nice try on Mattie's part, but Honest Rob refuses to play along. "I told you there was no reason to worry, Mattie," she clucks. "Raven had angels with her last night, watching and protecting. She was an instrument of Light."

That's *not* what it felt like to me, but I hold my tongue. Mattie rushes in to fill the silence that overtakes us.

"What were you doing at Green's last night anyway?" she asks, like I'm still a kid with a ten o'clock curfew. "We thought you were arriving today."

"I caught an earlier flight, thinking that I'd give everyone a little surprise," I say. "On the drive home, I stopped at Green's for cigarettes."

My mother's nose crinkles. "I wish you'd quit that nasty habit, Raven. It's so bad for you."

Her mild nagging flings me back into last night's bowels. I almost laugh like I did then, and almost for the same reason. At the last moment, though, I catch myself and try to outcast the memory with a less terrible joke.

"Did you get that from the angels, Mom?"

"No, dear," she says, perfectly deadpan. "That came from the Surgeon General. Now come and help us with the groceries. We're stocking up for Christmas."

I follow them back to the car, then gargle with surprise as Mattie pops the trunk. It's brimming with frozen turkeys. "Good grief! Who are you expecting—the army?"

"No," Mom says, smiling that secret, disengaged smile of hers, "not the army. But I wouldn't rule out the National Guard."

If anybody else in the world had said that, I might've laughed. But while it's rarely acknowledged by anyone other than Mattie, the fact remains that my mother often knows things that no one from H-C has any business knowing. And like I said, it's hard to tell what's going on with her even when she's looking right at you.

"So what are we waiting for?" she asks. "Let's put these birds away."

The freezer is in the barn. I would've thought nothing of trudging there and back, there and back, two turkeys at a time, until the trunk was empty, but Mattie has a better idea.

"When you get to be our age," she says, as she comes shuffling up to the car with a wheelbarrow, "you need to make the most out of every trip."

A dismissive as-if leaps to my lips only to crumble away unspoken as three years worth of new details catch up with me. Mom's a bit more stooped in the shoulders these days. Her hair is grayer than I remember it, and her Easter-Island face is florid. And Mattie's got range of motion problems from the waist down. Arthritis, I guess, more than a touch of it. I hope it's not as painful as it looks.

"I can handle this job by myself," I say, feeling guilty for being so much younger than them. "Why don't you two go inside and take it easy for a while?"

"Oh, we couldn't do that," Mom counters. "There's too much work to do." She turns to Mattie then and says, "Mrs. Burk and her children went back home this morning, you know."

Mattie makes a sour face. "But only until the next time that worthless husband of hers gets drunk and starts smacking her around."

Mom shrugs, refusing to involve herself in that part of Mrs. Burk's life. I grab the now-brimming wheelbarrow by the horns, then start to muscle it toward the barn. Neither Mom nor Mattie tries to stop me. Indeed, I get the feeling that they've forgotten all about me already.

Oh, well. Some things never change. I console myself by humming a Christmas song.

What child is thi-is, who laid to re-est…?

The barn's located maybe twenty yards to the rear of the house, past the empty clothesline and the withered remains of Mom's extensive garden. It's a friendly-looking place with a prancing-pony weather vane on the roof, a lucky horseshoe over the double doors, and snow-white aluminum siding all around. In my grandpa's heyday, it used to house horses and cows and even a pig named Bo, but by the time our family came to live here, it was well on its way to becoming a huge storage shed. As kids, Jay and I played in there on rainy days; as teens, we found other uses for it. Then Dad died, and the heavenly hosts came calling; and now it's Angelhaven: a place where people in need can come for shelter and food.

I bulldog the wheelbarrow up to the barn's double doors, then into the open space beyond. There's a TV and three well-worn easy chairs in one corner here, and a couple of picnic tables in the other. I take a deep breath through my nose, hoping to catch a stray whiff of animals and hay, but the smells are all human this morning. That makes me think that the Burks were here for more than a day. Either that, or they weren't the only ones who spent the night.

In which case, somebody could still be here. The thought makes me nervous.

"Heads up," I call out. "Woman with frozen turkeys on deck."

No one replies. Even so, I enter the sleeping section with an eye out for strangers. The last thing I want to do is spook some latent loon at the wrong moment. We've never had that kind of trouble here at Angelhaven, but they say bad things happen in threes, and I've only got one under my belt.

There are twelve sleeping compartments, all of them converted stalls. They aren't glamorous in any sense of the word, but they are clean, warm, and mostly private. Two of the roomettes are in disarray, a jumble of sleeping bags, blankets, and army cots. I make a mental note to come back and straighten up later—after that plate of chicken. My stomach rumbles as if to second the thought.

I wheel the barrow into the tack-cum-utility room, and begin loading turkeys into the freezer. Halfway through the job, my visions of roast chicken are shattered by a faint scraping sound to my rear. I pivot—pure reflex. It's not until I see the astonished look on Jay's face that I realize that I'm poised to chest-pass a turkey at him.

"Christ, Raven," he says. "What's with you?"

"Sorry," I say. "I guess I'm a little edgy." I pitch the bird into the freezer, then add, "My blood sugar is probably low, too. That never helps."

"Here." He reaches into his coat pocket and pulls out a roll of Cherry Life-Savers. He always has something like that on hand—for his daughters, he says, but just check his breath sometime. "You're going to need these."

"Why?"

"You've got company—a television crew plus a couple of newspaper reporters. I told them I'd go and see if you were home yet. Are you?"

I crunch a Lifesaver between my molars like a tiny bone, and think: *friggin' Kyle*. Why does he always have to be right? But what I say is, "Oh, I suppose so. If I get it over with now, maybe we can enjoy the holidays. Finish up for me here, will you?"

"Gladly."

I do a quick visual on myself. Fly shut? Jacket clean? Nothing hanging from my nose? Everything checks out, so I square my shoulders and go marching off to meet the ravening hordes.

"You're a better man than I am, Charley Brown," Jay calls after me. I guess he hasn't forgiven the press yet, either.

The driveway is crawling with people now. It's the same mob I saw at Green's: I know because I recognize the Barbara Walters wannabe in the trenchcoat. She's already taping her intro. As I draw near, I hear her say, "...This quiet little farm is home to Raven Middlefield, the woman who brought Clifton J. Dupree's violent interstate crime spree to an abrupt end last night. Ms. Middlefield was on her way here after a lengthy overseas engagement when she stopped at Green's Market to catch up with a close friend—"

I curl my lip, thinking that I'll strangle Junior Mayhew the next time I see him for billing himself as something more than a pernicious acquaintance. Then I butt in on Miss London-Fog before she can record any more misinformation.

"Excuse me," I say, "but I'm Raven Middlefield. I was told that someone wanted to talk to me."

The reporter's pale, telegenic face blanks for a moment. Then recognition and opportunistic delight kick in. "Oh! Yes! Hello, Ms. Middlefield. My name is Laura Lacey. I'm with the Channel 4 News crew." She tucks her mike under her arm, then offers me that hand. Her grip isn't as wimpy as I thought it would be. "Do you mind if I ask a few questions?"

"Fire away," I say.

Laura Lacey takes up the mike again, then nods at her cameraman. An instant later, she turns to me, all somber drama and says, "Tell us what sort of a woman takes on an armed robber and wins."

"I'm no one special," I reply, accent on *special*. "I have a family, friends, and a job—just like you."

"You also had a gun pressed to your head last night," she reminds me. As if I could forget a thing like that. "What was that like?"

"I thought I was going to die," I say. "I thought the guy was going to blow us all away."

"So you decided to try and disarm him, is that right?"

"It wasn't nearly that cut-and-dry," I say, declining to be cast as some bad-ass Amazon. "I knew I didn't want to lay down on that floor and let Dupree pump a bullet into my head. But I didn't make a conscious decision to try and get the gun away from him. It just sort of happened, you know?"

"Indeed." Her eyes are as shiny as fresh-minted pennies now. She looks at the camera and says, "No one special? I beg to differ. This is Laura Lacey reporting from Hobson's Corner, a place where one brave woman made all the difference in the world."

An instant after she signs off, she hands her microphone to a crewman and then turns my way again. Her eyes are still shining. She's smiling now, too.

"You're an inspiration, Raven," she says, "not just to me, but to women all over the country. I'd love to have you on 'Wake Up, Connecticut!'" I take a step back. She pursues me. "Have you seen the program? It's Channel 4's morning talk show. Unlike the competition, we try to stay on the cutting edge of our viewers' lives. Would you be interested in making a guest appearance in the near future?"

"Sorry," I say, "but I'm only in town for the holidays. And my schedule's already fairly tight."

"It wouldn't take that long," she cajoles. "Three hours tops. And we'd be happy to pay you an honorarium."

"Thanks, but no thanks. It was nice meeting you."

"Likewise," she says, then pulls a business card from her breast pocket and hands it to me. "If you change your mind in the next couple of days, give me a call."

"Sure," I say, another whopping as-if, and slip the card into a pocket in my jeans. Before I can make my escape, though, a small swarm of men bearing notepads closes in on me.

"Miss Middlefield," one of them calls, "a few minutes of your time, please."

I roll my eyes, then heave a nasal sigh of resignation. The newshounds proceed to lob questions at me. Do I know karate? Do I work out? Do I know that Dupree's having exploratory surgery even as we speak? "No," I reply. And: "Not really." And: "So I've heard." I sound like a seasoned crank, but some of that is my blood-sugar levels talking. All I want to do is go inside and eat my mom out of house and home. No one asks me that, though. Instead, it's: how do I feel about Dupree? And: what's my opinion on gun control? I tell them that Dupree's a coward and a bully who deserves a nice, long prison sentence; and that guns have no place in civilized society. Then someone says something that I don't quite catch.

"What was that again?" I ask.

"I said—" The speaker is short and oily-looking, with slicked-back brown hair and hooded eyes. "Did you get any help from the family angels last night?"

Ah, so that's his angle. Bastard. Twenty years ago, I would've chased him clear into the next county for daring to tweak my nose with Mom's eccentricities. These days, though, I'm not so easily flushed out of my hole.

"I'd like to think that God and His underlings were on my side last night," I say, "but I've got no proof of it either way, so I'll just have to take it on faith. And now, since the serious journalists seem to have vacated the premises, I think I'll do the same. Good day to you, gentlemen, and Merry Christmas."

With that, I turn on my heel and walk away. Behind me, I hear one reporter say, "Nice going, asshole." A visceral pang of satisfaction courses through me.

As soon as I'm in the house, I make for the fridge. The plate of chicken comes out, as does a bowl of macaroni salad; I feed from both while standing over the sink. The phone rings somewhere in the middle of this frenzy, but I ignore it, and it eventually goes away.

As I'm licking the last delectable molecules of chicken grease and what-not from my fingers, the kitchen door swings open and Jay comes walking in. His cheeks are pink from being outside.

"So," he says, looking me up and down like I'm something he's never seen before. "How'd it go?"

I glance toward the kitchen window. Although the blinds are half-closed, I can see that the mobile news unit is gone now. So is the rest of the circus. I feel like a new woman, or perhaps just my old self.

"Could've been worse, I guess," I say, and then remember the card in my pocket. "Some woman named Laura Lacey wants me to appear on her show."

"You gonna?"

I snort. "No way. I'll leave that scene to Abby."

"Good." He makes the word sound like a door being shut. "So what're you doing for the rest of the afternoon?"

"Beats me," I admit. "I've been too busy trying to get home to make any plans. I guess I'll unpack and maybe make a few calls. Why? What's up with you?"

"I have to go and pick the girls up from school in a few minutes," he says. "If you're going to be here, I'll get Sally, too, and bring them all by for a visit."

"I'd like that," I say, although I'm in no great rush to see my sister-in-law. "Let's order pizza and make a party of it."

"You got my vote."

He starts patting himself down for his keys. As he does so, a thought occurs to me, and I blurt it out. "Can you drop me off at Green's on your way out?"

"Returning to the scene of the crime?" he asks. I can almost hear him wondering if that's a good idea.

"Not really," I reply—to both questions. "I just want to pick up my rental. I left it there last night."

"Oh." He has his keys in hand now. He gives them a thoughtful jingle, then says, "OK. C'mon, let's go."

I snag my jacket, then follow him out of the house and into his Explorer. I can't believe how loaded this great, metal beast is. It's got a friggin' CD *changer*, for Polly's sake. The last car I owned didn't even have a radio.

"Got any holiday music?" I ask hopefully.

"Just 'Christmas With The Alvin and Chipmunks,'" he say. "And don't you even dream of putting it on."

Bah, humbug.

As we're pulling out of the driveway, a brown Nova comes pulling in. The man behind its wheel acknowledges Jay with a raised hand in passing. Jay responses in kind.

"Who's that?" I ask.

"Ted Cartwright," he tells me. "His trailer burned down four nights ago. He, his wife, and their two little girls are staying at Angelhaven until their insurance check comes through. Helluva way to spend the holidays, if you ask me."

"Oh, I don't know about that," I say, trying to be glib. "There's a certain poetry to a poor man and his family spending Christmas in a barn."

"Maybe," he grunts. "I just wish it wasn't Mom's barn."

Uh-oh. Fire in the hole. And before I have a chance to duck and cover, he goes off.

"It's just too much for her these days, Raven. She's not getting any younger, you know. And the farm's not getting any safer. If she were to fall from the loft, or zone out while she's chopping wood, or hell, just lift something that's too heavy for her, she could end up miserable for the rest of her life. And that's not even the worst that could happen. She's on her own most of the time—"

"That's not true," I say. "Mattie's with her. So is Dex."

His scowl deepens. After all these years, there's still something about Mattie that he doesn't quite trust. Maybe it has to do with the fact that she was a poor, single mother on the run from an East Hartford slum when she first approached Mom about working at Angelhaven in exchange for room and board. Or maybe it has more to do with what she's become since then: Mom's constant companion and major domo, the keeper of all keys. Or—and I hope to God I'm wrong on this—it could be that Mattie always has been, and always will be, a black woman. Bigotry is as common as clam chowder in this corner of the world, so common that most people don't even realize they're prejudiced. Just ask Mattie. Over the past seventeen years, she's been pulled over ten times just for driving the sedan solo. In that same span of time, Mom has never been pulled over—and she's as flaky behind the wheel as anywhere else.

"I've got nothing against Mattie and Dexter," he says, "but he's a teenager, and she's getting slower every day. The only thing they'll be able to do if some whacked-out transient drops a stitch and starts taking his problems out on Mom is call 911. And clean up the mess afterward. And please don't try and tell me that it can't happen, Rave. You of all people should know it could after what you went through last night."

"I'm not saying it can't happen, Jay," I growl back, peeved at him for dragging my misadventure into the debate. "In fact, disaster could strike anywhere: at the supermarket, on the road, even in a friggin' retirement home. Were you planning on locking Mom in a padded cell and throwing away the key?"

The Explorer surges forward: Jay stepping down on the gas pedal as if it were my neck. "You know damn well I wouldn't do that. Even if she *does* believe that angels are whispering in her ear."

There's that angry, aggrieved tone again. I understand: those astral busybodies embarrassed the hell out of me for a long time, too. But over the years, I've learned to straddle realities that don't quite mesh with my own. And therein lies one of the bigger differences between my brother and me.

"I just think it's time for her to move into something smaller," he goes on to say. "A place where she can live in safety and comfort."

"It won't work," I insist. "She won't go. Angelhaven isn't just her home, it's her whole life."

"Just talk to her, Raven. Make her understand that it's for her own good."

I snort—a surprisingly bitter exhalation. "Like she's really going to listen to me, Jay."

"All I'm asking is—" He makes the turn into Green's parking lot. The sight of that boarded-up front window makes him forget what he was about to say. "Holy shit," he murmurs instead, as he coasts to a stop beside my rental. "That's really something."

I, too, am transfixed. Last night's events don't seem real anymore—leastwise, not in any sense that pertains to me. A headache that I didn't even know I had begins to pulse behind my eyeballs. I raid the cache of butterscotch candies that he keeps in the ashtray, then climb out of the Explorer. Jay does the same.

"I'm going to run in and pick up some more Lifesavers," he says. "You wanna come along?"

"Not today," I reply, knowing full well that he's more interested in scoping out the details than buying sweets. "I'll see you back at the farm."

"OK," he says, and takes off. I fish my keys out of my purse and head the other way.

As I'm coming around to the driver's side of my car, I see a fold of paper beneath a wiper-blade. I snap it up with a sizzling curse, thinking ticket all the way, only to realize that it's ordinary notepaper. The message inside is neatly printed in pencil. It reads:

I'd Really Like To See You Again

I crunch the paper into a wad and stuff it into my pocket. At the same time, I grumble to myself: *friggin' Junior*. You'd think he would've learned a new trick by now.

The rental is cold, inside and out. It takes a long moment for the engine to catch. An instant after it does, the radio blares to life—a rousing rendition of 'Hark, The Herald Angels Sing'. I fire up a cigarette, more to counteract the lemony miasma of air-freshener than to satisfy a craving, then shift out of park. On the drive home, the headache I didn't know I had goes back into hiding.

Back at the house, I catch Mattie alone in the kitchen. She's sitting at our ancient Formica breakfast table, cutting up potatoes and carrots for what smells like chicken stew. The hat she was wearing earlier is gone now. Her graying hair is close-cropped, a nappy skull-cap that flatters her perfectly shaped head.

"Hey baby-girl," she says, as I come straggling in with my various bags. "Where'd you get to?"

"I had to go and get the rest of my stuff," I tell her, and then set said stuff down on the floor with a sigh of relief. "What's up with you?"

"Nothing much." She's back to work now, chopping away. "Just giving my legs a rest while I get supper ready." Chop, chop, chop. "Abby called while you were gone. So did a man who wouldn't give me his name. He wanted to know if you were married." Chop, chop, chop. "Abby says to call her at home after eight tonight. I told the man to get a life."

"Thanks, Mattie."

I wander over and poach a slip of carrot. When I go for seconds, she gently raps my knuckles with the flat of her knife. "Save some for dinner."

"I'm having pizza for dinner with Jay and company. You, Mom, and Dex are welcome to join us," I add, before she can scold me for choosing take-out over one of her home-cooked meals.

"In that case, help yourself," she says, and flips me a grin as well as another bit of carrot. "Just remember: no anchovies or pineapple."

"Whatever. Can I help in any little way?" I add, as she gets up and hobbles over to the stove with her bowl of hacked vegetables.

"Thanks, but I can manage." The veggies disappear into a huge steel stock-pot that's churning out fragrant steam. "Especially since the Cartwrights are the only ones I have to worry about tonight. You go on and put your bags away before those nieces of yours get here. Lisa has developed quite an active curiosity since the last time you saw her."

"Thanks for the warning."

My bedroom's on the other side of the house—through the living room and down the hallway, first door on the right. As I bulldog my bags down this oh-so-familiar path, I look around to see what's new, but it's same-old, same-old all the way. The TV has been in the same corner on the same stand for almost thirty years now. The slip-covered couch and matching arm-chairs are in their usual places, too. Even the fresh-cut Christmas tree by the fireplace seems like it's been there forever. I haven't always liked or appreciated Angelhaven's immutability. But at the moment, it feels reassuring.

I stash the two present-laden suitcases beneath my double bed, agitating a whole warren of dust-bunnies in the process. My camera-case goes in the closet. I turn to my duffel, meaning to unpack, but wind up meandering across the hallway to Jay's old room instead. This is the place where presents, souvenirs, and other what-nots that fail to catch my mom's capricious fancy go to collect dust. The mask that I shipped back from Papua New Guinea is here, as is the silver service set that Mattie got her for her fiftieth birthday, the pink-lipped donkey that Sally made for her in ceramics class, and a whole boatload of angels made from just about every conceivable material. Here's one made of porcelain; over there, we have one carved from mahogany. I wander from one memento to the next like some dime-store museum-goer until I happen upon the five-by-seven frame that holds my parents' wedding portrait. As soon as I see that, I know why I am here.

"Hey, Dad," I whisper. "How's it going?"

Martin Middlefield was a handsome man, big-boned and hazel-eyed like Jay and me, with a master's degree in electrical engineering and excellent prospects. Yet even on his wedding day, there was a shadow of sadness about him, some undefined potential for tragedy that would come to fruition some eighteen years in the future. It started out as a bruise behind his knee—I remember him complaining about it at the breakfast table as he read his newspaper, and me being more upset by the lumps in my oatmeal. Thirty-six hours later, he was dead.

"So there you are."

I start guiltily, then half-turn toward the door. Jay's leaning against the jamb. His hands are in his pant-pockets. One leg is crossed over the other. It would have been a nonchalant pose if not for the solemn look on his face. I know he knows what I've been doing.

"It's funny," I say, taking one last look at that photograph, "but even after all these years, I still need to see him when I'm home."

"Not me," he says, a blunt conversation-stopper. He doesn't like to talk about Dad, not even when he's half-loaded and oozing sentimentality. I can't really hold that against him. Martin Middlefield left this world too damned fast and too damned soon; and some scars stay tender forever.

"Ready to meet the troops?" he asks.

"You betcha."

The troops are waiting in the living room, and as soon as I happen into range, they attack—a giggling, squealing assault on my ankles and knees. I cry out in mock-surprise, then let them topple me to the floor. The smell of them, all soap and silky brown hair, reminds me of puppies.

"Guess what, Aunt Raven?" nine-year-old Gail trills, as she bounces up and down on my stomach. I cough up a clot of air that sounds like "What?" She proudly replies, "I got all A's on my report card."

"That's great!" I woof out, and then roll her off of me. But before I can catch a proper breath of air, baby Lisa races in for her turn on the abdominal trampoline. She'll be seven on the eleventh of January, but she's already a solid kid.

"An' guess what else, Aunty Waven?" she says, seemingly intent on outdoing her sister. "Mommy took me to see Santa Cwaus today. He's gonna bwing me a pony."

"Oh, I wouldn't count on that," I hear Jay mutter under his breath.

"Girls!" The sharp voice freezes all three of us in mid-cavort. "That's no way to treat an elder! Get off your Auntie Raven before you hurt her."

An elder? Me? She has got *to be kidding.* I push myself up and onto my elbows to see my brother's wife standing over me with her hands on her hips. She's got a pale, round face and a hair-do straight out of the sixties. As usual, she's dressed for something better than a visit to the farm.

"They weren't hurting me, Sally," I say. "We were just having a little fun."

"They're getting too big for those kinds of games."

I'd gladly argue that point if I thought it would make a difference, but we both know that the real issue here is sex, not size. Girls are supposed to sit quietly with their hands folded in their laps while the boys of the world make all the noise. I tell little Lisa it ain't so with a conspiring wink and then lift her out of my lap. She paddles over to her dad and tugs on his sleeve for a piece of candy.

"Not now," Sally says, before he can oblige. "It's too close to dinner."

"Grandma's not cooking, is she?" Gail asks suspiciously.

"Not tonight," Jay replies, smiling because Mom's cooking truly is something to dread. "Tonight, we're having pizza."

Both girls jump up and down at that, and start shouting out requests: pepperoni! Pineapple! Ham and double cheese! Suddenly hungry, I spring to my feet and head for the phone.

"Is Victorio's still in business?" I call out.

"Yep," Jay calls back. "Not only that, he delivers now."

Civilization comes to H-C.

We settle on two extra-large pies—one with everything but pineapple and fish, the other plain pepperoni and cheese. The girls are so excited, they can't contain themselves, so Jay tells them to go and wait outside.

"Make sure you wear your mittens," Sally calls out, as they go scampering off.

In the ensuing silence, we wander back into the living room and sit down: Jay and Sal side by side on the couch, me in what was once Dad's favorite chair. I wonder if Gail and Lisa hunt for loose change beneath the cushion like Jay and I did when we were kids. I seed the creases with coins—just in case.

"So," Sally says, "how was Australia? We got your postcards. They were all lovely."

"It was fabulous," I reply, slipping into a bit of an accent for fun, "especially the Great Barrier Reef. The only thing I didn't like was the endless onslaught of flies." I demonstrate the Aussie salute, which is a windshield-wiper motion used for clearing flies away from your face, and then remember something else I wasn't so crazy about. "That, and the fact that it's so far away from everything. The trip home took twenty-four hours, and that was all air."

Jay winces. He doesn't like to fly. He says it has to do with his ears, but I think he just can't handle not being in control for that long.

"But the good news is, our next shoot's in the Caribbean," I say. "So if all goes according to plan, I'll be able to come home for Easter and Labor Day this year. Or," I add, suddenly inspired, "maybe you all could come down and visit me for a change."

"Mmm," Sal croons, as if she can feel herself toasting in the tropical sun already, "that would be wonderful." Then a thought upends her Pina Colada smile. "We can't afford it, though. Not unless—" She cuddles up to Jay. "—your mom offers to pay for some of it."

"Sal," he says, wringing her name into a warning. "Let's not get started on that again, OK? Mom's money is Mom's money."

"It was just a thought, hon," she tells him, and then chases that lie with another one. "But it would be nice to see Raven more than once every three years or so. Don't you think?"

"Absolutely," he says. "It would be even nicer if we didn't have to go halfway around the world to do it." He freezes me in his sights then. "So when are you going to get married and settle down?"

Fuckin' A! Talk about not getting started on a subject! We must've had some variation of this conversation a billion times over the last fifteen years. But instead of getting cranky about it like I usually do, I try a different tack.

"Because I don't want to," I tell him pertly. "And why should I buy the bull when I can get seamen free?"

Disapproval deepens the ridges of his patriarch's scowl. Like he didn't do his fair share of fooling around before Sally sunk her hooks in him. "I hope to God you're taking precautions."

"Damn right I am. Otherwise, I might have to get married and settle down."

Actually, I'm not into casual sex. For one thing, it's not a good idea when you're the only woman living on a boat because the guys you're not sleeping with tend to cop an attitude, and that can lead to all sorts of hard feelings. For another, I'm just not that keen on intimacy. I've only had three "serious", sex-included relationships in my whole life—none of which began or ended in the past two years. And I'm pretty much OK with that. In a pinch, there's always hardware. But I'm not telling Jay that, not after the motherlode of double standards that he just tried to dump on me. He deserves the strangled look that he's wearing now. And before he can figure out a way to pass it back to me, Mom comes strolling into the room. Mattie and her teenaged son are right behind her.

"Dex!" I exclaim, jumping up to greet him. "How's it going, dude?"

"OK, I guess," he says, with a blasé shrug that's so typical of teenagers. "How's it going with you?"

"OK, I guess." I give him a quick hug. He doesn't know where to put his hands anymore, and so keeps them limp at his side. "I'm keeping busy anyway."

"Look at them, Rob," Mattie gloats. "How on earth did two pipsqueaks like us manage to have such big children?"

Dex rolls his eyes—an embarrassed repudiation of such motherly admiration. But Mattie has a right to be proud. He *is* big, as tall as I am now, and buffed in the arms and shoulders from working here on the farm. Not only that, he's cute. He's wearing his hair in dreadlocks these days. It's a good look for him, very Lenny Kravitz.

"We had big husbands," my mom says, matter-of-factly.

The kitchen door creaks open only to bang shut an instant later. Then Lisa and Gail come racing into the living room, squealing, "Pizza's here! Pizza's here!"

Jay starts to reach for his wallet, but I wave him off. "I got this, bro'. You can do the dishes."

I head for the door with plenty of cash in hand, but the pimply-faced kid who's standing there won't take any of it. Instead, he hands me a pen and an empty pizza box, and hits me up for an autograph.

"Victorio says to tell you that he thinks you're a hero, and that he's proud to live in the same town as you," the kid says. "He's going to hang this box up over the cash register so everybody can see it."

What the hell am I supposed to say to that—*get a life, Vic*? Nope. Can't do it. So I write my name and best wishes on the box, then give the kid a huge tip and go back inside with my two pies. I feel very naughty, though, like I'm taking advantage of people who don't know any better.

"Hey!" I call, because there's no one waiting at the kitchen table for me. "Where is everyone?"

"In the living room," my brother calls back.

And sure enough, there they all are, arrayed in front of the television like a spray of hot-house flowers. As I come striding in, Sally flashes me a smile and says, "Jay said you might be on the news tonight, so we decided to eat in here."

"Oh."

I'm not thrilled by the prospect of seeing myself on the tube, but if that's what they want to do, then fine, that's what we'll do. I dish out the pizza: one of each kind for everybody. Then I stretch out on the floor between Dex and my nieces, and dig in. Jay clicks the remote. The TV blips on. As it does so, a disembodied voice says:

"One man's interstate crime spree comes to an abrupt end in a small Connecticut community. That and more coming up on the early edition of Channel 4's award-winning nightly news."

Intro music blares. A handsome, middle-aged man appears on-screen. His top story is Clifton J. Dupree. A mug-shot of the creep comes up in the background: he looks scruffy, wan, and mean, much as he did last night. The anchor describes him as a career criminal with a drinking problem. Then a map of the east coast displaces Dupree's photo. It's pocked with red exes, a dirty bird's tracks. Nine towns, nine stick-ups, we are told, and each heist more violent than the last. At a liquor store in Maryland, he shot a seventy-year old man in the leg for moving too slowly. In a deli on the New York border, he shot a pregnant waitress in the belly for no reason at all.

"This vicious outlaw tried to strike again last night, this time in our own backyard. Channel 4 has obtained exclusive video footage of the attempt from the market's hidden security camera." My jaw drops. *Camera? What camera?* "Parents, be warned," the anchor adds, in an ominous tone. "Some parts of what you are about to see may not be suitable for young eyes."

"Christ," Jay croaks, and flashes me a look of horrified wonder. "What the hell did you do?"

I don't know. I don't really want to find out, either. But I can't stop myself from watching as the clip is rolled.

It starts with me and Junior at the register. You can tell we're talking. He looks massive. I look like a cross between a bag-lady and The Terminator.

Lisa gasps and points at the television screen. "Auntie Waven, Look! That's you!"

Clifton Dupree skulks in with his hands crammed into his pockets. Three steps later, he grabs me by the neck and presses a gun to my head.

"My God," Mom murmurs. "Oh, my dear sweet God."

My thought, exactly.

There's no sound to go along with the clip, but you can tell what's happening just the same. Dupree orders Junior to fork over the money, then sends the Hobson boys for food and beer. My eyes are wide-open and showing much too much white; I can see hysteria taking root even before I start to laugh.

"Dear Lord," Mom murmurs again. "I had no idea."

The boys are back with the goodies now; Dupree is waving them onto the floor. I watch my face go hard and blank. It's the look of a person who knows she has nothing to lose. My left elbow slams into Dupree's breadbasket. The gun goes off with a soundless flash. I grab his wrist before he can get another shot off. At the same time, I reach down with my free hand and give his testicles a vicious twist.

"Squirrel grip!" Mattie crows. "Way to go, girl."

As Dupree struggles to free his balls, I body-slam him onto the floor. He lands on his back, whacking his head in the process. I soccer-kick him in the side, then vault over his suddenly motionless body and boot the gun from his hand.

The anchorman reappears then, but I don't hear a word he says because I'm crying into my pizza like I never cried last night. The next thing I know, I'm being held from all sides. Jay has my hand, Gail is stroking my hair, Lisa's got me by the neck. I shift to take them all in my arms only to tense again as Mattie looses a little cry of alarm.

"Sweet Jesus," she says. "There's something wrong with Robin."

CHAPTER 4

St. Francis Hospital, Intensive Care Unit: oh, how I hate this waiting room and its hushed, haggard atmosphere. I hate the indelible smells of astringent and vending-machine coffee, too. But most of all, I hate the suspense. It propels me back and forth across a strip of ashy gray carpet that has long since had the nap scuffed out of it.

The last time I paced this threadbare floor, my dad was in one of the rooms down the hall. The bruise behind his knee hadn't been a bruise at all, but gangrene. His doctors lopped that leg off at the thigh, hoping to rid him of the rot, but they were too late—it had already gone systemic. He spent the last day of his life in unspeakable agony despite a constant morphine drip. Mom and Jay and I were with him when he died. He had no last words for any of us.

Oh, Mom! Is that the way it's going to be with you?

I turn the thought aside with a scowl. It's different this time, I tell myself. It has to be.

Just then, Dr. Kay appears in the doorway. He's a tubby Irish mongrel with wavy brown hair and kind eyes. His mouth is a straight line that gives nothing away. He waves Jay and me toward a nearby conference room. I invite Mattie to join us. She seizes my outstretched hand. For such a small woman, she has a killer grip.

"I know you're all worried," the doctor says, "so I'll get right to the point. Mrs. Middlefield has had a stroke." Mattie wrings my hand.

Gravity plucks at my gut. "The good news is, she's already starting to bounce back from it."

"Thank God," Jay says.

"Before you get too excited, though," Kay cautions, "you need to know that while she *is* recovering, she is by no means a well woman. She's sustained some paralysis—mostly to the right side of her body. She's also suffering from dysphasia, a condition that scrambles a person's ability to express his or her thoughts clearly. These are typical side-effects of a stroke, and temporary in most cases, but they aren't going to go away overnight. Please bear that in mind."

"We will," Mattie says. "Can we see her now?"

"Of course. But go in one at a time and only stay a few minutes each. Otherwise, the duty nurse will have all of our heads in a basket."

Mattie looks to me and Jay, acknowledging our right as kin to go first. But I'm not ready to visit just yet, and neither, it would seem, is Jay.

"You guys go ahead," he tells us, as he digs through his pockets for loose change. "I'm going to call Sal and let her know what's up."

"I've got to hit the head first," I say, "so the honor falls to you, Mattie."

We all go our separate ways. But while I do indeed stop at the restroom to splash cold water on my face, my final destination is the patio on the fourth floor. I want to have a cigarette and stare at the stars and maybe for a moment escape the sense of culpability that's bird-dogging me.

Bad Raven. Bad girl.

The patio is a strip of cement rooftop studded with white resin tables and chairs. It's cold out here, and the wind is everywhere, but I don't feel a thing because I'm already numb through and through. I'll bet anything that Jay is saying 'I told her so' to Sally even as I stand here neck-deep in guilt.

I could say that I didn't believe him because I couldn't see beyond the image of Mom that I'd crafted for her over the years: strong and self-contained, serene in her eccentricity; the eternally middle-aged woman who didn't need anything from anybody, especially not her own daughter. I could say that I didn't believe him because I couldn't bear to put the farm up for sale and so lose the last tenuous ties to my father. But the ugly truth is, I didn't want to believe him because doing so would've spoiled my fun. As long as Mom didn't need me, I was free to live my life as I pleased, where I pleased. And it pleased me to live far, far away from this landlocked part of the world and its blackwater memories.

Oh, Mom! I didn't mean to hurt you. At least, I don't' think I did.

I grind the cigarette out with the heel of my boot, then head back to the ICU. I'm supposed to check in with the ward watchdog before I stray into her domain, but she isn't at her desk when I get there and I'm way too restless to wait around for her return, so I go prowling down that too-quiet corridor on my own. All of the doors here are shut. I open one at random and tip-toe over to the bed. But that's not my mom laying there with tubes running from her nose, mouth, wrist, and nether-regions. That's not my mom breathing to the mechanical wheeze of a ventilator.

Thank you, God.

I start to back out of the room only to be wrenched forward again by a pang of sudden, incredulous recognition. Oh. My. God. The man in that bed is Clifton Dupree.

I'm standing over him now, staring into his vacant face. He looks old and pale by the thin, red light of his heart monitor. His stubbled cheeks are slack. I did this to him, I think—and I'm still not sorry. This is the bastard who held a gun to my head. This is the man who gave my mom a stroke. He ought to be put down. Strangled in his—

"What are you doing in here?" a voice demands. "This is a restricted area."

I start guiltily, and then pivot toward the sound. There's a nurse standing in the doorway. I wonder how long she's been there, and if she saw my fists clenched around the corners of Dupree's pillow.

"I'm sorry," I say. "I was looking for my mother's room, that's Mrs. Middlefield, she's had a stroke. Dr. Kay said it would be OK if I paid her a quick visit, but I picked the wrong door and wound up in here. Ordinarily, I would've turned right back around again, but the thing is—I sort of know this guy, too. He—" *The fucker put a gun to my head!* "—I was there when he tried to rob that market in Hobson's Corner."

"Of course," she says. "You're Raven Middlefield." Her round face sheds its shadowy suspicions. "I thought you looked familiar. That was a very brave thing you did."

"Thanks." Embarrassed by her misplaced praise, I avert my gaze. It chances to land on Dupree. "How is he, anyway?"

"Not very good, I'm afraid." She takes me by the elbow, but it's a kindly hold, like she's trying to protect me rather than him. As she leads me into the hall, she adds, "His liver was so cirrhotic, it just about disintegrated when you, ah, resisted. Without a transplant, his chances for survival are very slim.

"Now, this is your mom's room," she goes on, as if we've been talking about that all along. "Go on in and see her if you want, but please don't stay very long. She's had a tough day."

"Thank you," I say. "I won't."

My head is spinning with thoughts that have no beginning or end as I step into that room. I can't believe what I have done, or what part of me wanted to do. Then I see my mother and forget everything else. She looks so small in her hospital bed—small and wan and misshapen. The right side of her face looks like a cheap candle that's been left to burn overnight. I prowl over to her bedside, and then touch her hand. Her eyelids twitch, but do not open.

My fantasies are in tatters. I am standing on the brink of a cliff. The life that I have loved for almost twenty years now is at my elbow, urging me to come away. Yet I cannot bring myself to turn my back on this woman and the part of me that she still holds in her stroke-frozen hand. She needs me. The farm needs me. I must take the step; pay the piper. I must—make amends.

"I'm here for you, Mom," I whisper. "And I'm going to stay here for as long as it takes."

At that, I leave her to her post-stroke dreams. I feel like weeping, but the tears won't come. The voice in my head that sounds like Jay says there's nothing to cry about anyway.

🍁   🍁   🍁

The next morning, I drag myself out of bed and back over to the hospital long before my body is ready to start the day. In the few hours that I've been away, Mom has been moved out of ICU and into a private room on the third floor. Dr. Kay is delighted with her 'rapid' progress. He says she might be ready to go home by the end of the week. I wish I knew what he's seeing that I'm not.

Her face still looks semi-molten on one side, and while she's awake this morning, she can't talk yet. Or if she can, she's not letting me in on the secret. So we sit there—she in her bed, me in the adjacent chair—and stare at each other like two goldfish in a very small bowl. I know I ought to try and fill this silence with chatter—you know, to keep her spirits up and maybe stimulate the part of her brain that has to do with talking. But I can't think of a thing to say that she might want to hear. Eventually, she nods off. I'm happy to follow suit.

The next thing I know, someone's shaking my shoulder. I come awake with a start, thinking that something's wrong, but it's only Jay. He's brought flowers and a bag of donuts. My stomach lurches at the smell of glazing sugar.

"Come on," he says, urging me to my feet, "let's take a walk. It's time for Mom's therapy session, and Dr. Kay says it'll be easier on everyone involved if we're not here."

I turn my still-bleary gaze toward the bed. Mom's awake and staring at me again. No telling how long she's been like that. Guilt nips at me with its blunt, yellow teeth. I feel like I've let her down again somehow.

"We'll be back," I say, and then follow Jay out of the room.

We don't go very far—just down the corridor and into the waiting room. This one's much brighter than the one on the fifth floor. There are Monet prints on the pastel pink walls, and fake plants in all the corners. I think I prefer the ICU lounge. It treats a person's reasons for being in this place seriously.

"So," Jay says, as I scarf one of his donuts down, "how is she this morning?"

"Your guess is as good as mine," I admit, with more acid than I'd intended. "Kay seems to think she's doing well." I take another bite, then add, "How are Sal and the girls?"

He shrugs. "They're upset, but hanging in there. Sal's going to drop by after the girls get out of school. I figure we can sit with her in shifts: you in the morning, me and Sal in the afternoon, Mattie at night. If that's all right with you, that is."

"That's fine," I tell him. "I'll look after Angelhaven, too."

He lowers his eyebrows like he's getting ready to butt heads with me over the farm again, but before he can get started, a dark-haired woman strides into the room. Although she's average height and size, she's so stylish, she looks like a runway model. Her fingernails are long and perfectly polished; her coat is cashmere. As soon as her sky blue eyes meet my muddy browns, she breaks into a smile and comes clickety-clicking toward me with open arms.

"Oh, Raven!" she exclaims, and folds me into an embrace. "I came as soon as I heard. Why didn't you call?"

"I'm sorry, Ab," I murmur into the hollow of her scented shoulder. "I guess I just wasn't thinking straight."

"I guess." She gives my cheek a loud, forgiving smooch, then wipes the lip-print away with her thumb and moves on to hug Jay. As he pats her awkwardly on the back, she asks, "How is she?"

"OK," Jay replies. "It's going to take time, but the doctor thinks she'll make a full recovery."

"Then how come you're both sitting out here?"

"Her physical therapist just kicked us out," I say.

"Well then." Her smile returns. She loops her arm around mine with a schoolgirl flourish. "That leaves you with no excuse not to join me for lunch. Right?"

"Uhm—"

It's not that I don't want to go. That donut that I just had didn't even come close to filling me up. But I feel guilty for being hungry. And for wanting to leave my brother here on his own. And for thinking about myself instead of Mom.

"Come on," Abby cajoles. "We don't have to go anywhere special—the cafeteria will do. And I have a one-thirty showing in Manchester, so we can't be gone long. What do you say?"

I look to Jay, hoping that he'll make the decision for me. Because I've never been much good at turning Abby down, not even when I think I should.

"Go on," he tells me, with a wave of his hand. "We all gotta eat."

Now that I have my dispensation, I waste no time getting out of the gate. "OK, then. I'll see you later."

We make for the fifth floor—Mutt and Jeff on the loose once again. We talk about her parents while we're riding the elevator; and what sounds good for lunch while we're cruising through the cafeteria serving line; and afterward, where we'd like to sit. We opt for a table for two by the window. When we're finally settled, she freezes me in her Cover Girl sights and smiles.

"OK," she says, "honestly now. How are you holding up?"

"I'm fine," I tell her. "Just fine."

"Yeah? Then how come you look like shit? Nicely tanned shit," she notes, as she looks me up and down, "but shit just the same. Who's cutting your hair these days?"

"A one-armed Samoan," I quip, trying to shake her off my case. "And there's nothing wrong with me that a good night's sleep won't cure. The flight home was a real bear."

"I'll bet landing in the middle of an armed robbery didn't help matters, either."

I affect a sudden interest in my chili-cheeseburger and French fries, hoping she'll drop that subject, but Abby's very selective when it comes to taking hints.

"The story went national last night, you know," she says. "All the major networks weighed in. That shit-bag Dupree was the main course, but your name definitely came up on the side." She forks a hunk of tuna into her mouth, and then lets the other Gucci loafer drop. "They showed the video clip, too.

"If I were you, I'd burn that coat."

"If you were me," I fire back, "most of my wardrobe would be in one ash-can or another."

The space behind my eyeballs is throbbing now—a slow, rhythmic pulse that's more distracting than painful. I pinch the bridge of my nose, trying to squeeze the feeling off, but it doesn't seem to help.

"Why is this shit happening to me?" I whine. "All I wanted to do was come home and have a nice, quiet Christmas with my family and friends."

"Slow news days will screw you every time," she says.

And if anyone would know, it's Abby.

One August night back in 1989—the year I did my stint in a decompression chamber—Ms. Abigail Cox left her office to scope out a remote site for a prospective client. Twelve hours later, a tobacco farmer found her Audi parked on a dirt road with the key still in the ignition. He called the state police. They issued an APB, then brought in bloodhounds to hunt for the body. A week later, she turned up at her parents' house, disheveled and disoriented, but otherwise unharmed. When the police questioned her, she told them that a beam of soft white light had engulfed her car that night while she was driving. The radio slurred to a stop, then the engine. The next thing she knew, she was sitting in an egg-shaped thing that felt like a suction cup, and six amoeba-like beings were hovering over her. Via a tiny, pulsating blob that they had attached to her wrist, they told her that they meant her no harm. They only wanted to conduct some tests.

"I'm sure the worst is over, though," Abby says. "Come tomorrow, the world won't know you or Dupree from Adam anymore."

"One can only hope," I say, and then filch an olive from her salad Nicoise. She retaliates by stealing one of my fries. As she does so, I spy the tiny, faded scar on the pulse-point of her left wrist. It looks like something she acquired as a child, but I know for a fact that it's only been there since August, 1989, because we make a point of showing these things to each other. "Now let's just drop the subject, OK?"

"No problem." She nabs another fry, then dangles it between her fingers like a cigarette and drawls, "How's your love life?"

"Nonexistent," I reply, with an oy-vay roll of my eyes. "Unless, of course, you want to count that brief encounter I had with a shower massager before I left Adelaide." As she chuckles, I remember the note I found on my windshield yesterday and add, "Oh, yeah, I almost forgot. Junior Mayhew has started sending me love-notes again, too."

She crinkles her perfect little nose. "Ook. Time for a cootie booster shot, don't you think?"

We giggle at Junior's expense—just like old times. It feels good to be laughing, even if the dutiful daughter in me does think that now is not the time or place.

"OK," I say, when our mirth subsides, "enough about me. "Who are you seeing these days?"

"Oh—" She flashes me a look of coy surprise that's as bogus as a thirty dollar bill. "Didn't I tell you? Bruce and I are sort of back together."

"Christ, Ab." Bruce is a big, machismo, melon-head who thinks the mirror was invented just for him. Abby likes him because he's great in bed. "Didn't you get enough grief from him the last time around? And puh-leeze don't try to tell me he's changed. He thinks he's perfect just the way he is."

"I know," she admits, almost sheepishly. "But don't worry, it's just a temporary reconciliation. You know, to get me through the holidays. I hate waking up all alone on Christmas morning. And he does look good on my arm at parties."

I shoot her a look chockful of mockery. "Whatever you say, Abby. But when February rolls around and you're still picking his dirty underwear up from your bedroom floor, don't be calling me up at three in the morning to cry and complain."

"I won't," she says. But she will. When it comes to men, Abby has a history of repeating herself. "How's your burger?"

"Good," I tell her, even as I down another mouthful of meat and beans. "You can't get good chili in Australia. It either winds up as a kind of kidney bean curry, which is OK, or a sweet, chunky catsup, which is totally gross."

"Oh, shit," Abby grumbles in a low voice. She's staring at something behind me. The corners of her eyes are fletched with sharp lines. "Fenton Davenport."

I glance over my shoulder, expecting to see a doctor or male nurse bearing down on us with what can only be bad news. Instead, I catch sight of the weaselly-looking reporter from yesterday. His mouth is turned upward in the semblance of a smile, but his eyes are flat and shiny. I've seen that look before—I was in the water with a great white at the time. "You know him?"

She nods. "He's the sonuvabitch who crucified me in the tabloids."

Now, I know that Ab's explanation for her disappearance sounds like an Isaac Asimov acid trip, and if anyone else in the world had come forward with it, I would have said that he or she deserved whatever treatment the media dished out. But this woman has been my best friend since the last day of second grade. She's not psychotic, neurotic, or alcoholic. As far as I know, she's never done hard drugs. And while there is no denying that she enjoys attention, she always goes for the kind that invites admiration and respect, not ridicule. So when she says she was abducted, I cannot disbelieve her. And I firmly believe that people should *not* be punished for the bizarre facts of their lives.

Unfortunately, not everyone shares that opinion.

"My my," Davenport gloats, as he comes to a stop beside our table. "Angels and aliens at the same table. This must be my lucky day."

Abby's frown enters her eyes, turning them to glare ice. "If you're looking for Elvis," she says, "he's already on his way to a Seven-Eleven in central Pennsylvania. If you leave now, you might be able to catch up with him."

He stretches his thin, liver-colored lips into a parody of amusement, then shifts ever so slightly to freeze her out of the picture.

"I was sorry to hear about your mother," he tells me. "A stroke, was it?" I nod curtly. He shakes his head and sighs. "My father had two before he passed away, so I know what you're going through. I hear she was watching that video of you and Dupree when it happened. Is that true?"

A bright white ball of resentment flares within me. I'd love to open my mouth and let him have it square in the face, but Abby warns me against it with a surreptitious kick in the shin.

"Good lord," I rasp instead, "just look at the time. We have to get going, Abby."

She's on her feet in an instant. Davenport stays where he is, tenacious as a tick and twice as loathsome. "If your mother doesn't recover," he says, as we gather up our purses and trays, "you'll be a wealthy woman, won't you?"

"My mother," I growl back, truly outraged now, "is going to be just fine."

"Of course she is. But you do stand to inherit a chunk of her estate when she dies, don't you?"

In my hurry to get away from this odious little man and his odious insinuations, I catch a toe on the leg of my chair and pitch forward. The remnants of my lunch go flying onto Davenport's white shirt. His jaw drops. His eyes go round. Abby rushes in with a napkin.

"You'll have to forgive her," she says, as she smears streaks of chili and cheese into a nice, greasy stain across his chest. "She gets a little clumsy when she's upset."

He shoots me a venomous look, then snatches the napkin from Ab's hand and goes storming off. As he disappears from view, she breaks into a tight-cornered smile that she tries to pass off as reproving.

"You shouldn't have done that, you know."

"It was an accident," I say, although I hardly believe it myself. "Or karmic comeuppance. Either way, the little prick deserved it."

"I won't argue with you there," she tells me, "but like Uncle Jerry used to say: never get into a pissing match with a skunk."

I'm in my mother's room again. Abby's gone, off to her showing, and Jay's on a soft drink run, so it's just us two Middlefield women. I wish I knew what to say to her. I wish I could think up some magic words that would make her good as new or even better. But Davenport has sent my head into a tailspin.

"I don't want your money, you know," I say. "I never have, and I never will."

She blinks as if to say, 'Message received'. An instant later, she's asleep. Dr. Kay says she'll do a lot of that in the next few days. He says it's part of the healing process. Even so, it makes me nervous: mind over matter carried one step too far.

I wish my dad were here.

To be fair to all concerned, he wasn't the world's best dad. In fact, he was a lot like my mother: quiet and remote, almost reclusive at times. He didn't have a lot to say to me or Jay unless one of his rules had been broken, and he didn't go out of his way to get involved in our lives. If we wanted his company—and please God, maybe a dab of approval—we had to hitch our wagons to his likings. Jay began to read the newspaper with him in the morning. And I—I learned how to swim.

One of my last stand-out memories of him comes from one of our sessions at the reservoir. We were treading deep water, resting up for another round of laps. I had just turned fourteen, and was taller than all but one of the boys in my class. He asked me if I was going to join the high school swim team in the fall. I sneered, and said I had enough people calling me a geek already. He reached over and shoved me underwater, an angry slam-dunk; and when he let me back up a moment later, me sputtering with surprise and childish resentment, he told me that daring to be different was the biggest favor I could ever do for myself. I demanded to know what he meant by that, but he just swam away.

I joined the swim team that fall. And the photography club. A year later, Dad died and the angels came knocking, and being different became a permanent way of life with me.

Jay comes striding back into the room. He's got a diet cola for himself, and the real, sugar-rich thing for me. Mom's eyelids snap open as we pop our tops. She glances from Jay to me and back again. Her left eye's doing all the work. I'm ashamed to admit it, but the sight gives me the willies. She looks so fucking weird.

"Strings," she croaks. "Strong and bright."

"What is it, Mom?" Jay asks, hurrying toward her. "What can we get for you?"

But it's too late, she's nodded off again. Jay turns to me with suddenly shimmery eyes and says, "This is going to take some getting used to."

"No kidding."

"I wonder what it's like for her—popping in and out of consciousness like that."

"Maybe it's like diving in the open ocean at night," I say. "You're never really sure where you are until you surface, and even then it's strange because there's nothing familiar for your eyes to grab and hold onto until the boat comes gliding out of the dark. It can be a mind-expanding experience. It can also make you feel very, very small."

Jay grunts. I get the impression that that wasn't what he wanted to hear.

We settle back into our seats and sip at our sodas, but the subliminal roar of surf is in my head now, and I cannot seem to relax. I'd love to be in the water right now, fifty or sixty feet down on some unnamed reef, hanging with the local fish-life. The rules down there are easy. *Breathe. Swim. Don't tease the eels.* Life on dry land is too complicated.

"Did I ever tell you about the time I swam with a pod of dolphins?" I ask Jay, because talking about being in the water is the next best thing to being there.

"Not that I recall," he says.

It's not the most enthusiastic opening I've ever heard, but it'll do. "I was doing a freelance job in The Bahamas at the time. Me and this guy named Walt were on our way up from this cargo ship called Theo's Wreck when I saw a flash of silver in the distance. A heartbeat later, there were dolphins all around us, dancing and playing and showing off like a bunch of circus clowns. I was spellbound; utterly fascinated. If they hadn't gotten tired of us and taken off, I might've run out of air and never noticed until it was too late."

Jay breaks into a puzzled, semi-annoyed scowl. "I don't get it. What could be that great about swimming with a bunch of big fish?"

"Dolphins are mammals, not fish, Jay," I reply, appalled by his ignorance, and worse, by the narrowness of his spirit. "They're capable of curiosity, mischief, and joy. I felt like I was among long-lost friends while they were there with me."

He shrugs. The remnants of his scowl make it clear that he's still doesn't get it.

"I guess you had to be there," I say, and then wash my disappointment down with the last of my drink. "Anyway, I should be getting back to the farm. Are you going to drop by later?"

"I don't think so," he replies. "Sally wants us to stay home tonight."

"All right then, I'll see you tomorrow."

I drop my can in the wastebasket by the bed, then take a last look at Mom. She's still asleep. I'm glad of that, but to be honest, I'm not sure why.

❦   ❦   ❦

It takes me thirty minutes to get back to Angelhaven. I consume two cigarettes and six cherry Lifesavers along the way. The airwaves are clogged with Christmas ads. *Buy now! Don't wait! Give that special someone in your life the gift of a lifetime!* My stomach feels hollow and sore. All I want for Christmas is my mom's return to health. And I want that to happen *now*.

Any questions, Santa Baby?

"How is she?" Mattie asks, as soon as I set foot in the house. Her tone is hungry. Worry shines from her eyes.

"She's tired," I tell her, "but getting better. Dr. Kay says she might be ready to come home by the end of the week."

"Praise the Lord," she says, and then turns immediately practical. "We'll move her into Jay's old room. It's bigger and brighter than that cubbyhole of hers, and I'll be right up the stairs from her."

"Sounds like a plan. I'll get on it right away."

With a shake of her close-cropped head, Mattie tries to pull rank. "You'd better let me do that, Raven. I know how she likes everything. Besides, you have other stuff to do."

"Oh? Like what?" I demand, refusing to be treated like a guest in my own home.

She half-turns and points toward the telephone. There's a long list of names and numbers taped to the wall beside it. "Most are strangers who called to congratulate you," she says, "but there's more than one reporter in the bunch, and a couple of names that I recognized, too."

"Thanks, Matt. I'll see if I can scare up an answering service to keep the kooks at bay."

"While you're at it, see what you can do about these," she says, and leads me into the living room. There are flowers everywhere: mums and roses and three different kinds of poinsettia. My immediate thought is that it's all a huge mistake, but then I read one of the accompanying cards. It's addressed to me instead of Mom, and says: *Best Wishes From The People Of Latham, MD.*

"I'm as proud of you as the next person is," Mattie says, "but I have to tell you—all of this hoopla is getting to be a pain."

"I think the worst is over now," I reply, hoping to God that I'm right for a change, "but I'll call all the florists in town anyway and beg them to send anything else that comes along in my name to the nearest nursing home."

"Good idea." She gives me an affectionate pat on the rump, then adds, "I'm going upstairs to get cleaned up for the hospital. If you get hungry, feel free to polish off that chicken stew. The Cartwrights are eating elsewhere tonight, God bless 'em."

In her absence, I turn my attention back to the flowers that I neither want nor wholly appreciate. I mean, they're pretty and all, and I know they were sent with the best of intentions, but that doesn't change the fact that I'm being honored for pulping a man's liver. Nevertheless, I go from one arrangement to the next, collecting the attached cards for—I don't know, posterity, I guess. One is from Ms. Laura Lacey, and reads: *For The Heroine of Hobson's Corner*. Another says, *Thanks From the Folks At Green's Market*. Then I come to a single red rosebud caged in baby's breath. The unsigned note says: *I Can't Stop Thinking About You*. Something lurches within me: a moist, raunchy pang. Then the image of a soulful-eyed Junior blows it away.

Shit.

If this were any other Christmas, I'd just grit my teeth and ignore the big doofus until either he or I finally went away. But like it or not—and I'm still struggling with the idea—I'm not going anywhere after the holidays this year. I'm home, maybe for good, and avoidance won't work in a pond this small. So I slip Junior's card into my back pocket, officially adding him to my list of places, people, and things to straighten out.

Just as I'm finishing up with the flowers, the phone rings. I jump at the sound—it seems louder than it should. I always forget how quiet this house is compared to a boat at sea. The phone rings again. I answer it in the kitchen. "Hello?"

"Hello there!" a deep, creamy voice replies. "I'm Chuck Blaine from 'Connecticut Talks Live on WTYX'. I'm calling for Raven Middlefield. Is she in?"

"I'm afraid not," I tell him. "May I take a message?"

"Sure, why not," Chuck says. "Tell her that we here at WTYX would like her to be the guest of honor at a Bad-Boy Barbecue that we're throwing for Clifton Dupree."

"Why on earth would you want to do a thing like that?" I ask, instantly annoyed. "And what makes you think that she'd be interested in attending?"

"Well, my listeners and I believe that three-time losers like Dupree should fry for their crimes," Chuck says. "So we're going to barbecue a couple of pigs in effigy, then donate the proceeds to Brian McNalley's campaign fund. He's running for governor of this state, and his position on crime is hard-line. Since Ms. Middlefield is pretty tough on crime herself, we thought she'd appreciate the chance to help him out."

"Well, you thought wrong," I growl, and then hang up the telephone. An instant later, I'm thumbing through the Yellow Pages for an answering service.

I spend the next hour trying to return things to normal around here. When I'm done, the answering service is on-line, the florists have been called, and Junior is next on my list. As I'm looking for his number, a knock sounds at the back door. I scowl, thinking, *What now*, then sneak a peek through the kitchen blinds.

"What the—?"

I look again, but I'm not hallucinating. There really is a flat-bed truck loaded with mint-green portable latrines in the driveway.

An instant later, I'm standing on the stoop with a guy dressed in green cover-alls. There's a white Porta-San patch sewn to his breast pocket.

"Mrs. Middlefield?" he asks.

"I'm her daughter," I tell him, hoping he won't make me go into further detail. "What can I do for you?"

"Sign here." He hands me a clipboard with a triplicated form on it, then adds, "You'll have to tell me where you want them, too."

I glance from the paperwork to the truck and back again, clueless as to why Mom would want three more latrines for the property. It's bizarre. Unnecessary. Extreme. I wonder if she knew what she was doing when she ordered them. I wonder if this was really her first stroke.

"I don't mean to rush you or anything," the delivery guy says, "but I have another delivery to make this afternoon."

Resentment snarls to life within me. Like I really want to be out here in forty-five degree weather without a jacket, agonizing over a bunch of goddam toilets. Like I really want to believe that my mom doesn't know what she's doing anymore. I'm not ready to admit that—to myself or anyone else. So I scribble my name on the dotted line like a big 'Fuck You' and then point The Tidy-Bowl Man toward the barn.

"They go over there. Left side, toward the rear. Set them up side by side with the one that's already."

Just then, a police cruiser pulls into the driveway. My pulse does a sickly little jig as Kyle's features emerge from the windshield's glare. I run my fingers through my hair and then head down the drive to meet him. I'm hoping to God that he won't make any wisecracks about the toilets.

"What's the problem this time, Hobson?" I joke. "Did I forget to dot an 'i' or—" The look on his face turns that fluttery feeling within me to lead. "Uh-oh. What's up?"

"Dupree is dead," he says, all somber regrets. "We got the word from St. Fran's about an hour ago. I tried to call, but your line was busy." He swallows hard, like he's trying rinse a bad taste from his mouth, then squares his shoulders and says, "I'm sorry, Raven, but I have to take you in for questioning."

CHAPTER 5

I'm so blown away, I forget to breath for a second. And the thing is, I don't know what has me more stunned: the fact that Dupree kicked the bucket, or that the cops want to question me about it. My thoughts bungee-jump back to last night—me with my hands knotted in an ICU pillow. I wished that bastard dead, and now he is. Does that make me guilty of something?

"Raven?" Kyle asks. "Are you all right?"

The question irritates me. Like he really gives a shit if I'm all right or not. I want to thump my fist into his chest and shout: *go away, dammit! I didn't do anything wrong.* But I'm not as sure of that as I would like to be, and so shove my hands into my pockets instead.

"I'm fine," I say, and then scourge the Porta-San guy with a look for still being here. "I thought you had another delivery to make this afternoon."

"Huh?" Mr. Quick-On-His-Feet says, and then blushes all the way down to his Scandinavian roots as it dawns on him that he's been busted. "Oh, right. I was just on my way."

As he hustles off, I swivel my gunboat-turret of a head back toward Kyle. "May I go and get my gear before you take me in? I promise not to run away."

His freshly shaven face reddens just like the Tidy-Bowl Man's did, but the color looks more aggressive on him. He freezes me with a look of pure confidence and says, "Raven Middlefield, there's no running from me. I'd find you no matter where you went. So go and get whatever it is that you need. I'll wait right here."

No running from him, aye? Just who in hell does he think he is—Dudley Freakin' DoRight? Part of me is tempted to make him put his money where his handsome mouth is. I've been places he's probably never dreamed of—Micronesia, New Guinea, Guam. He wouldn't even know where to start looking. Fortunately for him, though, I don't need to run. Because. I. Didn't. Do. Anything. Wrong. Dammit. I give my head a haughty toss and then go inside. There, I grab a couple of mini-Snickers bars along with my bomber jacket and purse because I can feel the beginnings of a headache stirring behind my eyeballs. As an afterthought, I leave a note: *to whom it may concern*.

"All right," I drawl, as I come stepping back out of the house, "I'm ready. Do you want to handcuff me now or later?"

"Come on, Rave," Kyle says, "quit with the attitude. This is just a formality."

"Oh. Well then." I let my outstretched arms fall limp by my sides. "Where do I ride—in the front or in the back?"

He opens the passenger door to the front seat with the sort of brusqueness that often accompanies a kick in the pants. His tight-lipped scowl makes me feel better in a tiny, spiteful way. I sit as close to my door as I can get. He jams the car into gear and takes off. A long time passes in rigid silence.

"I was sorry to hear about your mom," he says finally. "How's she doing?"

I answer him with a teenager's sullen shrug. He clams up for a moment, then tries again.

"How's Angelhaven doing without her?"

"Everything's under control," I say then. "Or at least it was, until you came along and dragged me away."

"I'm just doing my job, Raven."

He doesn't know how freakin' lucky he is.

I think back to Australia, with its blue-for-months sky and Technicolor reefs. How I wish I were there now, doing my job, what I do best. It grieves me to think that I may never have that luxury again. But I made a promise, dammit. Things are going to be different. I have to accept that and move on.

A roadside tobacco barn snags my attention. Its roof is swaybacked, on the verge of collapse; its sides are slathered with graffiti. *TTHS 2001*, one pumpkin-colored tag reads. *Go, Pats.* I always wondered who decided to make that noxious shade of orange our school color.

"We sure had fun in those days, didn't we?" Kyle says.

I glance at him out of the corner of my eye, curious as to what prompted him to climb into the Way-Back Machine. Was it the graffiti or the tobacco? He'd had a hand in both back in his young-Turk days. But the *we* part was peripheral at best—me looking on from a wistful distance while he had his way with the world.

"If you say so," I reply.

"No, I mean it." He's smiling now, a nostalgic bend of the mouth. "I'll admit, the work itself sucked—picking tobacco is right up there with cleaning latrines as far as work goes. But you have to admit: we made decent money for our age. And at lunch, me and Bobby Clark and Will O'Malley used to sneak off behind a barn and drink vodka or whatever else we could snake from my old man's liquor cabinet. If we were lucky, we'd get a girl or two to join us."

Lucky, my ass. I can name at least a dozen girls who would've cheerfully stripped in front of the whole school in return for one of his lesser smiles. I know, because at one point, I was right up there at the top of that list. But he never thought to try his so-called luck with me. In fact, he never thought of me at all unless he needed quick answers to a homework assignment. I played that game with him for more than a year in the hope that it would eventually get better, but it never did so I wised up and got proud instead.

"Jay tells me there isn't much tobacco left in the valley," I say. "He says most of the old-timers are selling out to land-developers."

"Jay's right," Kyle says. "The only one in my family who still grows the stuff is Uncle John, and even he's talking about cashing it in. When he quits, there won't be a tobacco farm within twenty-five miles of Hobson's Corner. And that's a shame, really, because then a lot of teenagers are going to lose out on summer jobs. That means more kids getting drunk in the woods by day and getting into trouble by night."

"Like they'd be better people for getting drunk behind a tobacco barn, right?"

He sneaks a quick peek at me, as if he's wondering what has him by the tail. But he's lithe as an otter, and cagey, too. He can get out of any trap.

"OK," he cheerfully admits, "so maybe we got out of line every now and again—that's to be expected at that age. But we also worked ourselves into a man-sized sweat five days out of seven. Kids these days don't know elbow grease from a jar of Vaseline. They want everything quick and easy."

"That's because most of them have grown up in front of a television," I say. "And in TV-Land, quick and easy isn't just real, it's a friggin' rule of thumb."

"Maybe so," he counters, "but—"

I steam-roll right over him. "There are no 'buts' about it, Kyle. Kids are kids—they mostly want what they've been taught to want. And this generation has learned to want sex, drugs, and a happy, feels-good ending with their closing credits."

He shoots me a squinty, scrunched-up, sideways look of mostly mock-irritation. "Something tells me this isn't the first time you've had this conversation."

His expression is so comical, I have to laugh. And just like that, my hard feelings for him dissipate like the last wisps of a morning ground fog. "You're right," I say. "My brother and I have gone one round after another on the subject of 'kids these days'. He thinks everybody under the age of twenty-five ought to be fitted with an electronic tracking device. I say: quit using the TV as a pacifier and see what happens. If I had kids, I wouldn't even allow a set in the house."

"I'll bet your husband would have something to say about that," Kyle says. "I'll bet he'd want at least one in the bedroom so he could snuggle under the covers with you while you watched the late-night news."

It takes me a moment to realize that he's teasing, and when it finally does sink in, I get flustered. I think it has something to do with him picturing me in bed with a man.

We're pulling into a state police barracks now. It's a sprawling, single-story building tucked away in the middle of nowhere, unimposing except for the number of cruisers parked in the lot. My schoolgirl flutters give way to major league palpitations.

I don't want to be here. I don't, I don't, I don't.

But nobody's interested in my druthers.

Kyle takes me in through the back door and down a long hallway. The carpeting here is the same dark-blue and gray as his uniform. The smell is a perfusion of Lysol and cement. Working in such an uptight space, with its multitude of closed doors and air of subliminal tension, would drive me right out of my skull in a matter of hours. My brain's starting to squirm as it is.

We end up in a room full of cubicles and computers. No perps in sight here—except for me, I guess—just a handful of troopers going about their day-to-day business. A few of them glance at us as we pass. I can tell by their eyes that they know who I am, and that they don't wholly disapprove of me. That's something, anyway. I think.

"Here we are," Kyle says, as he steers me into his cube. It has a desk, two chairs, a computer and a filing cabinet—just like every other cube. He pulls the second chair out of its corner and then gestures for me to sit down. As I do so, he asks, "Can I get you anything? Coffee? Soda?"

"A Coke would be nice," I reply, thinking of the sugar.

"Back in a flash," he tells me.

In his absence, I check out his stuff. There's not much to see, just a ragged pile of papers in his in-out basket, an old Doonesbury comic strip taped to the side of his computer, and a white, oversized coffee mug. That's OK, though, because I'm more interested in what's not here—a photograph of a spaniel-eyed little woman, crayon drawings of dinosaurs and dogs dedicated to daddy from the gap-toothed kiddies. I don't know why I'm so happy to learn that he isn't married yet. It must be *schodenfrueda*. Hans turned me on to the word. It's German for taking a perverse pleasure in another person's misfortunes. That feels about right.

Kyle breezes back into the cube with my soda. As I pop the top, he reaches into a drawer and pulls out a folder that has *Dupree, Clifton J*, written on the index tab. The file isn't as thick as I thought it would be.

"Now," he says, as he extracts a paper from it. "Here's the statement you gave me on the night in question. The problem is, it doesn't quite jibe with what's on the video. You have seen the video, haven't you?"

"Yes," I say flatly, lapsing back into sullen-teenager mode.

"Well, what I'd like to do is run it by you again, frame by frame, and ask you some questions about what you're seeing along the way. I'll compare your answers with your statement and go from there. Is that OK with you?"

"Do I have a choice?"

"None that won't expire sooner or later."

Which is pretty close to what I thought he'd say. So I push myself out of my chair and make a sweeping, lead-the-way gesture.

"I didn't mean to hurt him, you know," I say, as we head back into that stifling hallway. "It just happened."

"I believe you," he tells me, momentarily slipping out of his lawman's persona. "Just about everybody else here does, too. But as soon as this story went national, it became a whole new ball of wax. Politics are involved now. Things aren't all as they might seem.

"Do you understand what I'm saying here?"

"I suppose."

We come to a door that's labeled 'Conference Room III'. He lets us in, then heads over to the audio-video unit that's obviously been wheeled in just for the occasion. As he loads a cartridge into the VCR, he says, "The tape's cheap and kind of old, so I'm going to turn the lights out so you can see it better. Is that OK?"

In another lifetime, I would've been thrilled to find myself in black-out conditions with Lady-Killer Kyle, but not now. All I want to do is go home and burrow under the covers after a long, hot shower. I feel like someone has shit in my head and neglected to flush.

"Why not?" I sneer. A moment later, the lights go out. A moment after that, a body settles down in the chair beside me. It smells of starch and aftershave.

"OK," Kyle says, "let's get to it. And just so you know, this interview is being tape-recorded."

"Hi, Mom," I say.

The television comes on with a click. Stripes of static sizzle across the screen, then phase into a scratchy image of yours truly striding into Green's Market. Ab's right, I think, as I study my unsuspecting image—I really should burn that coat.

"Could you please state your reason for entering this establishment on the night of December twelfth?" he asks.

"I stopped in to buy some cigarettes," I reply woodenly, trying to keep a distance between what I'm seeing and myself. "Speaking of which, I could sure use one now."

"Sorry, but there's no smoking in the building," he says, then fast-forwards me and Junior through our first hellos and over to the check-out counter. For a moment, we look like we have cerebral palsy with our jerky, high-speed movements, but then the tape slows down, we stop shaking, and Dupree walks in. The hair on the back of my neck stands up as I watch him pull the gun out of his pocket. A shiver courses through me as I watch him put it to my head.

Kyle hits the pause button and asks, "What were you thinking at this point in time?"

Dumfounded by the towering stupidity of the question, I swivel around to gape at him. There may be tears in my eyes; I can't quite tell.

"What was I thinking?" I echo biliously. "Christ, Kyle, take a good look at the gray thing that that scruffy-looking mongrel is holding to my head. See it? That's a gun. Guns kill people. And I am not immune. So to answer your question, I wasn't thinking anything at all at that point. I was too goddam scared."

"And yet, a few seconds later—" He advances the tape, then hits pause again. "—it looks like you're laughing."

"Believe me, it was strictly involuntary."

"You weren't trying to bait Mr. Dupree?"

"No. Absolutely not."

He breaks to jot something down, leaving me to stare at the frozen frame. I hate seeing myself like I am there, all wild-eyed and hopeless like a cow in a slaughter chute. And I hate seeing Dupree's ugly puss, too, with its frozen snarl and slack, bewhiskered jowls. Miserable, greasy bastard. I want to reach out and grab him by the scruff of his neck. I want to shake his teeth loose and shout in his face: asshole! What the fuck were you thinking?

Kyle advances the videotape a few frames, then freezes it again. My expression is different here: still wild-eyed and hopeless, but cornered-rat-hard, too. Dupree is waving his gun around like a Tombstone cowboy on a Saturday night.

"Can you tell me what was going on at this point?" Kyle asks.

"He was ordering Junior and the boys to get down on the floor. I thought he was getting ready to kill us all."

"OK, now we're coming to the part where your statement gets vague." The tape flicks forward at half-speed. "Here you are, elbowing Dupree in the side." I give him a good shot, too; or at least it seems that way in slow-mo. "The gun goes off, shattering the window." How odd that looks without any accompanying sound. "You grab his gun-arm with your left hand and his testicles with your right.

"Is any of this coming back to you yet?"

I shake my head. "It's all Memorex."

"Meaning?" he prompts, pencil poised.

"Meaning this isn't the first time I've seen this goddam video," I reply, growing more and more irritated with his deliberate obtuseness. "I *know* I elbowed Dupree. I *know* I crunched his privates. I know because I saw myself do these things on TV. However, the only thing I actually *remember* is not wanting to die." I chase the terrible taste of that memory out of my mouth with a swallow of Coke, and then ask, "Are we done here yet?"

"Just a few more questions," he says, and starts the tape again. An instant later, Dupree goes sprawling onto the floor and I kick him. Kyle throws the VCR into reverse, then replays that part. Blam! I catch him squarely in the brisket with the toe of my boot. I guess that's why they call those babies shit-kickers.

"A few people are saying you didn't need to do that," he tells me. "They're saying he was already unconscious."

My resentment reaches critical mass. As it boils up and over, I wring one of the candy bars that I'd pocketed earlier into the semblance of a state cop's neck. "Is there a point to all of this, Hobson? Aside from trying to make me feel even worse about this whole goddam business than I do already, that is? I don't know if Dupree was conscious when I kicked him. I don't know what I was thinking at the time, either, but I'm fairly sure that I was more concerned for my health than his. If that's a crime these days, then you'd better lock me up because I'm guilty as charged."

"Settle down, Raven." Kyle says. "You're getting a little out-of-hand."

"Can you blame me?" I caterwaul back. "I mean, knowing that I've contributed to a person's death is traumatic enough as it is." The figure sprawled on the still-frozen TV screen catches my eye. It's funny, but some terminally naive part of me half-expects it to get up and walk away. "But for you to suggest that I might have done so deliberately—well, that's just too much." Dupree's image stays where it is. He's dead, I remind my idiot self. Deceased. Defunct. "He's the one who had the goddam gun. He's the one who put it to my head. All I wanted to do was spend a nice, quiet Christmas at home with my family."

An image of Mom pops into my head. She mocks all of my desires with her half-molten face and unwavering stare.

I pull that mangled candy bar out of my pocket and choke it down in three quick bites. I'm crying now, outraged tears that are all for Kyle. I'm furious at him for trying to make me out as something other than a victim in this case, for reducing me to tears, and for not having the decency to leave the room while I try and pull myself back together. So when he hands me his fresh, white hankie, I blow the contents of my nose into it with a loud, spiteful honk.

"Hang in there, Raven, we're almost done," he tells me in a soothing voice, and then fast-forwards the tape to the part where I tear into the bologna. "Just tell me what you were doing here. It seems a little odd of you to be so hungry after such a harrowing ordeal."

"I was hypoglycemic, not hungry," I sullenly reply, and then hold out the empty candy wrapper like exhibit A. "If I don't eat when my blood sugar levels bottom out, I get dizzy. In extreme instances, I even pass out. Call my doctor if you don't believe me. I've got his number in my purse."

"That won't be necessary, Ms. Middlefield," a deep new voice says.

As I swivel around in my seat to see who has stolen into the room, the overhead lights snap on. I blink back a bright, white afterflash and a fresh wave of resentment; the man with the bald, pointy head and compact, hard-shelled body does not apologize for either.

"I'm Colonel McNalley," he says, as he struts toward me. "I'd like to offer you my thanks for your cooperation in this investigation."

The name rings some distant bell, but I can't figure out why. I've never met this ammo-shell of a man. He acts as if he knows me, though. He's all smiles as he invades my space, and he takes my hand before it occurs to me to offer it. His grip is strong and leathery—like a python's. It disagrees with me.

"I hope you understand that any inconvenience The Connecticut State Police might have caused you was done to uphold and preserve the law," he tells me, as he wrings my finger-bones.

"So I've been told," I say, countering his chumminess with a liberal dose of frost.

He half-cocks an eyebrow at me, a look of minor surprise and something more that lifts the hackles on my neck. In the next instant, he's all smiles again.

"At any rate, you're free to go now," he tells me. "I'm convinced that your role in Clifton Dupree's death was purely accidental." I reach for my purse, meaning to set a new land-speed record on my way out of this place. But before I can do so, he lets the other spit-shined boot drop. "Just so you know, there's a small press conference waiting for you in the parking lot."

I paste Kyle with a dirty look, silently accusing him of setting me up, but he just shrugs as if to say it was none of his doing and then closes his file.

"If you'd like," McNalley offers, "I can make an opening statement that'll get all of the legal jargon out of your way."

All of a sudden, I realize why this guy's name sounds so familiar—he's the gubernatorial candidate that that talk-show jock from WTYX was blathering about this morning. And an instant after I make that connection, Kyle's veiled warning about politics being involved in this case becomes breathtakingly clear. The smoldering bank of resentments within me flares to fresh, white-hot life. No way am I serving as this man's battle standard or poster child. I killed a man, dammit! Only a true-blue bastard would want to exploit such an unhappy fact.

"Or maybe you'd rather address the press by yourself," he says then, a seemingly polite little prompting.

"Don't be silly, Colonel," I reply, all saccharine-coated sarcasm. "This is your show. Please, conduct it as you see fit." I do not, however, promise to play nice.

The three of us hit the road: McNalley to my right, Kyle Hobson to my left, and me in the middle like a slice of sun-tanned turkey. I pay no attention to the way we take; I'm too busy imagining punishments for this would-be governor. One of them involves a hot curling iron to his privates. Another has him staked out over a nest of angry fire ants. The next thing I know, we're striding out of the building and into frosty darkness. That confuses me, because I'm not used to the days being as short as they are. And before I can get my bearings straight, a round of camera flashes goes off and people start shouting questions.

"Ladies! Gentlemen!" McNalley says. "Please. Let's show a little decorum here. I have a statement."

A thicket of microphones crops up in front of him. Questions fly fast and furious. What's Miz Middlefield doing here? Is she being charged? What would the charges be? Herr McNalley waits until the frenzy dies down and then clears his throat like a seasoned speechmaker.

"As most of you already know," he says, "Clifton J. Dupree died this afternoon at Saint Francis from complications stemming from injuries he sustained during the Hobson Corner armed robbery attempt. The circumstances surrounding his death were unusual enough to warrant an investigation. Part of that investigation involved questioning Miz Middlefield. That's the reason she's here now." He pauses dramatically. A few more flashes go off. "The good news is, she's been cleared of all wrong-doing. No charges will be pressed."

More shouting ensues. I hear some clapping, too. Then McNalley hauls me into the limelight and starts hamming it up for the cameras.

"Raven," he says, as he glad-hands me, "please allow me to commend you for your heroism. You're a credit to your community, the state of Connecticut, and all of America. I hereby pledge to do everything in my power to make this great state a safer place for you and all good citizens."

Yeah, right.

"Raven," one of the reporters shouts. "Do you have anything to add to that?"

I look at Kyle, Kyle looks at me; and although it's only there for an instant, I see a plea in his blue eyes. *Please, Raven*, it says, *pretty please with sugar on top, don't make a fool of my opportunistic prick of a boss.* Which is, of course, exactly what I'm so tempted to do. *Bad Boy Barbecue, anyone*? But the thought of Kyle Hobson begging for favors appeals to me more than roasting McNalley's nuts, so I grant my old classmate his wish.

Sort of.

"Yes, as a matter of fact, I do," I say, beaming green cheese at the sea of faces beyond the microphones. "I'd like to take this opportunity to express my appreciation for Connecticut's real-life heroes—the men and women of the state police. Trooper Kyle Hobson here has been a particular inspiration throughout this entire ordeal."

Now it's Kyle's turn to blink back his surprise. As he does so, I lean in close and smooch him soundly on the cheek. Camera flashes go off like rounds of artillery.

I can hardly wait to see the photos.

CHAPTER 6

"Christ, Raven," my brother says. "Now you've really gone and done it."

We're sitting in the hospital cafeteria, stoking up on coffee and donuts before our conference with Dr. Kay; and as usual, Jay has a stack of newspapers with him. He flips the one he's been reading in my direction. A picture of me kissing Kyle's cheek is sitting front and center. I smirk at first, because it looks like I've finally paid my old heart-throb back for ignoring me in my formative years. But then I catch the accompanying headline and my smugness turns to sour ashes in my mouth.

Cover-Up Involved In Outlaw's Death?

The byline is Fenton Davenport's.

I snatch the paper out of Jay's hands with a sputtered curse, then dive into the article. It starts by overstating the relationship that Kyle and I shared back in high school, then goes on to sling unsubstantiated words like 'prejudice', 'impropriety', and 'possible collusion' at us.

"This is bullshit!" I say. "How in hell could we have covered anything up? The whole damn thing is on video!"

Jay doesn't reply. His gaze is locked on the TV that's been bracketed to the far wall. At the moment, Laura Lacey's head and shoulders are on-screen. That picture of me and Kyle is in the background.

"In response to questions raised by reporters," she is saying, "Commander Brian McNalley held a press conference this morning, and vowed to review the case personally. He also told Channel 4's roving reporter that Trooper Kyle Hobson had already received an official reprimand for failing to disclose his relationship with Raven Middlefield, and that further punitive action may be forthcoming. Those details as they develop."

"Oh, shit," I say.

"See what happens when you try to be a smart-ass, Raven?" Jay says, totally unsympathetic.

"Shut up," I snap. "Just shut up."

For once, he does as he is told.

We set off for Kay's office, but once we get there, I hardly hear a word of what the doctor has to say. My thoughts are circling like buzzards around the dead meat that I've made of Kyle. All I wanted to do was make him squirm a little, dammit! Instead, I sucker-punched him right where it hurts. An official reprimand? What does that mean, exactly? And what about that bit about further punitive action? Lord, if he loses his job because of me, I'll never forgive myself. And as for him forgiving me, well, I don't think that's going to happen in this lifetime.

"…so we're going to keep her here for a few more days just to be sure," Dr. Kay says. "But all things considered, you have reason to be optimistic. Any questions?"

Jay shakes his head. I follow his lead. Kay wraps the session up with a promise to see us again on Friday, then sends us on our way. We head for Mom's room. Neither of us says a word until we see the pair of state troopers standing guard in front of Mom's door.

"Uh-oh," Jay says, under his breath.

"No shit," I say, in the same exact tone.

"Raven Middlefield?" the taller of the two asks me, as we approach.

"Ye-es," I say, stretching the acknowledgment into two wary syllables. "What can I do for you?"

"Commander McNalley wants to speak with you," he tells me, as stern-faced as a hanging judge. "We're here to escort you to his office."

I look at Jay. He looks from me to the two troopers and back again. "Go ahead," he says, all big-brotherly now. "I'll call my lawyer. His name is Dick Frenchette. He'll meet you at the barracks."

"That won't be necessary," the second policeman intones. "Miss Middlefield isn't under arrest."

Jay holds my gaze, waiting for me and me alone to accept or decline his plan. I'm grateful for the unflinching show of support, and just a little bit wistful, too. If only he could be like that all of the time!

"Hold up on that call for now," I say. Because the way I see it, I started this mess. The least I can do is try to put it right again. But I'm no fool, either, so I hastily add, "If I'm not home by supper, though, send Dick and every other lawyer in the county to my rescue."

"Will do," he says.

The Staties march me out of the building and into their cruiser. This time, I am required to sit in the back. And this time, no one makes the mistake of trying to be nice to me. I don't blame them for this ten-foot-pole treatment, but still, it makes for a long, uneasy ride to headquarters or wherever. All I can do as the miles fly by is gnaw at my hangnails and worry about the reception I'll get from Bullet-Head McNalley. I'm sure it will involve a thorough grilling. A rubber hose-job might be included, too. I don't intend to put up a fight. I deserve everything he has to dish out.

When we finally arrive at the barracks, my escort takes me in through a side door, then down a series of hallways. I try to make eye-contact with the few people we run into along the way, but no one wants to look at me. *Not* a good sign. I wish Kyle would turn up now so I could throw myself down at his feet and grovel for forgiveness. If he's in the building, though, he stays well out of sight.

We come to a firmly shut door at the end of an ell. One of the troopers knocks at it with his chapped, winter-white knuckles, and then draws it open as a voice within says, "Enter."

The office is small but showy: dark wood paneling on the walls, a bookcase filled with honors and awards, an outsized desk made of exotic wood. Colonel McNalley is sitting behind that chunk of murdered rainforest. Despite his welcoming half-smile, he looks like a fist poised to strike.

"Ah, yes; Miss Middlefield. Please, sit down," he says, and gestures at the plush leather chair across from him. As I do as I am told, he asks, "Would you care for something to drink? A Coke, perhaps?"

When I decline the offer, he heaves a bland, as-you-will shrug and then dismisses his men. They leave silently, like trained circus cats, and shut the door behind them. The room seems larger in their absence.

"So," McNalley says, peering at me over the steeple of his fingers. "What am I going to do with you?"

"Do whatever you need to," I say. "Just don't take my stupidity out on Kyle. He did absolutely nothing wrong."

"I know that," he quietly assures me.

My eyebrow goes up, an arch of surprise. "Then why are you punishing him?"

"You and Officer Hobson were long-standing friends—"

"*Acquaintances*," I say. "We went to the same schools when we were kids. That doesn't make us friends."

"Regardless. You two had some form of a relationship prior to the robbery. He should have disclosed that and handed the case over to a fellow officer, especially when it went high-profile."

"But why?" I press. "I didn't get special treatment from him. He conducted his investigation with the hard-nosed but fair professionalism that you'd expect from a state trooper."

"It's not enough for an officer of the law to avoid the act of impropriety," he says. "He must also avoid the appearance of it."

I give him a frustrated once-over. He's still sitting prim in his high-backed chair, his hands folded in front of him. I'm reminded of a giant Komodo dragon. Their mouths are so putrid, all they have to do is bite their prey once and then wait for septicemia to set in. I wonder if McNalley has chomped Kyle yet, or just lipped him.

"So what can I do to make that appearance of impropriety go away for Officer Hobson?" I ask. "I'll be glad to go over my statement with one of your other men. Or I could make a new one, if that'll help."

"That won't be necessary," he says. "I've reviewed all the material on this case, and have found no evidence of bias or collusion. The coroner's verdict stands: Clifton J. Dupree died by misadventure."

"You could've told me that over the phone, Colonel."

"Ah, but then I would've missed out on the pleasure of your company," he says, showing a little tooth in his smile now. "And we have things other than Kyle Hobson to discuss."

"Such as?" I ask, trying to match his casual tone. But I feel like I've just been air-dropped into uncharted waters.

"Such as your stance on gun-control, for instance. I'm all for taking guns out of the criminal's hand, too. And as the governor of this fine state, I could put that vision and others like it into action. You could be a great help to me in that respect."

"How's that?"

"You're highly regarded by a lot of people around here, Miz Middlefield. A well-placed word here, and a public appearance or two there would do it."

Ah-ha. I thought as much. This sonuvabitch has more balls than a one-legged bull-fighter. I'd like to come right out and tell him to stick his public appearances where the sun don't shine, but for Kyle's sake, I try to be more diplomatic. "Politics has never been one of my interests," I say. "In fact, I didn't even vote in the last election. You'd be better off with someone who's committed to your cause."

He leans forward. His smile becomes even more unctuous. "All I ask is that you sleep on it. It could mean good things for you; and for Kyle Hobson, too. I'll need smart people with me in Hartford."

"You'd promote a man with a big red flag in his jacket? I'm no expert, of course, but that doesn't sound like a politically correct thing to do."

He shrugs. It's the deceptively mild gesture of a man who has made things more substantial than a red flag disappear in his day. I'm definitely in water over my head here. And I don't like the way the currents are starting to run.

"And if I can't bring myself to drop those well-placed words for you?"

He shrugs again. His smile returns to its original set position. "It's your choice, of course. But you should know that friends aren't the only people I'll remember when I move into the governor's mansion. I may have to get tough on people who are breaking Connecticut's zoning and health codes. The worst offenders, even those with the best of intentions, may have to be shut down to protect the innocent.

"Oh, and by the way—how's your mother feeling?"

The hairs on the back of my neck stand straight up, and not from fear, either. This Fascist turd has really pissed me off! How dare he threaten my mother and Angelhaven? How dare he try to use the so-called innocent as a human shield? What an underhanded, self-serving creep! I'd love to scratch his scaly back right now, scratchscratch-scratch till I strike a bone, but the voice of reason intervenes. This is still his swimming hole, and he's still got lots of bite in him.

"She's fine," I say, forcing the words past a too-taut smile. "Getting better by the hour, in fact, thanks so much for asking. And speaking of which, I'd best be getting back to the hospital now. Your troopers intercepted me just as I was going in for my morning visit. She'll be wondering where I am."

"I'll have them return you at once," he says. Then, as I snap to my feet, he adds, "I'll have my campaign manager call you in a day or so. He's a very nice man. I'm sure you two will get along famously."

My only reply to that is a soundly slammed door.

🍁   🍁   🍁

I fume about McNalley's strong-arm tactics throughout the day: in the morning while I'm sitting with Mom; in the afternoon while I'm cleaning up the barn; and now, as I'm getting ready to go out to dinner with Abby. As I ram myself into my dress slacks, a thought cycles round and round in my head: *I'll get you, my pretty, and your little dog, too*. But I don't know if that's McNalley talking, or me. No doubt about it, I'd park a house on his pointy head in a heartbeat—if I could do it cleanly.

And that's a freakin' big 'if'.

A knock rattles my bedroom door. An instant later, Ab comes strolling in like she owns the place. She's dressed like a movie starlet: cashmere coat, silk stockings, high-heels. Her mouth acquires a lemony pucker as she checks me out.

"You're wearing *pants* to Michelino's?"

"I don't own a dress at the moment," I growl, "and I didn't have the time to shop today. You wanna go to Pizza Hut instead?"

"Not even in my nightmares," she says, and then looks me up and down again. As she does so, her scowl recedes. "It's not the worst outfit you've ever worn. And luckily, I know the owner. So if you're ready, let's go. Our reservation is for seven sharp."

"In Australia," I say, as I follow her out of my room, "no one even starts thinking about dinner before eight."

"Yeah well," she says, "welcome back to the civilized world."

We hit the road. It's a pretty evening, clear and crisp, with an almost full moon sitting low in the sky, but I'm too restless to enjoy the drive. I surf from one radio station to the next, looking for Christmas music, but all I can find is classic rock: Aerosmith, Led Zeppelin, Heart.

"Christ," I grumble. "When is this friggin' state going to crawl out of the '70's?"

"Are you planning to be like this all night?" Abby asks. "Because if you are, I'm going to turn this car around and drive your crabby ass home. The whole idea behind this dinner was for us to go out and have some fun."

"I'm sorry," I say, stung by her disgust. "It's just that I have a lot of things on my mind."

"Want to talk about them?"

Not really, I think, but the words come fountaining out of me just the same. I tell her how I got Kyle in trouble with that smart-assed kiss, and how his boss is now holding that over both of our heads. She is properly appalled.

"The rat-bag," she says, and then lights up a cigarette. The inside of her Audi turns blue-gray from the smoke. "You ought to turn him in."

I sneer at the suggestion. "And what would I say: 'Excuse me, but a Connecticut State Police commander is trying to blackmail me into endorsing him'? Nobody is going to believe that without proof, and McNalley wasn't dishing out any of that."

"Then just avoid him until the new year," she says. "After that, you'll be out of here, and that'll solve everything."

"I wish," I say, meaning it in a dozen different ways. "You're forgetting Kyle and maybe Mom."

"Oh. Yeah," she replies, and lapses into silence. But I cannot seem to do the same.

"The supreme bitch of it all is, he only wants me to help him because I killed a man."

She grinds her cigarette out in the ashtray, then looks at me out of the corner of her eye. "How are you doing with that anyway? You sleeping right yet?"

"Nah, I still have major anxiety dreams and flashbacks." I have one right now, in fact, for no reason at all: the feel of gun-metal at my head and a rank forearm around my neck. I banish the memory with a frown, then add, "I also seem to be on edge a lot these days."

"Maybe you should see a therapist," she says. "You know, like the cops do after they shoot someone."

"I don't need a shrink. All I need is a little time to forget. But no one will let me do that. They keep on bringing it up and up and up."

"Oops. Sorry."

"Oh, I'm not talking about you," I say, although I'm sure she'd never guess it by my tone. "It's the rest of the damn world—people I don't even know. Like freakin' Jay Leno. Did you catch his act the other night?"

I'm talking about the show that aired the day after Dupree died. My brother had invited me over to his place for dinner that night, and I was late getting home. The house was Amityville-quiet, and I was wired from a double dose of Sal's hair-raising coffee, so I turned on the TV. *The Tonight Show* was on; Leno had just started his monologue. He took a couple of cheap shots at the president, then clasped his hands together and tried to look solemn.

"There's been another development in the Clifton Dupree saga," he said. "You know who I'm talking about, don't you—the guy who was well on his way to robbing a mom-and-pop shop in every state on the eastern seaboard when he finally met the girl of his dreams? Well, he expired yesterday. And according to my sources, the last thing that went through his mind before he died was Raven Middlefield's boot."

I jumped up to turn the TV off. At the same time, Leno raised his hands as if to protect himself, then added, "Heh, heh. Just kidding, Rave. I know you didn't kick him in the head. Thanks for doing your bit to stomp out crime. And I do mean *stomp*! Man, did you *see* that video?—"

Click.

Very funny, Jay. Friggin' hilarious.

"Yeah, I saw it," Ab says, and then adds, "I'm switching to Letterman."

She pulls up in front of Michelino's. It's a swank little place, long and white like a stretch limousine, with a covered entryway and sculptured shrubs that have been strung with white Christmas lights. A valet opens our doors for us, then whisks the Audi away. The night air is crisp and full of flavors: I can smell tomato, garlic, and the sharp tang of lime. Somewhere in the background, I can hear the Connecticut River whispering in its winter bed.

A burly, bearded man in a black suit is standing at the hostess's station when we walk in. As soon as he sees us, his would-be professional smile broadens into a thing of pure joy.

"Bella!" he exclaims, and comes gliding toward us. "As always, it is pleasure to see you." He kisses Abby's hand with imported suaveness, then turns his dazzling smile on me. "And this can only be Signorina Middlefield.

"May I?" he asks, and kisses my hand, too.

"I am honored that you have chosen to grace my humble establishment with your presence this evening," he tells me. "You are a goddess in my eyes. Nothing but the best for you and Signorina Abby tonight, I promise. If you desire anything, anything at all, you need only to ask your friend, Michelino."

"You're very kind," I reply, thoroughly embarrassed by his enthusiasm. "Thank you."

"Before I seat you," he goes on, "I have a favor to beg. You see on this wall—" He gestures at the panel behind the hostess' station. "—an assortment of photographs. I would very much like to add a picture of you to the collection."

I check out his rogue's gallery. Paul Newman is in it. So are two ex-governors and several senators. I must say: I'm impressed. And though I'd never admit this aloud, I'm more than a little flattered, too.

"If it'll make you happy, Michelino," I tell him, "get your camera. But Ab has to be in the picture, too."

Abby has absolutely no problem with that. Neither does Michelino. He fetches a clunky old Canon that's seen better days, then tells us to say 'pecorino'. Arm-in-arm, we do so. The flash leaves ghostly afterimages floating on my retinas.

"Perhaps the next time you are here, you could sign it," he says, as he returns the camera to its hiding place.

"It would be my pleasure," I say, although I'm sure my autograph won't mean diddly to him or anyone else in a couple of weeks.

He shows us to our table. It's in the back of the dining room, next to an oversized window. There are no other customers in the area. Fresh bread appears, as does a bottle of Barolo. As we sample these offerings, we admire the view. The river is just down the embankment from us. The moon's ashen winter reflection dances in place on its surface. It's a peaceful vista, very serene. For some reason, it reminds me of my mother. Guilty pangs pulse through me then like little cramps. I resent her for each one of them.

"Ever dive in a river?" Abby asks.

"Nah," I say, grateful for the distraction. "They're usually too murky. The closest I've come is a fresh water spring in Florida."

"See anything good?"

I nod. "Manatees. They're just about the ugliest of all God's creatures, but they sure are graceful underwater. And gentle? Hell, I was no more than two feet away from a mother and her calf, and she didn't even bat an eye at me. Try that with any other one-ton mammal and see what happens."

"No thanks," she says. "I'll leave the Wild Kingdom escapades to you." Then she returns to the menu in her hand and asks, "So what are you going to order?"

"I think I'll start with oysters on the half-shell, then move on to a primavera salad and the rack of lamb."

"I'm leaning toward the osso bucco, it's terrific here." A moment later, she adds, "But the duck is awfully tempting, too."

Michelino himself appears at our table to take our order. Abby flirts with him in fluent Italian. As she does so, my gaze wanders across the dining room—and slams right into another of God's ugliest creatures. Fenton Davenport! He's standing at the hostess's station, studying a menu. His appearance can't possibly be a coincidence. He's all alone, and much too casually dressed for a place like this. Indeed, as I'm staring daggers at him, the sleek, black-gowned hostess hands him a pre-tied necktie. I grind my teeth against an urge to curse. It's getting so I can't even take a shit without that man cropping up.

"Is there a problem, Signorina?" Michelino asks me.

My first impulse is to deny it. Davenport's my problem, my plague, my goddam albatross. And I've been taking care of myself for a long time now. But I don't want to handle that little weasel tonight. I'm sick and tired of seeing him in the rear-view mirror. So I swallow my pride with a silent what-the-hell, and give Michelino the lowdown.

"See that man over there?" I say, discreetly pointing to Davenport. He's slipping the tie over his head now. I wish it were a noose. "He's a tabloid reporter. And at the moment, I'm his favorite target."

"I'll have him thrown out immediately," Michelino promises, and starts to crook a finger at the muscle-bound giant who's tending the bar.

It's a grand idea. Inspiring, in fact. All it needs is a tiny twist.

"No, wait," I say. "Let's give him a chance. Just seat him at an out-of-the-way table where he can't see or hear us. If he minds his manners and leaves us alone, fine, we'll all have a nice dinner and you'll make money on him. But if he so much as pokes his nose in our direction, feel free to see him to the door in spectacular fashion."

A sly grin slices across Michelino's face, giving him a wolfish aspect. "You are indeed a goddess, Signorina. Excuse me while I see to the arrangements."

"Oh, and one more thing," I add, as he turns to go. "No matter which way this thing goes, please tell your valet that I'll give him ten bucks to put a potato in that man's exhaust pipe."

"That won't be necessary, dear lady," Michelino says in parting. "I'll do the job myself for free."

Ab and I exchange a grin. She looks like a cat with a mouthful of brown feathers. I feel like a cross between King Solomon and a Huntsman spider.

"You know there's no way he's going to leave us alone," she says.

"I know," I say. "I'm counting on it. Care to bet on when he'll make his move?"

She predicts that he'll wait until we're halfway through our main courses. I say he won't be able to restrain himself that long. As it happens, though, we're both wrong. The moment arrives at the end of the night, while we're lingering over double espressos and tiramisu. It starts with a warning rumble from Michelino.

"You don't understand," we hear Davenport protest then. "She's an old friend of mine."

Michelino rumbles again. The bartender leaves his post at a leisurely pace. At the same time, a mountain of a man in a white chef's hat emerges from the kitchen.

"This is outrageous!" our roving reporter says. "I demand to see the manager."

"I'm the owner, you fool!"

We turn and stare—just like everybody else in the room. The bartender and the sous chef are now bulldogging a thoroughly red-faced Davenport toward the door while Michelino hovers on their heels, ranting in raucous Italian. And—the hostess is standing ready at her station with the old Canon in hand. The flash goes off again and again and again—lightning to go with Michelino's thunder. I'm agog, aghast, and delighted all the way down to the tips of my toes. I can't remember the last time I enjoyed a floor-show so much.

"And don't come back," Michelino booms, as his men sling Fenton out into the cold like a sack of rancid grain. "If you ever set foot in here again, I'll have you arrested for trespassing."

Moments later, our perfectly composed host saunters over to our table with the dignity of an affronted cat. "So," he says. "How was that?"

"Wonderful," I reply, embracing him with a smile. "Absolutely wonderful." A heartbeat later, I add, "I hope you got his money before you turfed him, though."

He disdains Davenport with a sniff. "I didn't lose much on that one. Can you imagine? All he ordered was spaghetti and coffee. Not even a glass of wine. Feh! The man has no soul."

"I'll pick up his tab, such as it is," I say. "And I'll pay anything you want for a set of those pictures."

"You shall have it, Signorina Middlefield," he vows, and then orders us all a glass of vintage port to consummate the deal. While we're waiting for it to arrive, he and Abby flirt with each in Italian, and I sit back to enjoy the view. The moon is still dancing on the river. The stars sparkle just like they do at sea. A voice in my head says, *you could get used to this*. And I do not disagree.

CHAPTER 7

The smells of frying eggs and bacon seep into my dreams. A moment later, my father makes an appearance, too. He's been to the mailbox to collect the morning paper. His cheeks are flushed from the cold. As he heads for the breakfast table, he gives his wife a peck on the cheek in passing. She's hovering over the stove with a spatula in hand, but she's not really paying much attention to what's cooking there. She's off in her own little world; and it must be quite a place because she goes there a lot. Maybe that's because she hit the big four-oh recently, and life with two teenagers and an emotionally detached man isn't what she thought it would be. She would like to have a job, perhaps something community-oriented, but she isn't qualified to do much. Besides, her husband wants her to stay at home, even when nobody else is there. She doesn't argue the point. That's not her style. Instead, she tunes out. Or in. Or maybe sideways. She can do it anywhere, anytime: at the supermarket; in the garden; while her only daughter is trying to talk to her. A person who didn't know better might think that she was stoned. She's not, leastwise not in any familiar sense of the word. For whatever reason, she's just *not there*.

Jay comes strolling into the room, downy-faced and ready for school. In an age where long hair and bell-bottoms rule, he's wearing a button-down shirt, straight-legged denims, and a fresh crew cut.

He filches a blackened twist of bacon from the frying pan as he greets Mom, then joins Dad at the table. As they trade sections of the paper, Mom flips the eggs and butters the burnt toast. Conversation is limited, news-related: Nixon is a crook, the Russians are insane, the Celtics look good this year. Then Dad glances at his wristwatch and calls my name. I answer the summons in a hurry, like a good daughter should, shuffle-shuffle-shuffling into the kitchen in my disheveled pajamas. Although my eyelids are still mostly swollen shut from sleep, I can see something is wrong. Dad is turning the eggs now; and Mom is nowhere in sight.

"Good Lord, Raven," Sally says, "the very least you could've done was put a robe on. What if somebody you didn't know was here?"

"What would somebody I didn't know be doing here at this hour?" I say, growling because I can't stand being nagged the first thing in the morning. "Besides, I thought this was a dream." I scuff my way over to the stove and rest my chin on Jay's shoulder. In a gentler tone, I add, "I thought you were Dad."

"Sorry," he says, flashing me a complicated half-smile.

"Don't be."

I'm eyeballing the contents of his frying pan now. The bacon is on the rubbery side, just the way I like it, and the eggs are runny-side-up. Happily, there seems to be enough for everyone. "What's the occasion—your stove on the fritz?"

"Nah," he says. "We just felt like spending a little time over here with you before we went to pick Mom up."

Is that today? Mercy, how the time does fly.

It's been a week since that itty-bitty blood clot lodged itself in Mom's gray matter, and Dr. Kay says she's making great progress. She's finally starting to *look* better. The two halves of her face are almost entirely back in phase with each other now. She can sit up in her bed without help, too. But she can't manage more than a few faltering steps yet, not even when she's clinging to a walker, and while she can talk, all that comes out of her mouth is gibberish. Kay assures us that this, too, will pass, but I don't quite believe him. To my way of thinking, false hope is worse than none at all.

"She's scheduled to be discharged at eleven-thirty," Jay adds, as he relieves the frying pan of its contents. "Do you want to come along for the ride?"

"No thanks," I say, and then hasten to justify myself before he can turn the high-pressure hose on me. "The fewer people there are milling around her, the less chance there'll be of her getting overexcited."

"Hmm, good point. I never thought of that."

He hands me a plate heaped with eggs, bacon, and buttered toast. I head over to the table and take the seat to Sally's left. A moment later, Jay sits down across from me. To my surprise, he's neglected to bring a plate for his wife. I look in her direction. She's dunking a teabag into a mug and looking much aggrieved.

"None for you?" I ask.

"I'm trying to watch my weight over the holidays," she says, and then arches a holier-than-thou eyebrow at my heart-attack special. "You ought to be more careful with your diet, too. All the fat on that plate is going to go straight to your hips."

"A little extra blubber will keep me warm in the water," I say, then tear into my breakfast. And I do mean *tear*. A slapdash sandwich of bacon and egg disappears in a half-dozen ravening bites. The other egg goes down in two. I wipe up the leftover yolk with crusts of toast, and then wash it all down with a gulp of sugared coffee.

"Jay-bird," I croon then, "you are one helluva cook."

He and Sal are staring at me like I'm an accident on the freeway. His plate is all but untouched; her teabag is still steeping in its mug. Only then does it occur to me how I must look—me with my wildly uncombed hair and 'Get Stuffed' nightshirt hunched over a spit-shiny dish with both elbows on the table. *Here be troll.*

"Oops," I say sheepishly, and then slowly draw myself up into a more civilized position. "Sorry about that." As I scrub the corners of my yolk-smeared mouth with a napkin, I try to explain. "We don't get much time for breakfast on the boat. There's too much work to do, and only so many hours of daylight to get it all done. So as you may have noticed, I've fallen into the habit of inhaling my brekkie." I think of Hans, who eats with his dive-knife, and Raymond, the juniormost camera-man who seldom bothers with flatware at all, then add, "Dining day-in and day-out with a bunch of dedicated bachelors doesn't help matters, either."

"I don't know how you can live like that," Sally says. "It sounds worse than a college dormitory."

"It's not all that bad. Really," I insist, as she lobs me a skeptical look. "I get a cabin of my own and plenty to eat. And getting paid to do a job that I love is more than adequate compensation for the few inconveniences that I have to endure."

She affects a delicate shudder. "I wouldn't have your job for all the money in the world. Salt water leaves my skin scratchy. And I get sick just thinking about that gooey, green crud on the bottom. When the girls want to go to the beach, I make Jay take them."

I know it's pointless to argue with her. When she makes up her little mind about a thing, no force on earth can bring her around. But I can't hold myself back. This is the love of my life we're talking about here.

"You simply can't compare wading along a shoreline to swimming in an ocean," I say. "Depending on where you are, the floor can be sandy, or crusted over with coral, or forested with kelp. There aren't any waves down there, just currents that whisk you along like Peter Pan in a wind. You fly, you float, you frolic with the fish. And if you're really, really lucky, you come face to face with something that very few of your fellow human beings will ever see first-hand. I'm telling you, it's like being in a whole 'nother world."

"I like *this* world just fine, thank you," she says, as she nibbles mouse-like at the strip of bacon that she filched from Jay's plate. "And you probably would, too, if you'd just give it half a chance. There's plenty of stuff to photograph here, especially in the fall, and you could do some studio work, too. Everyone who sees them adores the pictures that you took of the girls the last time you were home."

Like I really want to spend the rest of my days snapping pictures of antsy kids and lap-dogs, right?

I can see it, though: a studio in the back of the barn, me scheduling appointments around my chores. It won't be exciting, but it will keep me sane, and maybe I'll get to see more of my nieces. I'll teach them how to use a camera and handle film. When they're a little older, I'll let them into the darkroom, too, and show them how to develop their photos. Meanwhile, Mom will get better, and I'll keep her that way. I can do this, I tell myself. I can, and I will.

Suddenly restless, I excuse myself from the table and start collecting dirty dishes. There's no dishwasher in the house, so I fill the porcelain sink with hot, soapy water and go to work.

"You should do the plates first," Sal advises, even as I dunk the greasy frying pan beneath the suds. "The water will stay cleaner that way."

I'm in no mood for housekeeping tips at the moment, so I ignore her. Never one to take a hint, she grabs a dish towel and starts to dry.

"You should use hotter water for rinsing," she tells me. "You know, to sterilize any germs."

"I've been washing dishes for twenty years now," I say. "And so far, nobody's keeled over from food poisoning."

"Not yet anyway," she says. A moment later, she makes another scornful sound and shoves a pair of forks under my nose. One has a bit of egg-yolk stuck between two tines; the other seems perfectly fine. "You have to do more than swish them around in the water, you know."

I roll my eyes, then give the stupid forks another swish and throw them back into the drying rack.

"Now I know why you're not married yet," she says. "No man would want such a lousy housekeeper."

The resentment that's been building within me suddenly bursts its banks. "Like that's all that's standing between me and wedded bliss. Right, Sal?" I sneer. "Like I've had dozens of relationships that could have amounted to something if only I had taken a sponge to the forks instead of swishing them! Did it ever occur to you that I might not want to be married?"

I yank the stopper out of the sink with a gesture that could double as a Sicilian obscenity. The water drains away with a lurid slurp, leaving a ring of greasy soap scum behind. I do not clean it up.

"I'm going to take a shower," I inform Sal then, biting each word off at the knees. "Would you like to tag along and comment on my technique?"

Cheeks flushed, she backs away. I storm off toward the bathroom like a hurricane in search of dry land.

After I all but run the hot water heater dry, I retreat to my bedroom and shut the door with enough force to let my brother and his brainless wife know that I want it to stay that way. I'm in such a foul mood, I'm sure I could spit blood and fire if I tried.

To be fair, it's not just Sally's fault. Everybody seems to be on my case for one thing or another these days.

The biggest offender by far is McNalley. I got a special-delivery from one of his toadies yesterday—an 'invitation' to attend a New Year's Eve banquet being held in the bastard's honor. No RSVP, no permission to bring a date, just a handwritten *See You There* with an elephantine 'or else' lurking between the lines. The length and breadth of that man's arrogance infuriates me. How dare he assume that I'll roll over and play Dixie for him like some SeaWorld sea lion? He may have me by the air-hose now, but I can go a long time without a breath. And I'll take in water and drown before I climb aboard his friggin' ship.

But McNalley isn't the only sleaze-bag who wants a piece of me. The growing heap of mail and messages on my dresser is full of can-you's, would-you's and how-about-it's. Like: some guy from *Hard Copy* wants to buy the exclusive TV rights to my story—and do I happen to have any footage of myself in a bikini? And: some writer from Manhattan wants to talk to me about turning these last two weeks into an off-Broadway play. Laura Lacey is still pestering me to appear on her show, too. I throw those scraps of paper into the circular file, then begin to sift through the rest of the over-the-transom stuff. Most of it is benign: fan-mail, a few bills, a Christmas postcard from Hans that's written in German. Then I come to a message from Bailey's Surplus Supplies: the blankets that Mom ordered are in. I don't know why she wanted them because the barn is already well-stocked, but mine is not to wonder why, so I add a drive into H-C to my to-do list. The next message is from Abby—feel like going shopping tonight? She must be out of her mind. That goes on the can-wait list. Then I come to another message from Laura Lacey. I'll give her one thing: she's persistent. I start to crunch the message up only to smooth it back open when an unlikely word chances to catch my eye. After that, I can't help but read the entire note.

Any Comment On The Lawsuit?

The next thing I know, there's a telephone receiver in my fist and I'm on hold for Ms. Lacey. As soon as she picks up, I get right to the point.

"What lawsuit?"

A brief silence occupies our connection—her trying to decide what tone to take with me. Then she clears her throat and says, "Raven. Hi. How good of you to call back. Do you mean to tell me you haven't been served with the papers yet?"

"You catch on quick, Laura. Now do me a favor and tell me this is all about before I wind up in the stroke ward next to my mom."

"Well—" I can almost see her battening down the hatches for a big blow. "It's like this. Clara and Willy Dupree are filing a civil suit against you for the wrongful death of their son. They're asking for three million dollars."

"Wha—?" The world flashes red. "Are they insane? I don't have that kind of money."

"Your mother does," Laura points out, in a muted tone. "And according to some sources, she isn't long for this world."

"She's coming home today, dammit!" I roar, furious with her and that rat-faced bottom-feeder Davenport for daring to suggest otherwise. "She's going to be fine. And even if I inherited all of her money tomorrow, I'd sooner go to hell than give the Duprees a dime of it. Their son wasn't worth a gob on spit on a hot sidewalk."

"I know how you feel," Laura says. "But the Duprees don't see it that way. And they might just have that video on their side."

"I'm sick to death of hearing about that video," I say. "I'm sick of hearing about Dupree, too. I was his victim before he was mine."

"Maybe you need to remind the people of that. Maybe you need to tell them your side of the story." She pauses for a moment, then adds, "I can give you that chance."

I'm so pissed off, I don't even stop to think if this is a good idea or not. All I want to do is eat somebody alive. "When?"

A quick, satisfied intake of air scours the line. "How about this Friday? I know it's short notice, but—"

"The sooner, the better," I tell her. "Just tell me where I have to be, and when."

She starts to rattle off a string of instructions, then stops herself and says, "Never mind, I'll just Fed-Ex you a letter with all the details in it."

"Fine," I say. "See you Friday."

As I bang the phone back into its cradle, I hear a knock at the door. A moment later, it swings slowly open, and Jay pokes his head into the room like he's half-afraid he's going to get it bitten off.

"We're going to go and get Mom now," he says. "Is there anything I should know before we take off?"

Which is his way of telling me that he heard me shouting in here. I gladly treat him to a full volume encore.

"Can you believe it? Dupree's parents are slapping me with a wrongful death lawsuit! They're after Mom's money." I take a swipe at the air, wishing that I were swinging at Ma and Pa Dupree instead. "Assholes! Stupid, money-grubbing hillbillies." I take a deep, shuddering breath to still the threat of tears in my eyes, then add, "Christ, Jay! When's it going to end?"

"I wish I knew, Rave," he replies in a tired voice, and then gathers me into a rare embrace. "I wish I knew."

"I'm not sitting still for this one, though," I say, promising him or perhaps myself. "I'm going on 'Wake Up, Connecticut!' to tell my half of the story."

He groans, an almost involuntary sound of disappointment and reproach. Before he can elaborate on that sound, though, his wife pipes up from out of the blue.

"Are you, really?"

I slip out of Jay's embrace to look at her. She's got her coat and gloves on, so I figure she came in to haul Jay out of here by the ear, but at the moment, she doesn't look like she's in any hurry to go anywhere. Her eyes are shiny. Her expression is one of adolescent jealousy.

"You betcha."

"You are so lucky," she says. "Laura Lacey is wonderful. I'd love to be on her show."

I gape at her for a moment, amazed because she can't see the friggin' ocean for the fish. I mean, here I am, practically *forced* to go on the air to defend myself for killing a man, and she thinks I'm lucky. Oddly enough, though, I don't get mad at her. In fact, all I feel is pity. It makes me more generous with her than I might've been otherwise.

"I'm booked for Friday," I tell her. "You're welcome to tag along as long as you don't mind hanging out in the studio audience."

"Mind?" Her tone is incredulous. She turns to Jay with a plea in her eyes. "Is that OK with you?"

He shrugs. "It's entirely up to you, Sal. I'm off till the new year, so I can take the kids to school if you want to go."

A smile lights up her face like a sunrise. It brings out a beauty in her that I didn't know she had. "I'd love to come. If you want, we can take the Explorer. You can sleep while I drive."

"Whatever. Just be on time."

"No problem," she says, and then goes floating out of the room on a cloud of her own making. Although Jay ought to be going, too, he stays put. There's an unusual glint in his eyes.

"That was a nice thing to do, Rave," he says, in a quiet voice. "I know she tends to rub you the wrong way."

"Yeah, well." For some reason, his gratitude embarrasses me. "What can I say? It's Christmas. You're welcome to tag along, too, if you want."

"No, thanks." He pauses, and the glint in his eyes takes a solemn turn. "Just do me one favor, OK?" I cock an eyebrow at him, wondering what's up. He says, "Don't mention the lawsuit to Mom. She's got enough to deal with as it is."

Like I don't, right? But I don't say that aloud, I just shrug and say, "Whatever." As he relaxes, I add, "You'd better get going now. She'll be expecting you."

"OK. See you when I get back."

As soon as he's gone, I sink down onto my bed. The fury that had me throwing off sparks is gone now; its passing has left me drained. I would love to curl up and nap the rest of this miserable day away, but I can't because Mom's coming home and I still have work to do. So I reach for some instant energy: the two-pound box of chocolates that's sitting on my nightstand. It came four days ago, by special delivery. The note that came with it said: *Still Thinking Of You.* Now,

I know I ought to call Junior and tell him to quit playing these dopey, school-boy games. It's on my to-do short list, along with buying a moisturizer for my face and calling my boss, Marcos, to let him know that I'm retiring. But I'm in no mood to drop a bomb on either of those unsuspecting souls at the moment, so I pop a chocolate into my mouth and set off for the barn instead.

Just as I'm stepping out of my room, Mattie steps out of Jay's. She lets out a little yelp upon seeing me, then grins with relief and pats the place over her heart.

"Lord have mercy," she says. "You nearly scared me out of my skin. I thought I had the house to myself."

"I'm sorry," I say, grinning simply because she's so cute. With her tiny ears and nappy, close-cropped hair, she reminds me of a fieldmouse that's been caught out in the open. Then I notice the baggy half-moons under her eyes, and am reminded of something completely different. "It's been a rather rocky Christmas so far, hasn't it?"

"She's alive and on her way home," she tells me. "That's all that matters."

Easy for you to say, I think.

Even as the thought crosses my mind, she grabs me by the arm and hauls me into Jay's old room. It's brimming with flowers now, and the hospital bed that we've rented has been made up with a bright patchwork quilt.

"How's it look?" she asks.

"It's perfect, Mattie," I assure her. "Just perfect."

"I've got the door to the stairwell unlocked now," she goes on, "so don't fret if you hear footsteps late at night. It'll just be me coming down to check on her."

"Gotcha." My gaze drifts back to those circles beneath her eyes, and while I'm not much good at taking care of other people, I feel the urge to do so now. "It's going to take Jay at least an hour to bring Mom all the way back from the hospital. Why don't you use that time to catch a nap?"

The lines in her careworn face gather themselves into a stubborn refusal. "Oh, no. I couldn't do that. There's still the barn to take care of—"

"I was just on my way to do that," I tell her.

"—and dinner to get ready," she goes on.

"I can do that, too."

She snorts, a derisive sound. "The hell you can. You don't know paprika from pickling spice." Which is true, I'm ashamed to say. "Besides, I'm making all of Robin's favorites tonight, and the recipes are all in my head."

Mattie can be scrappier than a Jack Russell terrier when she's cornered, so I concede the issue without a fight in the hope that she'll make a few concessions in turn. "OK, OK," I tell her. "Dinner's in your capable hands. But won't you at least sit down while you're slicing and dicing?"

"Well, of course I will, you silly girl," she says. "I'm getting old, not stupid." As I stare at her, confounded by such cussedness, she laughs and throws her arms around my hips. "Oh, Raven, you're such a dear. I'm so glad you're home."

At that moment, so am I.

We go our separate ways: her to the kitchen and me to the great outdoors. It's colder today, maybe twenty-five degrees, and overcast. Although there's work waiting for me in the barn, I'm drawn into the six acre lot of oak and pine trees beyond it. These woods were a favorite haunt of mine in the old days. Abby and I used to come up here to smoke cigarettes on the sly and share our deepest, darkest secrets. One time in particular springs to mind. We were in the last few throes of eleventh grade, and Abby had just lost her virginity the night before to a jock by the name of Brett Williams. She was quite clinical about the details: the way the car's seat felt on her bare back; the heavy, sweet smell of rum on Brett's breath; that first, blind thrust; the tiny, tearing pain of penetration; seventy seconds of frantic pumping and then his heavy limpness on top of her. I was so repelled by what she told me, I swore that I'd *never* have sex. And as it happened, I kept that vow until I was twenty-three, and learning all sorts of ropes from a French photographer by the name of Francois. He wore a beret and Speedos, and very little else. He ate croissants in bed. I shake my head at the memory of that Burgundy-mouthed pirate. I thought I loved him. He taught me otherwise. We were both better off for the lesson.

The ground here is covered with leaves: gold, rust-red, brown. I wade through the deepest pockets I can find just to hear the dry, friendly rustle. I like trees, especially old, gnarled oaks. They remind me of retired prizefighters who know they have nothing left to prove. If Mr. Benedict from the high school Shutter-Bug Club hadn't turned me on to the idea of a career in underwater photography, I might have become a forest ranger. So when that first, faint whiff of smoke tweaks my nose, it triggers an immediate reaction. I suck in a breath, meaning to sound the alarm, but before I can shape the air into a sound, recognition kicks in. That's not woodsmoke I'm smelling. It's marijuana.

Thank God. The air in my lungs leaves me as a sigh.

My relief, however, is quickly ousted, overthrown by an alliance of curiosity and territorial defensiveness. Who the hell is smoking dope on my mother's property? I start to track the skunky smell. It leads me to a well-worn path that's too broad and straight to have been made strictly by deer. I follow that *and* the smoke to a cozy little hollow in the back forty. Three teenagers are quietly partying away at the bottom of that basin. Much to my surprise, I know all of them. Two are Hobsons—Joey and Mike, the boys from Green's Market. The third is Mattie's son.

"Aren't you guys supposed to be in school?" I boom, and then step boldly into view. Three heads swivel my way, jaws agape. The Hobson boys are poised to bolt. I chuckle at their panicked expressions, then say, "Psych."

"Raven," Dex says, giving my name a nervous little flutter. "What are you doing here?"

"Just checking on the property," I say, as I saunter toward him. "And I have to admit, I'm not crazy about what I'm seeing here."

He swallows hard, a guilty man's gulp, but his presence here doesn't concern me half as much as all the garbage does. It's everywhere: beer cans, broken glass, cigarette packs, even a few empty condom wrappers. Disbelief rockets through me. The younger denizens of H-C are turning my backyard into the next Hell's Last Acre.

You never think these things are going to happen to you.

"This is too fuckin' cool," Mike, the older Hobson says, as I join their little group. "We're, like, partying with a celebrity." He beams at me for a moment, radiating adolescent relish and semi-stoned awe, and then adds, "Oh, and by the way, thanks for saving our lives that night."

His cousin Joey seconds that with a "Yeah," and then offers me the joint that's been smoldering between his fingertips. "Want some?"

To tell the truth, I wouldn't mind copping a little buzz. It seems like ages since I've felt warm and tingly inside. But ever since Fenton Davenport took that photograph of me sleeping in a chair next to Mom's hospital bed—the one whose caption read, *Waiting For Mom's Money?*—I've become paranoid. I can just imagine the little weasel popping up out of nowhere just as I'm taking a hit. I also can imagine his next headline: *Dupree's Killer A Junkie!* So I refuse Joey with a photogenic shake of my head.

"That's cool." He takes a hit for himself, then passes the joint on. As he holds the smoke in his lungs, he croaks, "You were totally awesome that night, you know. I mean, you took that dude out just like Bruce Lee."

"No, sir," Mike says. "Bruce Lee would've never gone for the guy's nuts. That's more of a Steven Seagal move."

"No way, shit-for-brains."

"Yes way, maggot-boy."

"Let's just drop the subject, OK, guys?" I say. "I'm a little tired of it these days."

"Sure, Raven," Mike says instantly. "Anything you say."

But Joey starts to giggle.

"Did I say something funny?" I ask him, with a warning in my tone.

"No," he says, trying to hold his mirth in his lungs like it's a breath of marijuana smoke. "It's just that—" He looks at me and loses it again. "—I know someone who likes you."

I roll my eyes heavenward. Great. Just great. These boneheads spend half their lives at Green's. God only knows what they've heard Junior say.

"Good for you," I say, forcing the words past a too-taut smile. "Now why don't you and Mike go and tell him hello for me? I'd like to spend some time with my friend Dex here."

"Sure, Raven," Mike says. "Anything you say." Then he grabs his still-twittering cousin by the coat-sleeve and hauls him away. As they climb their way out of the hollow, I hear him hiss, "Shut the fuck up, dickhead. Do you want her to kick the shit out of you, too?"

Joey just keeps on laughing.

I turn to Dexter, who still hasn't looked me in the eye. He's scrunched up in his jacket like a sullen box-turtle. His hands are jammed in his coat pockets. He's obviously embarrassed, but I don't know if that's because of me or his friends. I tap a cigarette out of the pack that I'm carrying with me these days, then offer it to him. Maybe he thinks it's a test. Maybe it is. At any rate, he makes no move to take it. I shrug, then light up. The first drag feels good going down.

"So," I say. "What's up with you?"

All at once, the logjam within him breaks, and he begins to babble. "I didn't skip the whole day, Raven, just the two periods after lunch, and they're both study halls. You won't tell Mom, will you? She'll kill me if she finds out."

An image flashes through my head: Mattie flinging Dex to the floor and kicking his liver into school-boy pate. I take another drag from my cigarette. This one almost chokes me.

"Those boneheads aren't leading you astray, are they?" I ask, glancing toward the place where we last saw Laughing Boy and Mike.

His nervous, eager-to-please expression hardens on me. "Those boneheads are my friends, Raven. I won't have you dissing them."

"But I didn't—"

He doesn't let me finish, which is OK, because I'm not sure what I was going to say anyway.

"The big joke around school is—what's a six letter word for trash? Hobson. Even the teachers think it's funny. But you know what? As punky as Mike and Joey might be, they have more class than most of the people who are making fun of them. Like—they don't smile to my face and call me nigger when I'm not looking. They don't treat me like some kind of a freak-show, either. To them, I'm just this guy."

I'm glad to hear that, I really am. But that joke about the Hobsons has been around for a long time now; and like Dex said, they are, with one or two exceptions, a shifty lot. So he can just sue me if I press the issue.

"Good friends are special," I tell him. "I should know, I have a few of my own. But sometimes they can talk you into doing things that go against your better judgment—like skipping classes to get stoned in the woods. If you let them sway you that way too many times, you'll wind up doing chores at Angelhaven for the rest of your life."

A grin slices its way across his face. It makes me feel like my fly is down.

"What's so funny?" I ask.

"Nothing," he says. "It's just that you sounded like your brother just then."

"Hey, now! There's no need to get nasty."

But he's right, and we both know it. All I can do now is laugh along with him. He snickers a bit harder than I do, but I forgive him because he's young and stoned.

"Seriously, Dex," I say, as our mirth tails off. "I'd hate to see you get sucked into the wrong kind of action here."

"It's OK, Rave," he says. "I know what I'm doing. Honest. I don't cut classes very often. And I've made high honors every semester. I'm going to college."

I hear real conviction in his voice, so I let him off my hook. "OK, lecture's over. I've got to get back to the house and do some work before Mom gets home. And just so you know, your secret's safe with me."

"Thanks."

I take one last drag from my cigarette, then grind the butt out beneath my heel. As I do so, I notice the mess of other casually discarded filter-tips and remember my earlier snit.

"One more thing," I say, slipping back into an authoritative tone. He pays me back by slipping back into sullen teenager mode. "If you and your pals want to continue partying on this property, you're going to have to start cleaning up after yourselves. I'll put a barrel out here for you. It'll be your job to make sure it gets used—and emptied. Let everyone know that I'll shut this place down the next time I find it trashed.

"Does that sound unreasonable?"

"No," he says. He doesn't look exactly thrilled, but at least he's not trying to bore holes into my skull with his eyes anymore. "Not really."

"Glad to hear it," I say, and then huddle deeper into my jacket. "Now let's hit the road. I think I can get you into the house without your mom knowing it."

"I don't think she'd notice if I walked right past her," he says, as we start the hike homeward. "Everything's Robin, Robin, Robin these days."

"She's been worried," I say. Which is not, I know, a valid excuse to the teenaged mindset. But really, what else am I supposed to say? "I'm sure she'll be back to her old self once Mom's home again."

We walk in silence for a while. I'm thinking about Mom and how it's going to be when she's home: nice, I hope, but I can't quite believe it. We've never had much to do with each other. She prefers her own private swimming hole to the public pool, and I—well, I've learned to keep to myself. I don't know if one itty-bitty stroke can change all that. My stomach is achy; my palms, cold. Maybe I'm afraid she won't want me to stay. Maybe I'm afraid she will. It's all so very confusing.

"I got your postcards from Australia," Dex says. "Did you really dive with great white sharks?"

"You betcha. We shot a whole segment on them."

"Was it scary?"

"Yeah, sure."

"What was the scariest moment you ever had?"

Now, I know this is only a man-child's fascination with danger talking, but it bums me out just the same. Dex knows the scariest moment I ever had. He saw it on the tube along with the rest of the world. I don't tell him about the feel of gun-metal against my temple and the waxy smell of Junior's sweat, though. I go with something lighter—for both of our sakes.

"Well," I say, "that would have to be the time when me and my friend, Hans, got a little turned around during a dive and wound up coming up maybe a hundred yards from the boat. We were hanging out on the surface—you know, just catching our breath and little sun—when all of a sudden, this big ol' shark fin popped out of the water and came cruising toward us. Me, I dropped my camera and started swimming for all I was worth. But Hans stayed right where he was. 'Are you crazy?' he shouted. 'You can't outswim a shark!' 'I know', I shouted back. 'But all I have to do is outswim you.'"

I break into a big, 'Gotcha' grin at that. He gapes at me like he can't believe I just did that to him, then shakes his head and chuckles.

"You really had me going there," he says.

"Sorry," I say, "but I couldn't resist. You gave me a perfect lead-in."

We're out of the woods now, and heading toward the barn. "Want some help in there?" Dexter asks, as I ease a side door open.

"Nah," I say, and then glance over my shoulder at the house, "I can manage. Go and do your homework. You're going to college, remember?"

He tosses me a grin, then disappears. I get to work.

Angelhaven slept eight last night: the Cartwright family plus three college guys who spent all but their last ten dollars on a new fan-belt for their van. I start with their roomlets, because they're back on the road already, homeward-bound for the holidays. The only things they left behind are a trio of dirty coffee mugs and the receipt from the auto-parts store. I pick up after them, then break down their cots. As I'm rolling up their sleeping bags, I hear the muffled crunch of snow-tires coasting over gravel. By the time I get to the barn door, Jay is already lifting Mom out of the Explorer. She looks like a little voodoo doll in his capable arms: stiff and crudely carved, yet fragile. He sets her in the wheelchair that she'll have to use until she recovers her strength. An instant later, Mattie is all over her—laughing and hugging and crying glad tears. I'm touched by the sight, but abashed as well, because my eyes are as dry as old bones.

My family trundles into the house. I return to my chores, thinking that I'll give Mom a little time to get settled before I go and see her. She'll need a moment or two to get used to her surroundings again.

"'Bout time," Jay says, when I finally come in from the cold. He's hanging out in the kitchen, sampling the fixings for Mom's dinner. "I was beginning to think that you'd gone AWOL on us."

"I was putting the barn in order," I reply, as I shuck off my jacket. "You know she'd ask about it if she could."

His eyes narrow, as if he's trying to look through me. I wonder what he would see if he could. "Yeah, well. I guess we all have different notions about what's important to her."

Sal strides into the room. She's wearing her coat already, and is tugging on her gloves as she goes.

"Come on, Jay," she says, "let's get cracking. The kids will have to stand out in the cold if we're late." She looks up from her leather-encased hands then and smiles as she sets eyes on me. "There you are. We were beginning to wonder."

"So I've heard," I say.

"You haven't changed your mind about Friday, have you?"

"Not yet," I say, and then give my brother a clap on the shoulder. "I guess I'll go and see how Mom's doing. Are you coming back after you pick up the girls?"

"Maybe later," he tells me. "Those two can be a handful right after school, and I don't want them wearing Mom out on her first day home."

Meaning: he's had enough for now. Lucky bastard. Where am I supposed to go when I've had my fill?

I head for Mom's room only to stop at the door. Mattie is chattering away within, and she sounds so glad to have her old friend back, I cannot bring myself to intrude. So I duck into my bedroom and look around for something to keep me occupied while I'm biding the time. It's too late to call Marcos, too early to call Abby, and simply the wrong time to call Junior. Out of sheer, restless boredom, I start to unpack. It's been almost two weeks since I blew into town, but my clothes have yet to see the inside of a dresser or closet. Sal would be appalled. I take great pleasure in the thought.

As I'm hanging up a blouse that formerly festooned the doorknob, I spot a large cardboard box filled with old photographs on the floor in the back of the closet. Just for the hell of it, I bring it out and pick a picture at random. As it happens, it's of Dad. I took it with a Kodak Instamatic: the first camera I ever owned. My hands weren't very steady back in those days, so the background is a bit fuzzy, but Martin Middlefield came out OK. He's standing in front of his then-new Plymouth with his arms folded across his chest. His mouth is slightly crimped at one corner. That's as close to a smile as he ever got—for the camera or otherwise.

I don't know why he was like that. He wasn't what you'd call an unhappy man, and his life never seemed that hard. Or maybe I should say that it seemed no harder than that of any other middle-class family man. He went to work in the mornings and returned at night. He took out the trash on Tuesday, went to the YMCA to swim on Thursday, and mowed the lawn on Saturday. He had a shining star of a son; and if there was less to brag about where his girl was concerned, at least he could say that she was good at keeping her head above water. Maybe his old-world father had tauht him that smiling was a sin, or a show of weakness. Maybe he was ashamed of his slightly crooked front teeth. Or maybe, just maybe, he came into this world without a smile in him.

Poor Dad.

I toss the snapshot back in the box and dig out another. This one's of me in a string bikini, hamming it up for Francois. My hair was still long and straight back then. I look much younger than I remember feeling at the time. But my ex-lover got the lighting just right.

I'm about to dip into the carton yet again when Matt's voice filters into my room. "I have to go and take care of dinner now, Rob, but don't you fret. I'll be back. And if you want anything while I'm gone, just ring that bell."

Now I have no excuse. My mother's alone. So am I. I stand up, then catch the box as it bounces off the mattress after me. All at once, it dawns on me: this is something Mom and I can do together. The right picture might even jog her into remembering how to speak. So I tuck the box under my arm and go across the hallway. I knock before I enter the room, but there is no response.

I find her sitting up in bed, swaddled in Mattie's sunny quilt. She looks good, just a hair out of focus. She smiles when she sees me and makes a croaking sound. Although I have no way of knowing for sure, it pleases me to think that she's trying to say my name.

"Hello, Mom," I say, donning my best sickroom smile. "I would've come sooner, but I thought you'd like some time with Mattie."

She croaks again, then reddens in the face with what I hope and pray is only frustration.

"Please, Mom, don't try to force it. It'll come in its own time."

She glowers at me for a moment, then pitches a resigned sigh and settles down again. To my immense relief, her color subsides. I walk over and sit down in the chair that's next to her bed. The cushion is still warm from Mattie.

"Angelhaven is doing OK," I tell her. "The extra latrines have been installed, and I'm going to pick up the blankets you ordered this afternoon."

She nods approvingly. It's amazing how good that tiny gesture makes me feel.

"The place isn't the same without you, though," I go on. "The Cartwrights ask after you every day."

She nods again; and just like that, I run out of things to say. I look at her for a moment, waiting for I don't know what, then abruptly reach for the box.

"I brought some old photos with me," I tell her, as if she can't see that for herself. "I thought we might have a look at them." I drag my chair closer, then draw a picture out of the box at random. "Remember this?"

It's a grainy black-and-white of her in her garden. I have no idea who took it—it's way before my time. She's wearing a housedress and curlers; her apron is brimming with fresh-picked pea-pods. The look on her young face is one of distance and grudging surprise. I wonder who it was that snuck up on her that day—my dad? An earlier boyfriend? She doesn't seem too pleased to see whoever it is, but then, it's hard to tell.

Some things never change, I guess.

I take the photo away and replace it with another. She makes no move to stop me.

"Look," I urge her, "you took this one. See?" I point to a dark, fuzzy streak in the photo's upper corner. "That's your finger."

Dad, Jay, and I are clumped together beneath that fleshy smudge. The guys are wearing baggy swim-trunks; I'm clad in some frill-bottomed fright. I remember when this photo was taken—it was the day that Dad took me into the Atlantic Ocean for the first time. Mom stayed on the beach and did needlework until it was time to go home. I wonder if she has a thing about slimy ocean-floors like Sal does, and why it never occurred to me to ask until now.

I show her another picture, then another still. None of them provoke any reaction from her, so I set the carton down.

"Are you comfortable?" I ask. "Can I get you something? A drink of water? Or how 'bout a LifeSaver to sweeten your mouth?"

Although her expression remains composed, tears begin to roll from her eyes. Dr. Kay has told us about this, he says it's something she can't control. But it looks so weird, and so goddam deliberate, I'm tempted to reach out and shake her. I want to shout: What in hell do you want from me? And: What in God's name can I do?

Mom reaches for my hand. Startled by the movement, I shy away. And before I can rectify that mistake, Mattie's voice floats into the room with my name on its back. "I'm in here with Mom!" I call back.

A moment later, she snakes her head around the corner. Her face is still creased with worry and regret, but the bags beneath her eyes seem lighter. "I'm sorry to bother you, hon," she says, glancing from me to my mom and back again, "but there's someone at the door who says he has something for you. Another special delivery, I guess."

"Thanks, Mattie. I'll take care of it," I say, and then heave to my feet. On my way to the door, I brush my mom's arm with my fingertips. "This'll only take a minute," I tell her. "I'll be right back."

She waves me on like she's glad to see me go. Tears are still streaming down her cheeks. As I go trotting down the hallway, I thank God for getting me out of that room. I don't know how to act with her. I don't know what to *do*. I'd rather deal with Junior's love-sick antics, or even more of McNalley's bullshit.

As it happens, though, the man standing at the back door isn't bearing gifts from either of my not-so-secret admirers this time. This man is here with papers, the kind you get when you're being sued. I stare at them for a long, long time—until Mattie drags me back indoors.

"This ain't the tropics, babygirl," she scolds, as she rubs the heat back into my arms. "If you don't bundle up when you go outside, you'll catch your death of the cold."

I grumble at the thought. "Somebody would probably sue me for that, too."

Then I go to my room and sulk.

CHAPTER 8

Friday, six thirty-five a.m.: here I am, backstage at the Channel Four studio. My dressing room is on the chilly side, but it could be forty below and falling, and I wouldn't care. I've been waiting for this morning—waiting with clenched fists and gritted teeth for my shot at the Duprees. Money-grubbing trailer-trash. I'll bet they're swilling top-shelf moonshine for breakfast these days and cackling at how well Cliff provided for them in the end. This, when they're not kicking the dog or going through the neighbor's trash. Argh! Every time I think about their lawsuit, I bristle. If anything, it ought to be me suing them for raising such a scum. I mean to say as much when I'm on the air, too, even though Jay's lawyer-friend has advised me to hold my tongue. No way, can't do it. I'm on a mission from God.

I pop a last bite of complimentary danish into my mouth, and then wash it down with a swallow of lukewarm coffee. As soon as I set the mug down again, Sally rushes in to whisk a crumb from my lap. I try to be patient with her, but that's not easy at this point because she's been mommying me ever since we got into the car this morning.

"For God's sake, Sal," I say, "sit down already. You're making me crazy."

"I'm sorry," she says, looking wide-eyed and slightly nauseated. "It's just that I'm so terribly excited. I never dreamed that I'd actually be hanging out backstage at a Laura Lacey show some day."

"So make the most of it," I urge her. "Sit down, have a danish and coffee. Put your feet up on the furniture if you want to."

She glances at the tray of pastries on the coffee table, then nibbles on her lower lip. "I wish I could get away with eating like you do."

I flash her an exasperated, get-real look. "Do yourself a favor, Sally, and join an aerobics class. You'll lose more weight that way, and get to enjoy your food, too."

"Your brother doesn't believe in paying for exercise," she says. "He says taking care of a house and two kids ought to be enough of a work-out for any woman."

That sounds like something Dad would've said. I guess Jay is more of a chip off that old block than I had imagined. Which doesn't particularly thrill me. I mean, I loved my dad and all, but the plain truth is, he wasn't right for the part. If he hadn't died when he did, Mom probably would've divorced him as soon as Jay and I flew the coop. The thought makes me mad for all sorts of unnamed reasons.

"My brother isn't always right," I say. "In fact, he can blow more smoke than a three-alarm fire when it suits him. If you want to take an aerobics class, then go ahead and sign up for one. While you're at it, sign Jay up, too. He's getting a bit thick around the middle these days."

Sally's mouth rounds itself into a scandalized O which then flattens into a feline grin. "He says it's just winter fat. Like it's all going to melt away in the spring."

We snicker at that—me, because my brother would be mortified if he knew we were talking about his love-handles, and Sally for reasons she doesn't bother to disclose. Then a youngish woman with heaps of auburn curls and freckles pokes her head into the room. Her name is Beth, and she's tougher than she looks.

"Ten minutes till show-time, Ms. Middlefield," she says. "Do you remember what you need to do?"

I dutifully recite the instructions she drilled into me earlier. "As soon as I hear my name announced, I stroll onto the set and over to Laura. We shake hands and smile. Then I take a seat to her immediate right and be myself."

She flashes me the expressive equivalent of a pat on the head, then turns her gaze to Sal. "I'm going to need you to take a seat pretty soon, too, Mrs. Middlefield. Would you like me to show you where it is?"

"Thanks," Sal says, "but I think I can find front and center on my own. And don't worry," she adds, as Beth starts to draw herself up to her full, unyielding height, "I'll only be another minute or so. I promise."

"OK," Beth grudgingly concedes. "But if you're not out there when the show starts, you're going to have to watch it from back here. And believe me, that's not nearly as fun."

As soon as Beth withdraws, Sally shifts into hyper-fuss. First, she dusts nonexistent flakes of dandruff from my shoulder-tops. Then she picks at strands of my lacquered hair in an effort to make them stand just so. All the while, she chatters away like a squirrel on speed.

"Now don't forget, you're going to be on TV. Sit up straight and keep your legs crossed. Don't fiddle with your fingers or hair—that's very distracting. And don't swear. Ms. Lacey isn't one of your foul-mouthed sailor friends."

I bat her nit-picking fingers away, and then keep them at bay with a scowl. "You ought to start spending a little more time with people your own age, Sal. In the adult world, it's considered impolite to violate another person's personal space."

She laughs as if I've said something funny. "Oh, Raven, you and your personal space. We're family, for Pete's sake."

"Five minutes, Ms. Middlefield," a passing voice calls.

"Oops," Sal squeaks, "I guess I'd better go." She gives me one last once-over, then makes an excited, puppyish sound and hugs me. "Good luck. Break a leg. And remember," she adds, as she's heading out the door, "never look directly at the camera."

She disappears—Thank God. I feel like I've just done hard time in a wind-tunnel. But the funny thing is, now that she's gone, I'm suddenly nervous.

I check myself out in the room's big, backlit mirror. My hair looks great, thanks to Mitchell the Make-Up Man and his industrial-strength hairspray; and while my face is nothing fancy, it's still nicely tanned. Sal thinks I should've put on some eyeshadow and lipstick, but Abby's the glamour girl, not me. I'm happy with one coat of mascara for the lashes and a pat of cornstarch to keep the shine down. I must admit, though, I did dress to impress: black slacks; a black-and-white, cowl-necked sweater; and a pair of black heels out of Sally's closet. Hans would say: not bad for an American. I would have to agree.

As I'm congratulating myself, a pre-recorded theme song starts playing out in the wings. A moment later, I hear an outburst of applause and then Laura Lacey's buoyant, "Thank you, Connecticut! Thank you so much!" She goes on to say some stuff about the show that I don't quite catch, and then asks everyone to put their hands together for her very special guest, Miss Raven Middlefield.

Which is, of course, my cue.

The first thing I notice as I walk on-stage is the crowd. It's huge, a full house and then some. And every eye in the joint is focused on me. My throat goes dry. My armpits turn suddenly slick. What on earth are all of these people doing here at this ridiculous hour? Don't they have anything better to do—like sleep, for instance? Then I remember why I've come and buck up again. The more, the merrier.

Laura Lacey receives me like some long-lost friend. Her skin smells of expensive beauty cream. Her winter white suit and Christmas-y accessories make me think of dryer lint. She tells me what an honor it is to have me on the show, then invites me to sit down. As I do so, I see Sal. She's sitting in the front row, waving her head off like a starstruck teenager at a Britney Spears concert. I'm embarrassed, but oddly touched as well.

"As you know," Laura says to the audience, "we're going to take an up-close and personal look at the Hobson's Corner Hold-Up on today's show. Let's start by reviewing the case."

A newspaper headline appears on the studio monitor: *Local Woman Thwarts Hold-Up*. Other clips follow—TV, newspaper, video. We see Laura reporting *live* from Green's Market; me taking Dupree down; and then Laura again, reporting his death. *Middlefield Cleared*, the next headline says. The accompanying picture is of me kissing Kyle right under McNalley's ambitious nose. I raise my lip at his image and think: you're going to hit the fan today, too, hot-shot. Meanwhile, some of Davenport's garbage flashes on-screen: *Angels Come To Family's Rescue Again*. And: *Waiting For Mom's Millions?* I have no doubt whatsoever that this is the crap that whipped the Duprees into a greedy lather. I wish Davenport to the coldest part of hell for his yellow sins.

The montage ends with a last headline: *Bereaved Family To Sue Son's Killer*. A moment later, we break for a round of commercials.

"How are you doing?" Laura asks, leaning in close like a confidante. "That wasn't too upsetting, was it?"

"I suppose not," I say. "But I could've lived without seeing that video again."

"Sorry, but that's what made this story so notorious in the first place," she says. "We couldn't leave it out. Don't worry, though. In the next segment, you'll get to have your say."

A prompter flashes us the high-sign. Laura sits up straight. I do the same. Heartbeats later, we're on the air again. Laura welcomes the TV audience back in a lively tone, then proceeds to remind everybody concerned that the theme of today's show is the Hobson's Corner Hold-Up.

As if I could forget.

"Now that we've reacquainted ourselves with the case," she says, "let's hear from one of the saga's central characters. Connecticut, I give you Raven Middlefield."

A wild round of applause ensues. There's a bit of whistling, too. Laura smiles indulgently, then shifts in her seat toward me. As the noise settles down, she adopts a look of straight-faced compassion.

"So tell us, Raven," she says. "What have the past two weeks been like for the heroine of Hobson's Corner?"

Now that the floor's all mine, I don't know what to say. No, scratch that. The words are all there, all jumbled up in my head—I simply don't know where to begin. So I blurt out the first thing that makes it to my mouth.

"It's been a freakin' nightmare, Laura."

Down in front, Sal covers her face with her hands as if to hide her shame or embarrassment from the world. I clear my throat, a tacit apology for the slip, and then press on.

"What I meant to say is, it's been an ordeal—mentally, physically, and spiritually. Everyone in my family has suffered in one way or another. And, unfortunately, the situation has been getting worse instead of better."

"How so?" Laura asks.

"First, I was a victim. That in and of itself was bad enough, but then I was pressed into the role of a local hero, and then a national celebrity."

"Yeah, so?" a spectator shouts. "What's so bad about that?"

"It turns you into a target," I reply. "People you don't know begin to want more and more from you; and when you can't or won't give it to them, they take it anyway. Or else they make something up, and their lies take on lives of their own. Like that bit about me waiting for my mom to pass away so I can inherit her money—there's not a stitch of truth to that."

"And yet now you're being sued to the high tune of your supposed inheritance," Laura says.

"Exactly. And what's worse is, my image is being recast yet again. You saw that last headline—it referred to me as a killer instead of a hero."

"Don't let the turkeys get you down, Raven!" a female voice from the audience yells. "You did good. Damn good. If it were up to me, you'd be getting a medal for taking that piece of trash out."

"Thanks," I say dryly, "but I don't want a medal. I don't want to be anybody's bitch or poster child, either—especially not Colonel Brian McNalley's."

"What does the commander of the Connecticut State Police have to do with you, Raven?" Laura asks, with just a hint of hunger in her tone.

"A week or so ago, Colonel McNalley approached me about endorsing his run for governor. I told him I wasn't interested, but apparently he misunderstood because his campaign manager has been setting up engagements for me ever since. So I'd like to take this moment to clarify my position, Laura: I want nothing to do with the man or his politics. I can not, and will not, endorse him for governor, no matter what position he may take on zoning and health code violations in the future. That's as nice as I can say it."

"Fair enough," Laura says and then swivels toward the camera with a stern look on her face. "Are you listening, Colonel McNalley? 'No' really does mean 'no'." Then she breaks into a charming smile and adds, "Stay tuned, Connecticut, because there's still plenty of excitement waiting in the wings! We'll be back right after this word from our sponsors."

As soon as the prompter signals her, she swivels back to face me. She's grinning like someone who's just scored big at the race-track. The lights in her eyes are dancing. "You were great!" she says, "absolutely great. If you ever get tired of chasing after sharks and whatnot, you could take the world of broadcasting by storm."

I deflect her flattery with a snort. "I don't think so."

"No, really," she says, "I mean it. You've got this audience eating out of your hand."

I'm glad to hear that, because I'm not done yet—not by a long shot. I still have to do some damage control for Kyle, denounce Fenton Davenport as a lie-monger, and then give the Duprees the tongue-lashing of their miserable, money-grubbing lives. I only hope I have enough time to fit everybody on my dance-card in.

"Welcome back, Connecticut," Laura croons then, right on cue. "As you know, we're taking an in-depth look at the Hobson's Corner Hold-Up today. We've seen the media's version. We've heard from Raven Middlefield, the victim-turned-victor. Now, in this last segment, we're going to meet some people who have an entirely different take on the case."

Say what?

"They came all the way from Williamton, West Virginia to be here today," she goes on, "so please, join me in welcoming Clara and Willy Dupree."

Dupree's parents emerge from the wing's shadows. They're met by a smattering of uncertain applause. Neither of them seems to notice that, though. They're both staring at me. And I have to admit, I'm staring right back. They're both on the older and grayer side. Willy's got Coke-bottle bifocals and a slight hitch to his gait; Clara's got a widow's hump. As they approach the set, I notice that they're dressed neatly but frugally. Clara's sweater has K-Mart written all over it. Willy's brown loafers are beyond broken in.

"Thanks so much for joining us today," Laura says to them. "Won't you please be seated?"

Willy guides his wife into her chair before taking his own, and I can tell by the way he does it that it's routine rather than an act for the camera. Likewise, when Clara reaches for his hand, it's because she's used to having it there.

"Before we start," Laura says, "I'd like to express my sympathy to you both. It's never easy for parents to lose a child."

"Thank you," Willy murmurs. Clara just nods.

"And now, if you don't mind," she goes on, "I'd like to talk about your son for a few moments. We know from police reports that he was a troubled man with a tenacious drinking problem. What else can you tell us?"

"Cliff wasn't troubled," Willy says bluntly. "He was downright wrong-headed. I don't know why. I guess he musta been born that way. Me and the missus tried like hell to straighten him out, but it was like trying to tame the weather. He would take whatever punishment we gave him without a word, then turn right back around and do whatever it was that we'd punished him for all over again. I tell you truly, Miz Lacey: that boy could make a grown man cry."

Laura gives his arm a there-there pat, and then turns to Clara. "Would you care to give us a mother's point of view?"

There's an ocean-sized ache in that woman's brown eyes, but not a drop of it comes spilling out. All she does is sit there and stare at me. I think of my mom and her post-stroke gaze. It keeps me strong.

"You'll have to excuse the missus," Willy says. "She hasn't said a word since—" He glances at me. His eyes look huge, almost extraterrestrial, behind those tortoise-shell glasses of his. "Since we got the word about Cliff."

"Ah," Laura says, like that makes a difference, and then presses ahead. "So she and your son were close?"

"He treated her like dog dirt."

She arches a freshly waxed eyebrow at him. "You seem to have a rather low opinion of your late son, Mr. Dupree. That makes me wonder why you're suing Miz Middlefield." She looks my way for the first time since the segment began. There's a Mike Wallace gleam in her eyes. "Is it just for the money?"

"No, Miss Lacey," he says, "it's not that. Clara and I have lived on our own honest earnings for almost fifty years now. The money doesn't mean that much to us."

"Then why?" Laura presses.

"Because as mean as that boy was to my wife, Miss Lacey, he was the music in her heart. And as low-down as he was, he didn't deserve to die for his crimes. If the authorities had punished that woman—" He lobs another magnified look in my corner. "—for what she did to him, we probably would have been satisfied. Since they let her off scot-free, though, we had no choice but to sue. One way or another, we want her to pay."

"I see." Miz Lacey turns to me. Her expression is perfectly neutral. "What do you have to say to that, Raven?"

I look from her to the Duprees, who are both staring at me again. An angry inner voice wants me to turn all the vitriol that I've been stockpiling into napalm and firebomb the living shit out of them; and if they had been the blowsy, loud-mouthed alcoholics that I'd imagined them to be, I might've done just that. But I can't lambaste these people. I can't even be mad at them, not in the way I was before Laura pulled this nasty little stunt. They're too pathetic.

Pathetic or not, though, I'm *not* going to roll over for them.

"I'm truly sorry for your loss," I tell them, projecting firm sincerity. "But the way I see it, I've been paying for what happened that night from the get-go. I jump out of my skin every time I hear someone coming up behind me now. My privacy has been violated in a half-dozen different ways. And every night, I wake up in a cold sweat to the memory of a gun pressed to my head.

"The fact is, your son killed himself with his drinking and desperado ways. I just happened to be there when the poison pill finally dissolved."

The audience breaks into applause at that. There's some shouting, too. "You tell 'em, Raven!" And: "Amen!" Willy tightens his grip on Clara's hand and holds fast.

"You kicked the boy when he was down," he says. "You damn near turned him inside out. We know. We saw the video."

"What you saw," I fire back, "was one desperately scared woman fighting for her life. No more. No less."

Clara's eyes begin to drizzle. Laura the Ratings Whore waits until the cameraman get a close-up of that before wrapping the segment up.

"Well, friends," she says then, "that's our show for today. I hope you'll all join us on Monday when Cary Easton takes a critical, Wake Up, Connecticut look at the state of our roads and highways. Until then, be safe. And have a great weekend."

The show's pseudo-jazzy theme song starts up again. Credits start rolling across the studio monitors. Laura Lacey tosses the applauding crowd a cheesy wave, then turns to shake hands with the Duprees. As she does so, I unclip the mike from my sweater and exit, stage left. A moment later, she catches up with me.

"Great show, Raven," she says. "Thanks for joining us today." When I decline to take her outstretched hand, the dancing lights in her green eyes skid to a sudden standstill. "What's the matter?"

"How come didn't you tell me that *those* people were going to be here?" I ask in return.

Her mouth rounds itself into a 'O', as in oh-yeah, as if this was one of those silly little details that slip a working woman's mind. "At first," she says, "I wasn't sure if they were going to be available on such short notice. And afterward—well, to be honest, I didn't want you to bail on me."

Part of me wants to give her credit for owning up to the unadorned truth. The rest of me, however, wants to slam her pretty blonde head into the nearest wall for being such a high-handed bitch. She had no right to arrange such a confrontation without my knowledge or permission; no right to turn a simple, black-and-white grudge into something far more complicated. Her grab for higher ratings has earned her all of the resentment that I couldn't unload on Willy and Clara.

"You media people are all alike," I say, scorning her with the dirtiest look in my arsenal. "I don't know what made me think that you'd be any different."

Just then, Sal comes scampering onto the scene. There's an excited gleam in her eyes. She looks like a terrier who has jumped over or crawled under every fence in town to get here.

"Laura," she says, "I just have to tell you—that was one of your best shows ever. You were terrific. And Raven," she adds, as her heroine glad-hands her, "you were good, too. Except for one or two little slips."

"Yeah, well," I snarl, "that's me for you. Now let's get the hell out of here before I slip again."

Surprised ridges crop up across her forehead. A protest forms on her lips. Before she has a chance to dig her heels in, though, I hook her by the elbow and start hauling her toward the nearest exit. She bleats a hasty farewell at Laura, who wishes us both a merry Christmas, then falls into step alongside of me. A moment later, she jerks free of my tow.

"Raven," she hisses, "what's *wrong* with you? That was rude in a dozen different ways."

"She started it," I say.

"Who? Laura?" At my nod, she asks, "How?"

"She never bothered to mention that I'd be sharing the stage with those people this morning."

"With which people? The Duprees?" I nod again. "Oh." She gnaws at her lower lip for a moment, and then says, "They seemed nice enough."

"Didn't they, though." I can still see both of them staring at me: Clara with those shipwrecked eyes; and desperate, alien-eyed Willy, looking for nothing but his wife back. "Too bad they're suing me, huh?"

"Don't worry," she says. "They probably won't win."

Like that makes any difference.

We step out of the building then and into what's starting to look like tundra. It began to snow just before dawn this morning, and while the fall doesn't seem to have any sense of urgency to it, there's already an inch-thick crust on everything in the parking lot. On our way to the car, Sally tries to hopscotch over the worst patches of tire-striped slush, but I just plow right through them.

"By the way," Sal says. "You can have those shoes."

As soon as we're in the car, she cranks the heater up as high as it will go. I turn on the radio—not because I want to listen to music, but because Sal can't stand silence and I'm in no mood to talk. The final refrain of 'Grandma Got Run Over By A Reindeer' line-dances into the cabin, then the weather report. The news isn't encouraging. Every other word out of the forecaster's mouth is snow.

"Sounds like we're going to have a white Christmas," Sally says. "It's about time, too. I can't remember the last one we had. Can you?"

"No."

She slips the car into gear, and starts to drive in tight-lipped silence. Maybe she's pissed at me for ruining this little adventure for her. Maybe she's just concentrating on the slush-filled roads. Either way is fine by me, because I need some time to myself.

Three weeks ago, the prospect of a white Christmas would've thrilled me to no end. Snowmen, snow-angels, snowballs; red cheeks and runny noses; frosted eyebrows and mustaches—these would've been the icing on my homecoming trip. Oh, what fun to ride and sing a sleighing song tonight! I would have gone back to my job a happy diver, and if Hans or any of the other guys had asked how my holiday was, I would've said, "It was just right, thanks."

But things didn't exactly track like that, did they? If Hans were to pop up here and now with that same question, I'd have to reply,

"Well, they say I killed a man, Hans. Now I'm doing twenty to life for good behavior."

Is it any wonder that I'm really not that fired up about Christmas?

"Are you still mad at me?" Sally asks. Her tone is meek, like that of a child who's been made to sit in a corner for something she didn't do.

"No," I say, mildly ashamed of myself now for being so beastly to her. "And I'm sorry I spoiled your morning. It's not your fault that I'm being sued."

"I know," she says, "but I could've been a bit more sensitive about your feelings. Jay says I need to think more before I open my mouth."

"You and me both."

"Would it be OK if I stopped at the grocery store before heading home?" she asks. "I'd like to stock up on a few necessities—you know, just in case we get snowed in."

An image of home unfurls before my mind's eye: Mom clenching her teeth as she struggles, Jello-legged, to walk from the edge of her bed to the wheelchair two feet away. My offer of help is angrily waved aside—even in this condition, she has no time or need of me. Yet I cannot bring myself to leave her alone. The dutiful daughter must stay and watch, hoping or perhaps dreading that mommy might yet require assistance.

"Sure," I say. "Whatever you want."

The next thing I know, I'm pushing a shopping cart up one brightly lit aisle and down another, and marveling at the stuff my sister-in-law seems to regard as necessities: hairspray, hand cream, a bag of candy for the girls. Like anyone in their right mind would ply two housebound juggernauts with sugar. She picks up some toilet paper and a variety of fresh fruit, too, though, so I keep my thoughts to myself.

We're waiting in a check-out line that's four carts long when someone taps me on the shoulder. I half-turn around to find a short, moon-faced woman swaddled in Gor-Tex grinning at me.

"That's you, isn't it?" she asks, and then points to the magazine rack beside the conveyor belt. There, in a corner by the pocket-sized recipe books, is a copy of *World Weekly*. An awful cut-and-paste picture of me in my oilskin coat has made the front page along with cutouts of Sharon Stone, Jennifer Lopez, and some chick who's wrapped in cellophane. It seems that we've all made the top ten on some dickhead's worst-dressed list. "You're Raven Middlefield."

"No, ma'am," I say. "That's definitely not me."

And in a sense, that's true.

The line moves forward, once and then again. Sal puts the *Lady's Home Journal* that she's been flipping through back on the rack—*over* the *World Weekly*, God bless her—then starts to transfer her groceries to the conveyer belt. I am pleased to help. The line moves again. As I move with it, I notice the cashier for the first time.

"Junior," I blurt, trying to hide my surprise and a flurry of misgivings behind a flustered smile. "What are you doing here?"

"The pay's better," he says, and then starts to drag Sal's purchases across the bar-code scanner. There's something different about him today, and it's not the paisley necktie. I can't figure out what it is until I try to catch his eye and fail. That has to be a first.

"Greenie must miss you," I say.

"Yeah, well—" He shrugs, then scowls at the bunch of bananas that he's just set on the scale. "He'll get over it. We all will. Eventually.

"Your total comes to thirty dollars and fourteen cents," he tells Sal then. As she goes digging through her pocketbook for the exact change, he focuses on a spot beyond my right temple and says, "I never thanked you for saving my life."

"Don't sweat it, Junior. You would've done the same for me if you'd had the chance."

"I'm glad you think so."

Sally hands him the money. He hands her a receipt with a mechanical word of thanks, then glances at that spot to my right again. It's almost like he's scared of me. Or—wait, I know what the problem is. He's not scared. He's hurt. I never called him about the flowers or the chocolates, but I guess he got the message just the same. I should be relieved, but I'm not. I feel like a royal shit.

"Take it easy, Raven," he says.

"You, too, Junior," I meekly reply. "Merry Christmas."

Sally and I head for the exit. As we do so, I hear the woman who had tapped me on the shoulder exclaim, "Aha! I thought so!" I do not look back.

🍁   🍁   🍁

It's only a hop, skid, and a jump from the Big Y parking lot to Angelhaven; and I do I mean *skid*. The car in front of us spins out in the intersection after rounding a sloppy corner. Moments later, a blue minivan heading our way at unseasonable speeds begins to fishtail. Sally steers out of harm's way like a NASCAR pro, then scowls in the rear-view mirror and remarks, "Minivan-drivers are such morons."

My respect for my sister-in-law soars.

"I hope they don't wait too long to get the plows out," she goes on to say. "Jay and I are going to a party tonight."

I try to call up my agenda for the evening, but all that comes to mind is an image of Mom and me staring at each other. A tightness creeps into my ribcage. It feels like I'm wearing a wetsuit that's a half-size too small. A voice within begs to be let out.

"Need a babysitter?" I ask. "I'm available."

"Thanks," she says, "but we already hired Dex for the job."

The little "Oh," that I eke out then sounds pathetic even to my ears. Sally hastens to throw me a bone. "I'm sure he'll let you help out if you want to, though. The girls are spending the night at your mom's house."

"Super," I say. It's not exactly what I had in mind, but what the hell—I'm getting better at making the best of things. "We'll have a slumber party."

Sal pulls into my mother's driveway. Snow pops beneath the Explorer's tires like gritty Styrofoam. My rental car has acquired a thick, white toupee.

"How's that handle in the snow?" Sal asks, as she parks alongside of it.

"I don't know," I say.

The humid smell of boiling butternut squash hits us as we step into the house. An instant later, by Mattie hails us from the kitchen sink, where she's cutting up a chicken. "Hello, girls," she says. "How was the show?"

"Very exciting," Sal says, as she scurries off toward the bathroom. "Excuse me, but I've had to tinkle ever since we left Hartford."

Mattie and I exchange an amused look—it seems so very silly for a full-grown woman to be using that word to describe that process. Then Matt returns to her grisly task, humming as she goes.

"You're in a good mood today," I say, as I strip out of my snow-flecked jacket. "What's the occasion?"

"Robin spoke her first clear sentence this morning," she replies, all triumph and pride. "We were looking out the window, you know, just admiring the snowfall, when she turned to me and said, 'It won't be long now.'"

"It won't be long now for what?" I ask.

"I don't know," she says, still beaming. "I didn't want to frustrate her by asking for an explanation. The important thing is, she's making progress."

"Absolutely," I say, although I'm not as impressed with this would-be milestone as she is. I mean, what good are clear sentences if you can't make heads or tails of them?

She casts me a shrewd look like she's been eavesdropping on my thoughts. Then the left corner of her mouth shapes itself into a sly hook. "By the way, I didn't catch what you had to say about the show."

"That's because I'd rather not talk about it," I say. Then, because she's family, and because she'll find out sooner or later anyway, I give her a thumbnail sketch. "Laura Lacey invited Dupree's parents to do the show, too. I didn't know they were there until they walked out on stage."

Mattie hisses through her straight, white teeth. I know exactly what she means. "You stayed cool, didn't you?"

"Yeah. At first, I was too surprised to tear into them. And by the time the shock wore off, I was already starting to feel sorry for them. I guess that's why I'm so pissed off at the rest of the world at the moment."

"Oh, Raven, you're just like your mother."

"If you say so." I know she meant that as a compliment, but the way I see it, she just added insult to injury. "I'm going to go and get changed. That driveway is going to need shoveling pretty soon."

"You got that right," she says, and then blurts out an agitated, "Oh!" as I turn to leave. "I almost forgot. Abby dropped by earlier. She said if you didn't call her as soon as you got home, she was going to disown you as a friend. I think she meant it, too."

"Thanks, Mattie."

En route to my room, I stop to check on Mom. She's sitting up in bed. There's a folded magazine on her lap, but she's not looking at it. She's staring into space. Her face is slightly flushed. Her lower jaw is slack.

"Mom?" I ask, fearing the worst. "Are you OK?"

Her head slowly swivels toward me. As it does so, her color returns to normal. So much for my fears, I tell myself. She was just tuning into her own little world. Again. I don't know why that irks me so much today. Maybe it's a childhood gripe resurfacing, the Mommy-doesn't-need-me blues. Or maybe it's that damnable knack of hers. Why should she be able to slip away, at will, from the inescapable facts of her life, when I must slog through every waking moment of my own?

"Wrangle," she says then. "Crack sun eggs?"

"Matt's fixing chicken for lunch," I reply, trying to be pleasant in spite of the bug that's up my butt. "I'll be glad to scramble some eggs for you, though, if that's what you want."

She waves her hand—a distinct, negating gesture—then tries again. "No knots light later."

"I'm sorry, Mom," I say, "but I just don't understand. Are you in pain? Hungry? Tired?" She shakes her head after each question. Her color begins to rise again. "Don't stress yourself, OK?" I beg then. "I'll figure out what you're trying to say sooner or later. But right now, I've got to go and do some shoveling. The snow is starting to pile up."

"It won't be long now," she says.

Now I understand why Mattie was so thrilled. Those five little words are clear and full of promise, like church bells on Christmas morning. I want the ringing to go on and on. I want gay noises and glad tidings and a happy new year. All I get, though, is silence.

"I hope you're right," I say. Then, because I don't know what either of us is trying to say anymore, I sound a hasty retreat. "I'll look in on you again later, OK?"

She nods. I get the feeling that she's happy to see me leave.

I dash across the hall to my room, where I trade my Sunday-go-to-meeting duds for some heavy-duty sweatclothes. Then I grab the phone and punch in Abby's number. She answers on the first ring.

"Abby Cox here," she says, in her perky realtor's voice. "How may I help you?"

"Hey Ab," I reply. "It's me—Raven."

"Raven Middlefield, I can't believe you didn't tell me that you were going to be on Wake Up, Connecticut!" she says. "I would've rearranged my schedule so I could've gone with you. I've always wanted to meet Laura Lacey."

"Sorry, Ab. I didn't realize how freakin' popular that bitch is around here."

"Now why would you call her a bitch?"

I fill her in. Afterward, she honors my injuries with a moment of silence and then says, "You're right, she *is* a bitch. I still would've liked to have met her, though."

"Sorry," I say, for the second and last time. "Tell me what I can do to make it up to you."

"Well, for starters, you can come to the Christmas party that a client of mine is throwing tonight," she replies, with no hesitation. "Bruce is bringing an old college pal of his and—"

"Abby," I say, in a barely patient tone. "You know how I feel about fix-ups."

"This isn't a fix-up," she assures me. "This is just four adults going to the same party together. You don't even have to talk to the guy if you don't want to. So what do you say?" When I don't throw my hat into the ring immediately, she presses me as only Ab can. "Come on, Rave, it'll be fun. You could use a little of that after all you've been through lately. And if you won't think of yourself, think of me. Bruce and Vince are going to spend the whole night yammering about the old days. I'll be bored to tears if you're not there."

"I don't know, Abby," I say. "The weatherman's predicting snow for tonight, and it's been years since I've driven a car in bad weather."

She shoots that excuse down with a tsk. "Oh, you don't have to worry about that. We'll pick you up. Bruce's Durango handles like a dream in the snow."

There are other reasons why I shouldn't go. The biggest one is Mom, of course. I feel like the worst daughter in the world just for thinking about fun when she can't even make it to the bathroom on her own steam. There's also that proposed slumber party with Lisa and Gail; and Bruce, who's an active, first-class asshole. As plentiful as my excuses are, though, none of them have enough power to hold me back. I want to go to this party. I want to see Abby, and have a few laughs. But most of all, I want out of this house. Its walls are closing all around me, and I don't trust them to keep the bogey-men at bay.

"OK," I say, "you win. But I probably won't be able to get away until after eight."

"Eightish it is then," she says, magnanimous in victory. "Wear that outfit you had on this morning. You'll put all the other women at the party to shame."

"Yeah, right."

"Believe what you will, Rave—I've got to run. Catch you later!"

I hang up, wondering what I've let her talk me into this time. Then I go outside and get to work.

CHAPTER 9

Sally and Jay drop my nieces off at suppertime. Mom is eating in her room with Matt tonight, and Dex isn't hungry, so it's just us three Middlefield girls at the kitchen table for boxed macaroni and cheese. In the absence of adult supervision, we burp and giggle and flash orange mouthfuls of half-chewed pasta at each other. Little Lisa laughs at the wrong moment, and winds up with a snootful of milk. This is definitely one of the more enjoyable meals I've had in a long, long time.

Afterward, I pay the little darlings two bucks apiece to take a bath. While they're splashing around in the tub, I start on the supper dishes. I think I'm just about done when Mattie comes striding into the kitchen with more. Ain't that always the way?

"Robin ate everything on her plate tonight," she tells me, and offers up that dish as evidence. "If she keeps this up, she'll be romping in the loft again in no time."

"You're a fine nurse, Mattie," I say. "Much better than I am, I'm afraid."

"Don't be ridiculous," she says. "You're a tremendous help to your mother in a lot of different ways."

"Yeah, right."

She grabs a towel and starts to dry the dishes that I've put in the rack. Unlike Sal, she doesn't have a cow when she finds a bit of crud on the outside of a pot. She just scrapes the crud off with her thumbnail and puts the pot away.

"Small load tonight," she says.

"One of the benefits of having an empty barn," I reply.

A mild worry-frown rumples her brow. "I hope the Cartwrights made it to New Hampshire ahead of this storm. They're such nice people. And they've been through so much. Ted said he was going to use that insurance check as a down payment on a house.

"Your brother wants Robin to sell Angelhaven, you know," she says then, a shot from out of the blue. "He says she's going to be recovering for a long, long time; and that I'm not strong enough to take care of her, the farm, *and* an unending parade of hard-luck cases by myself." She clutches my arm. Her grip is as fierce as the look in her eyes. "He may be right about me, Rave. I'm not as young as I used to be. But I know this much—it would break Rob's heart to give up this place."

I grumble to myself: *friggin' Jay*. At the very least, he could've waited until the holidays were over before trotting out next year's wish list. I look into Mattie's dear old face: the worries I see there aren't for herself. My conscience wants me to tell her about my promise to Mom, but—I just can't bring myself to let that cat out of the sack yet. I'm not ready; it's too soon. I need more time to get used to the idea.

"Don't worry, we'll work something out," I say. "I'll talk to Jay."

She gives my arm a grateful squeeze, then pats my cheek. "Your mother's lucky to have you, Raven."

"She's lucky to have you, too, Mattie," I say. But what I'm thinking is: *friggin' Jay*.

The dishes are done now, so I go in search of the girls. I find them in the living room, sprawled on their bellies by the Christmas tree. They're playing with their trolls: ugly little dolls that look like a cross between a Pekinese and a Smurf. At the moment, these trolls are snooping around the presents under the tree. Then a felt ornament slips free of its branch and hits the tree-skirt with a soft plop. The trolls race over to check it out. Moments later, a wrestling match for salvage rights breaks out. Gail's doll knocks Lisa's to the ground and then stomps on the bun-like bulge of its plastic pot-belly. Lisa squeals a protest.

"That's enough," I say. My tone is so sharp, they both flinch. I have no idea why I snapped at them. "It's time for you to hit the hay," I say, in a gentler tone. "Tomorrow is Christmas Eve, you know."

The hurt in Lisa's eyes evaporates immediately. "Do you think Santa will bwing me a pony, Aunt Waven?"

"Hard to say, kiddo," I say. "He might have a hard time getting something that big down the chimney."

She turns toward the fireplace with a speculative glint in her six-year-old eyes. "Maybe you could help him. Daddy says you're stwong. And bwave."

"Oh, he does, does he?"

She nods solemnly. "I heard him say so to Mommy."

"And do you know what brave means?"

She nods again. "Bwave is what you are when you get a shot at the doctor's and don't cwy even though you want to."

"Exactly so."

I scoop her into a fierce embrace, then draw Gail in as well. Nothing seems more precious than these sweet-smelling darlings at this moment. I find myself wondering what it would be like to have a few of my own. They'd be as adorable as these two, I think, but scruffier, tomboyish. I'd let them be loud and just a little wild, especially in the company of their Aunt Sal. They'd proclaim me the best mommy ever, and I'd always be there for them. I'm so enchanted by this fantasy, I let the girls talk me into letting them stay up an extra half-hour to watch one last program on TV. As they snuggle on the couch, cozy as kittens, I steal into my room to get ready for the party. When I steal back out again, I find Dexter on the couch, too. The girls are cuddled up next to him.

"Aunt Raven!" Gail exclaims, as I join the crowd. "You look like a movie star!"

"Yeah," Dex adds, eyeing me with a mixture of teenage awe and surprise. "You could be on *Baywatch*."

Although it's only out of the mouths of babes, I get off on the praise. So I strike up my version of a movie-star pose and thank them profusely in my best, phony French accent. As I'm doing so, I see headlights flash through the curtains.

"*Mon Dieu*! That's my ride," I say, and rush in to give the girls a quick hug and a smooch. As they're returning the favor, I turn my smile to Dexter. "See you later, dude."

"Have a nice time," he says.

As soon as I step outside, my bouncy mood takes a sudden nosedive. For the driveway that I just cleared a few hours ago is filling up with snow again, and the vehicle that's waiting for me there isn't the promised Durango, but a puny BMW sedan. I'm tempted to pull a one-eighty and go back into the house. Before I can do so, though, the BMW's rear window whirs open to reveal Abby's smiling face. She's beautiful, as always. Tonight, she looks faintly Egyptian.

"Come on, Rave, get in!" she cries merrily. "You're in back with me!"

The next thing I know, I'm sitting next to her and she's brushing snow off my shoulders like it's dandruff.

"Raven Middlefield," she says then, "say hello to the guy in the driver's seat. His name is Vince Pescinetti."

Although I feel like Contestant Number Two on the Dating Game, I do as I am told. Vince twists around in his seat and offers me a civil, this-wasn't-my-idea smile and a handshake. He has classic Italian good looks: brown eyes and olive skin; thick, black hair and a chiseled jawline. His grip is European, too—firm but genteel, easy on the testosterone.

"Pleased to meet you, Raven," he says. "I've heard a lot about you."

"Don't believe everything Abby tells you," I say. "Otherwise, you're bound to be disappointed."

Ab deflects that barb with a girlish laugh, then goes on to present her lover to me. "And of course, you remember Bruce."

Of course. But I try to be nice just the same. "Hello, Bruce."

He runs his hand through his short, wheat-colored hair before turning to greet me. He's got stunning blue eyes, a forehead like Half-Dome and a weightlifter's neck. "Good to see you again, Raven," he says.

Yeah, right. The last time we were trapped in the same room together, he called me a ball-busting lesbian. In turn, I told him to lay off the steroids before they made him stupid and then added, oops, sorry, too late. Which makes me wonder why he agreed to let Ab play matchmaker tonight. Maybe Vince isn't the great friend he's supposed to be. Maybe this is Bruce's idea of a payback. Whatever. I'm just along for the ride.

And what a slow ride it promises to be! The road we're on has been plowed, but not recently, and Vince is trying to drive in the slushy ruts that other cars have left behind. Judging by the set of his jaw, he's thinking of his insurance premiums. I can't say that I blame him.

"Where is this party anyway?" I ask, hoping to distract myself from my fishtailing thoughts.

"Hell's Last Acre," Ab says, and flashes me a grin. "Just like old times, hey?"

An image from one of those foolhardy old times bubbles forth from my tarpit of a memory: her and me huddled around a smoky, barn-board fire, both of us swigging from a fifth of blackberry brandy to stay warm as we watched our dates put the moves on a pair of prettier party-goers. I shiver at the recollection. That night had been her idea, too.

"I can't even imagine doing that kind of shit anymore," I say. "My blood must've been a lot thicker back then." Then I lean in close and whisper, "I thought we were going to take Bruce's Durango."

"The blockhead forgot to gas it up," she whispers back, scourging the thick neck in front of her with a look of pure disgust. "Don't worry, though, we'll be fine." Then, in a louder, sunnier voice, she says, "Did either of you happen to catch Raven on television this morning? She was fabulous."

Bruce snorts derisively. "I don't have time to watch television in the morning. My job starts at eight."

"I'm afraid I missed it, too," Vince says. "I was on the road most of the day."

"Where'd you start out?" I ask, to keep myself from jumping on the blockhead's high-and-mighty case. "And where are you going?"

"D.C. and Hanover, New Hampshire respectively."

"That's quite a drive."

He shrugs. "I do it at least six or seven times a year. My folks would pitch a fit otherwise. If they had their way, I'd still be living at home in my old bedroom."

"I know what you mean."

"Raven is an award-winning underwater photographer, Vince," Abby says, doing her best to sell me as exotic goods. "You've probably seen some of her work on PBS."

"No kidding."

He asks me a few questions about the job, but I'm feeling sorry for myself now, so I keep my answers short and bland. Meanwhile, we clear Devil's Bend and the turn-off to Hell's Last Acre. A housing development looms out of the snow-dappled darkness. The sudden abundance of Christmas lights makes the storm seem less threatening somehow.

"It's that one up there at the top of the street," Abby says, pointing toward an enormous, cornflower-blue Cape Cod. "See where all those cars are?"

I see the house all right, but there really aren't *that* many cars in the vicinity: just four in the double driveway, and three or maybe four more parked on the snow-hedged roadside. Any decent party would have at least twice that many. I'm hoping Abby will realize this too, and tell Vince to turn around and take us home, but—no such luck. The next thing I know, we're all standing in a pine-scented foyer and handing our outer wear to some big-haired gal named Emily. Then Abby introduces us to our host, Gerry. His aging Boy Scout's face begins to glow like the Christmas tree in his bay window as soon he hears my name.

"You're a life-saver," he whispers to Ab, and then ushers me into the living room like some fatted calf. The sparse crowd turns our way as we enter. At Gerry's urging, it closes in.

"Everybody," he says, "this is Raven Middlefield. If you don't know who she is by now, then you need to start watching the news. I hope you'll all join me in a toast to this brave woman and her continuing good health."

Abby presses a glass of champagne into my hands. I down it all in one gulp as the crowd hip-hip-hurrahs me. Gerry immediately offers me more. Before I can decline, he says, "Don't worry, I've got plenty thanks to this darn storm."

The thing is, I don't drink much anymore. Overindulging can result in all sorts of unpleasant complications when you're a single woman living abroad. But I'm on my own turf tonight, and as safe as I'm ever going to get, so I recklessly accept one refill and then another. Before I know it, I'm laughing and talking and totally cool with being the center of attention. I tell my listeners about the time I dove with wild dolphins; and the time my soon-to-be ex-boss Marcos lured the grandaddy of all lobsters out of its bolt-hole with a pair of pantyhose; and then, the story about me and Hans and the shark, ha-ha, got you all, you silly gits.

Afterward, as I'm taking in a breather as well as yet another glass of champagne, a middle-aged woman strolls up to me. She's short but very fit—a high school gym-teacher would be my guess. Her hair and dress are cut to flatter her build. Although I'm sure that we haven't been introduced, I have the feeling that I know her.

"Hi, Raven," she says, almost coyly. "Remember me? We went to school together."

I look her up and down, waiting for recognition to kick in, but it remains a small, niggling voice in the background. "Sorry," I say, with a shrug. "My memory's not what it used to be."

Her smile takes a wistful half-turn. "That's OK, it's been a long time." She holds out a hand for me to shake. "The name's Diana, Diana Tate." At my puzzled scowl, she adds, "You knew me as DeeDee."

My first impulse is to drop her hand in mid-shake. My second is to crush it like a small-boned rodent. *Freakin' DeeDee Harcourt.* I *knew* I knew her from somewhere.

"My husband and I live next-door to Gerry and Em," she's saying now. "He's an engineer with Pratt. I teach aerobics at the Y—"

Stunned by the width and breadth of my ex-nemesis's nerve, all I can do is stare at her. She looks nothing like the snotty little misery-maker she used to be—and that's not just because she's twenty years older now, with faint worry lines fanning from the corners of her blue eyes and deeper ones bracketing her once-mean mouth. The superior attitude is gone now, replaced an aerobic instructor's ingrained perkiness. Her crowd of admirers has disappeared, too.

"I can't believe how much you've changed," she gushes. "You used to be such a shy, skinny thing. Now—" She shakes her head and gestures. "Just look at you."

"You've changed, too," I say, and a part of me wants to go into gory detail about what an absolute bitch she was—in a voice just loud enough to be overheard. Because I know that by doing so, I could pay DeeDee freakin' Harcourt back in spades for all the humiliation she ever heaped on me. I owe her. She owes me. "You used to be—" Shit. I'm all lined up for a shot that I've dreamed about for twenty years, and I can't bring myself to take it. It just wouldn't be right. Because she's *not* DeeDee Harcourt anymore, and I don't want to be the one to raise that Ghost of Christmas Past. "You used to be taller."

Just then, Ab catches my eye from across the room and presses two fingers to her lips—our private sign for a cigarette break. I respond with a nod, then wish Diana a merry Christmas and abandon her along with the desiccated remains of a twenty-year-old grudge. I feel surprisingly lighter now, but that could just be the champagne.

"So what did DeeDee want?" Abby asks, as she leads me away from the crowd. "She looked like she was trying to sign you up for something."

"She was telling me how much I've changed," I say, and then shudder as we step out of the house and onto the semi-sheltered deck. We have the space to ourselves. No one else is crazy enough to hang outside during a snowstorm. "She thinks I'm *cool* now."

"*Everyone* thinks you're cool now," Ab says, as she hands me a smoke from her pack. "You're the life of the party."

I light up. The first drag gives me a head rush that I could've done without, but I keep on smoking just the same. Between one puff and the next, I say, "Pathetic, isn't it?"

"What's that?" Ab asks.

"Me being the life of the party."

"How do you figure?"

"I'm still the same ol' boring Raven I always was," I say. "The only reason any of these people want to talk to me is because I'm a celebrity. When I'm no one again—and please let that be soon—I'll be lucky if they give me a moment's notice."

"I wish you'd stop putting yourself down all the time," Abby says, flashing me a reproving scowl. "You're smart, hip, and very good-looking. You also have one of the coolest jobs on the planet. People are going to want to talk to you regardless of whether they've seen you on TV or not."

"Yeah, right."

"OK, so maybe you *have* been getting a bit more attention than usual these days. What's so wrong with that? It's nice having a hero in the herd for a change."

"But that's just it! I'm not a hero. I'm just me—the good, the bad, and the ugly. I don't want any credit for what went down that night at Green's. And I don't want any blame, either. It's like waking up the morning after a big night on the town and having no clue as to how the stranger in bed next to you got there. You know?"

She knows. She's been there. Her mouth becomes a thin, red line.

I flick the remnants of my cigarette over the railing. It hits the snow-covered yard with a hiss, flares hell-fire red for a second and then dies. Abby still doesn't know what to say.

"Don't worry," I tell her, because there's no point in both of us being bummed out on the night before Christmas Eve. "I'll get over it—eventually. In the meantime, just be patient with me."

"Anything for you, girlfriend," she says.

We go back inside, but the house seems stuffy after my stint in the cold, and the thought of joining the crowd in the living room leaves me claustrophobic. So I head into the kitchen and begin to sample the hors d'oeuvres. Gerry and Em have gone all out for the occasion, and I try a bit of everything: shrimp with cocktail sauce, Swedish meatballs, mini-quiches. But while the food feels good going down, it doesn't fill me up. It's like a bad scar has broken open within me, exposing some vast and nameless void.

As I'm nibbling on a salmon canapé, Vince comes padding into the room with a champagne bottle in hand. He sheds his bored expression when he sees me camped by the buffet table. "Anything good?" he asks.

"Everything's fabulous," I tell him, gesturing at the extent of the spread. "But our host and hostess are going to have leftovers coming out of their ears."

"Champagne, too," he says with a grin, and holds up the bottle he's toting. "Gerry is starting to give these away as door-prizes.

"Want some?"

I know I shouldn't, but what the hell? T'is the season, and maybe alcohol will close that void. So I let him pour me another glass. Then I stick around to chat as he samples the grub for himself. He seems like a nice enough fellow—a little too yuppyish for my tastes, but nobody's perfect and at least he doesn't ask about the hold-up or its assorted byblows. We talk about Grand Cayman instead, because he's been there; and Australia, because he's always wanted to go. He tops off our glasses again. As he does so, he slops a bit of champagne on his shirt. I snatch up a cocktail napkin and try to rub the spot dry.

Just then, Abby pokes her head around the corner. When she sees Vince and me huddled together, she breaks into a triumphant smile and immediately disappears again. I curl my lip at her afterimage. Vince catches the look and chuckles.

"Did she swear on her grandma's grave that this wasn't a fix-up?" he asks. I nod. He chuckles again. "Same here. I must admit, though—if I *had* wanted to be fixed up, I couldn't have asked for anyone better than you."

His gaze strays from me to a point above my head. His mouth molds itself into a sensual curve. I look up to find myself standing beneath a sprig of wilted mistletoe.

"May I?" he asks.

I don't know what to say. He's easy enough on the eyes, but the only chemistry between us has to do with the Moet. On the other hand, it's just a friendly Christmas kiss, and maybe a bit of gratuitous male companionship is all I need to cure what's ailing me. As I flip-flop back and forth, too buzzed to decide, he leans in and presses his lips to mine. His breath smells of champagne yeast and crab dip.

Mine must smell even worse from the cigarette I had, but he steals another kiss anyway. Although it does nothing for me, I don't withdraw. It's like I'm twelve years old again—stuck with a voyeur's curiosity and no hormones to make the experience feel sexual. Somewhere in the background, I can smell candles burning. It's an odd, unsettling intrusion.

Vince nuzzles me one last time. Then, encouraged by my compliance, he moves in for a more serious taste of Christmas cheer. He pulls me in close, and then loops his arm around my neck. As he does so, the waxy smell that's in my nose acquires the sour tang of fear. My brain sounds an adamant retreat. In response, I shove Vince away with both hands. He staggers back a few steps, and then looses a wide-eyed bleat of surprise.

"Hey! What's up?"

"I'm sorry," I say, breathless now because I feel like I'm about to fly apart at the seams, "but I can't do this."

"You were doing fine just a moment ago," he says, amused now and maybe a little turned on. I realize then that he's drunker than I am. And I'm fairly shattered. "C'mon, Miz Underwater Photographer. There's no need to be shy."

He closes the gap between us, meaning to take what I do not wish to give. Creep, I think. He'd probably put a gun to my head, too, if he had one on him. The thought infuriates me. I grab a fistful of his shirtfront and pull him nose-to-nose with me.

"You stupid sonuvabitch," I say. "I've already killed one man this month. Did you want to be the second?" With that, I thrust him back into his own corner. An instant later, Abby comes flouncing into the room. I can tell by her smug grin that she thinks she knows why Vince is so furiously tucking his shirttails back into his pants.

"I hate to break up this tête-à-tête," she says, "but Bruce is in a dither about the weather and wants to go home."

"Fine by me," I say.

"Me, too," Vince mutters. Then, as Abby goes flouncing off to collect our coats, he trains his drunken sights on me and delivers the ultimate slam. "Looks like Bruce was right about you."

All sorts of nasty words rush into my mouth, but I can't seem to weave them into an insult scathing enough for the occasion. So I turn my nose up at him like he's dogshit or worse, then go in search of Abby. I find her with Gerry, who proceeds to thank me at length for deigning to attend his soiree. I'm beginning to feel sick to my stomach now, so I'm actually almost grateful when Bruce says, "Wrap it up already, would you, Raven? It's going to take us half the night to get home."

Outside, nothing's changed. It's still snowing, steady as she goes, and the roads still need to be plowed. We find the BMW chilling beneath an inch-thick blanket of fresh fall. Vince is in no condition to drive, so Soberer-Than-Thou Bruce takes the wheel.

He starts out at a cautious crawl, then works his way up to just plain slow. And I have to hand it to the nimrod—he gets us back onto the main drag and past Devil's Bend without so much as a scare. We all relax a notch after that. Ab starts talking about the party; I nod off somewhere during the dissection only to snap back to full, adrenaline-laced consciousness as the car begins a slow-motion slide toward the shoulder. Vince lets out a helpless yelp. Bruce swears and tries to stay on the road. But a BMW handles differently than a Durango; and with a sobering series of jolts, we come to a stop in a snow-filled drainage ditch. It takes us a moment to realize that we're all in one piece, and another to realize that we're stuck. Bruce The Butthead heaves an exasperated sigh, then orders everyone out of the car.

"OK," he says, after he sizes our situation up, "I think we can do this. Abby, get behind the wheel and crank it hard right when I tell you to. Vince, you're with me on the front end. And Raven—" He shoots me a disgusted look. Like I'm the one who forgot to gas up the friggin' SUV. "—just try to stay out of the way, OK?"

His overweening chauvinism ticks me off in a big way. I can heave-ho as hard as the next person, especially when the next person is a seriously trashed yuppie with a raging case of high-frequency hiccups. I tell Bruce as much, too.

"Fine," Butthead says, "have it your way. But if you break a nail or something, I don't want to hear about it."

Rather than dignify the comment with a reply, I simply take my place on the front bumper. And when he says push, I give him everything I've got. But we're nose-down, and axle-deep. The sedan's rear wheels spin hopelessly until Bruce tells Abby to stop. We try again. And again. And again. Then Bruce looses a string of curse-words and climbs up the embankment to see what the problem could be.

My toes are turning into icicles inside of my shoes. My nose can't decide if it wants to run or go numb. And to top it all off, my stomach is quivering from all of the hard work and champagne. I'm sure I'd feel better if I blew whatever ballast I have in me, but I'd rather live with the belly-ache than give Bruce the satisfaction of seeing me puke. I scowl in Butthead's direction. He's pacing furious circles in the roadside snow now, cursing Christ, the weather, and Abby as he goes. His bitching gets old in a hurry. I'm maybe a hair away from volunteering to hike back to Gerry's just to get away from him when a set of high-beams lights up the snow-spackled night. Moments later, a pick-up truck appears on the road. It begins to stop even before Bruce flags it down.

"Is everyone here OK?" the driver asks, as he steps out of his cab and into the nighttime shadows. "Anyone hurt?"

"Nah," Bruce says, sounding all disgusted. "We were going pretty slow when it happened. Can you help us out?"

"Maybe. Let's have a look."

Our would-be savior strides into view then, and although I recognized his voice as soon as I heard it, I'm still amazed to see him here in the flesh. Kyle is dressed in ultra-faded blue jeans, a sheepskin jacket, and cowboy boots rather than a state trooper's uniform. He looks good. Handsome—as always. I'm certain he's on his way home from a date. A blonde with big boobs, I'll bet. Or maybe a big-boobed redhead with nipples like bright red noses.

Then all the reindeer loved him, and they shouted out with glee....

Vince comes staggering back from a pee in the woods. His pants are encrusted with snow all the way up to the knee. He stumbles past me, seemingly intent on joining Bruce and Kyle,. As he does so, his left leg goes skidding out from under him. I catch him by the arm as he goes down. To my surprise, I find that I'm not mad at him anymore. All I want to do is go home.

"You'd better take a couple of aspirin and drink a gallon of water before you go to bed," I say, as he steadies himself. "Otherwise, you're going to be one seriously hurting unit in the morning."

"Good idea," he says, and admits me back into his good graces with a wobbly grin. "Thanks."

I turn him loose. As I do so, I catch Kyle staring right at me. His expression has disapproval stamped all over it.

"You and your friends could've picked a better night to go joy-riding," he tells me, in a tone as stiff as his upper lip.

"Oh, Kyle, don't be such an old poop," Abby scolds. She's leaning out the car window now, and doing the pretty girl pout. At one time, she was hot for him, too. "We weren't joy-riding, we were on our way home from Gerry Blair's Christmas party. And just so you know, Bruce was driving and he doesn't drink."

"Glad to hear it," he says, although you'd never know it by the look on his face. "Now please exit the automobile so I can tow it out of this ditch."

"Whatever you say, officer."

She and I remove ourselves to the side of the road. The menfolk get to work. This time, I do not offer to help.

"Oh, well," Abby says, as she huddles within her jacket. "At least the party was fun."

I do an impromptu line-dance, trying to stomp the chill out of my feet, but only succeed in driving it into my legs. "I can't remember the last time I was this cold," I say.

"Keep moving," she advises, and then goes digging through her purse for a cigarette. As she lights up, a sly smile slithers across her face. "So what do you think of Vince?"

"I'm sure he'll make some woman's mother very happy," I say, and then steal a drag from her cigarette.

Big mistake. My throat goes dry from the menthol in the smoke; my stomach clenches against the taste. The next thing I know, I'm doubled over a snowbank and barfing my brains out like a true-blue bulimic. Mac-and-cheese, shrimp and cocktail sauce, chunks of Swedish meatball—it all comes up in a hot, fluid rush. It's funny, but the only clear thought in my head is: *the fish would go crazy over this.*

When my stomach is finally empty, Ab hands me a tissue. As I'm wiping the lingering spools of bile from my mouth, she kicks snow over my mess. So Bruce won't see it. She truly is my best friend.

"Kyle!" she shouts then. "Can we camp out in your truck for a while? Raven's freezing out here."

"Yeah, go ahead," he shouts back. "There's a blanket in the back if you need it."

"Thanks."

By the time she gets me into the truck and all bundled up, my teeth are chattering like the world-record holders at a castanets convention. "I'll be—OK," I stammer, as she moves in close to share her body heat. "I just need—to sleep."

"You gotta warm up a little first, OK?" she says.

"Sure."

She begins to rock me, a gentle side-to-side motion that makes me feel like I'm on a boat. I think of bathwater and a sunlit beach. Eventually, a needling sort of pain creeps into my feet. I want to scratch the feeling away, but nod off instead. Abby jars me back to my senses twice: once, to make me chew a mint because she can't stand my breath; and again a few minutes later to tell me that I'm snoring. "So what?" I mumble, then immediately doze off again.

I'm on that beach again, basking beneath a tropical sun, when the world begins to shake. In the distance, I can hear a voice calling my name, but I'm down too deep, ha-ha, and it can't touch me. The shaking becomes more insistent. The sun and the black-sand beach begin to fade.

"Ab-by," I whine, "piss off."

"Dammit all, Raven! Wake up. You're home."

The voice is familiar, but it isn't Abby's. I bolt upright, then blink back a tsunami of confusion. I'm still in the truck, but the shoulder that I've been snuggling against belongs to Kyle.

"Where's Ab?" I ask. In my half-dazed, half-drunken state, I'm afraid the aliens have taken her again. "Where'd she go?"

"She's at her parents' house," Kyle says, "along with the rest of your friends. You wouldn't wake up, so I brought you home. Fortunately, I don't live too far from here."

"I'm sorry," I say. "I didn't mean to be a pain."

"Yeah well, you know how it is with the state police—we're here to serve and protect."

His tone is brusque, borderline sarcastic. I draw my head back to get a better look at him. His cheeks are starting to sprout reddish-gold stubble. His eyes are bloodshot. He wasn't on his way home from a date, I realize. He was coming home from work.

"I thought you worked first shift," I say.

"I volunteered for extra duty during the holidays," he says. "I'm hoping it'll make my record look better."

The memory of what I did to him comes rushing back to me, and it's as dazzling as a photographer's flash. I lift my face toward his, meaning to apologize from the very bottom of my tiny, thoughtless heart. As I do so, I notice that I drooled on his shoulder while I was sleeping. Oh, God, I probably snored, too. I'm doubly embarrassed now, so much so that I can't bear to look him in the eyes. I rest my eyes on the dashboard instead.

"Kyle," I say, all meekness and rue, "I'm really and truly sorry. I didn't mean to get you into trouble with that kiss."

For a moment, silence reigns between us, perfect and imposing. Then, to my amazement and surprise, he chuckles—a low, sensual sound like rolling thunder on a hot, midsummer night.

"That wasn't a kiss," he says, in a half-mocking tone. Then he takes my chin in hand and tilts my head back until our eyes meet. "*This* is a kiss."

And baby, is it ever! Hard, wet, deliciously insistent: it throws a powerful switch. My arms are around his neck before I know what I'm doing. My tongue is in his mouth. He tastes like coffee with two sugars. He feels like land after three weeks at sea. In no time at all, I'm squirming inside and out, and wondering how far I should let him go here and now in my mother's driveway in the middle of a Christmas Eve storm. But even as I grant myself permission to ride this rogue wave to its still uncharted end, a distant siren's moan steals into the cab. Kyle tenses. Suddenly, there's a space between our mouths.

"What is it?" I whisper, although a part of me remembers that high-low wailing from somewhere.

"It's the Hobson's Corner Volunteer Fire Department," he says, and turns back into a state trooper before my very eyes. "Of all the nights for a fire.

"I'm sorry, Raven," he tells me then, "but they're probably going to need me at the scene." As he presses me toward the door, he adds, "I'll call you."

An instant later, I'm standing out in the falling snow, and his pick-up truck is in full reverse down the driveway. To the west, the horizon is glowing orange through the snow-pocked tree-line. I feel sick. Like a fool. I head inside and go to bed.

CHAPTER 10

"*R*aven."

"C'mon, Rave. Rise and shine."

"Dammit, Raven. *Wake up.*"

The voice plucks me out of a sound sleep by the back of my neck. One moment, I'm down so deep, I'm as good as dead. The next, I'm gasping for breath on the bleary shores of wakefulness. Jay is standing by my bed. His look is one of aggrieved urgency. The first thought that comes to mind is: Oh, my God, it's Christmas morning and I've overslept. But even as I tense, preparing to launch myself out of bed, a more dire thought takes its place.

"What's wrong?" I blurt. "Is it Mom?"

"No, no," he hastens to assure me, "it's nothing like that. Mom's fine."

My fear subsides, but the little jolt of adrenaline that accompanied it has left me wide-awake; and not all is well in Denmark. My head is throbbing; my stomach muscles are sore; and my mouth tastes like Godzilla's ass. All I want to do is tunnel back under the covers and sleep until the pain goes away. But I can tell by Jay's unrelenting stare that he isn't going to let me do that.

"What's so freakin' important that it can't wait a few hours?"

"We got a call from the state police a few minutes ago," he says. "Fred's Motor Inn burned down last night." I recall the sirens then, and the glow on the horizon. "No one was hurt, thank God, but most of the guests have no place to go."

"No place but here," I guess.

"Exactly," he says.

Oh, shit.

My brain kicks into overdrive despite the hangover. All at once, I'm making a list of the things that need to be done and wondering how it's all going to get that way. "OK, give me a few minutes to get up and dressed. While you're waiting, you can turn the heat up in the barn. What's it like out, anyway?"

"Still snowing," he says, and then lobs a scowl at the world beyond my shuttered window. "Half the roads in Connecticut are closed already, and I'm betting the governor shuts the rest down before noon. I haven't seen anything like this since the year that ice-storm hit. Remember that? We were out of school for a week."

I remember all right: no power, no heat, no phone. It was a fun-filled adventure from a child's viewpoint, but now that I'm on the other end of the stick, I can appreciate what a pain in the neck it must've been.

"While you're out in the barn, start the coffee," I tell him. "Make it strong. I have a feeling everybody's going to need a little extra oomph today."

He nods, seconding the thought, then shows himself to my door. In his absence, I do a reluctant forward roll out of bed. I have no idea how I came to be wearing a flannel nightgown. The last time I saw this hideous, grandma's special, it was buried in my closet along with the other too-old, too-big, or just-not-me clothes that I keep meaning to donate to Good Will. Likewise, I don't remember hanging my slacks up to dry, or pulling three pairs of socks on my still-cold feet. I shake my head, silently swearing off champagne forever and ever, amen, then begin to dress. Several layers later, I shuffle off to the head to brush my teeth and my hair. The bathroom is unoccupied when I get there, but not quite empty. Three frozen, hunch-backed turkeys are having a soak in the tub. I cannot stop myself from keeping an eye on them in the mirror as I perform my morning rituals. Their presence is surreal, like a fragment of a Salvador Dali painting.

When I'm finished making myself presentable, I head into the kitchen in search of something that'll settle the tremors in my stomach and knees. There, I find another turkey thawing in the sink. I'm sure this wouldn't seem quite so weird if I weren't so hung-over. Ugh. Never again. I eat a banana, then go outside. The snowfall is so gentle, so quiet and peaceful, it's hard to think of it as dangerous. Then I look at Jay's Explorer, which looks like a big, white pillow, and remember that smothering is a form of violence, too.

I grab a shovel and begin to clear a path to the barn. I'm maybe a yard away from the door when Mattie and Dexter come up behind me. She looks like she's been up for ages already, but his eyes are still puffy with sleep.

"Sorry it took us so long to get our acts together," she says, "but this one had a hard time getting out of bed, and I had to go and check on Rob. She's very excited this morning. I think she was expecting something like this."

Hark, the herald angels sing. Again. When I was a kid, I always wondered who Harold was. I guess I should've asked Mom.

"Did she happen to mention anything about a head-count?" I ask, only half in jest.

"Sorry."

"Oh, well. I guess we'll just have to be surprised." I scrape a last bit of snow out of our way, then hand the shovel to Dexter. "Your turn, dude. The driveway has to be cleared and kept that way. Ditto for the area around the latrines. I'll come out and spell you later, OK?"

"Whatever," he says, and goes shuffling off like a lead-limbed sleepwalker. I know how he feels. Or at least I would, if I had the luxury of time to think about it.

The inside of the barn smells like winter and fresh-brewed coffee. There is no sense of urgency about the place; I have to manufacture it for myself. "We should ration space until we know for sure how many people we're putting up," I say, thinking aloud simply because it hurts less than thinking to myself. "Families with kids will need rooms to themselves. Singles will have to share. We should register everybody, too—just in case. Do we have a notepad or something like that around here?"

"Rob keeps a guest book in the back room," Mattie says.

"Where do you want these?" Jay asks, as he makes his way down from the loft with an armload of blankets.

My reply is cut off by the distant, mechanized growl of one snowmobile and then maybe two more. The three of us exchange an uh-oh look. The growling draws nearer.

"Put them on the picnic table," Mattie tells Jay. "And keep 'em coming."

Shortly thereafter, our first two arrivals come straggling into the barn. They're both bundled up in borrowed snowmobile suits and helmets, so it's hard to tell if they're men, women, or what. Then their helmets come off, one after the other, and astonishment slams into me like a furnace's breath. Because the person standing in front of me is Willy Dupree. And standing beside him is his tight-lipped missus.

"What are you doing here?" I ask.

"Clara wanted to spend the night in the town where Cliff was killed," Willy says, looking supremely uncomfortable. "The place we were staying at burned down."

Disbelief multiplies within me like a bad case of Salmonella poisoning. The only explanation I can come up with for this perverse turn of events is that I'm being punished for something I did in a former life. And Clara's accusing stare makes it clear that there's even more punishment in store. I give her a flat-eared look, drawing an uncrossable line between us. Then, because I have no other obvious choice, I let them into Angelhaven.

"The toilets are outside and to the left," I say, as I march them and their allotment of blankets toward the back of the barn. "Meals are communal. For now, we're asking people without children—" Clara winces at that. I grit my teeth. "—to share sleeping quarters. That may change depending on our final headcount. If you need anything, ask. My family will do its best to accommodate you."

I tell them to pick a roomlet, any roomlet, and then turn to head upstream again. As I do so, Willy steps in front of me. His humble expression leads me to expect thanks or maybe even an apology.

"We have a suitcase," he says instead. "One of the men back in town said he'd bring it in his truck later. Clara's heart medicine is in it."

"I'll keep an eye out for it," I tell him. And that's a promise, because the very last thing I need is another friggin' Dupree dropping dead on me.

The hours pass in a snow-capped blur. A family of four arrives by pick-up truck; the kiddies are still in their pajamas. As soon as I get them squared away, a puffy-looking woman with big, garishly red hair flags me down and demands a room for herself and her seventeen-year-old daughter. When I tell her that they may have to share their space with others, she pauses like she's weighing her options and then nods.

"So long as we're with our own kind, OK?" she says, and then casts a significant glance at Mattie. "They never wash, you know."

This isn't the first time that I've come face-to-face with an unabashed bigot. God knows, the world is full of them. But they're like piles of dogshit in a grassy park—you tend to forget they're there until one gloms on to the bottom of your shoe. And while I'd love to scrape my sole clean on her tiny curb of a brain right now, I simply don't have the time. The front room is filling up, and the coffee urn is nearly empty.

"That kind of thinking isn't welcome at Angelhaven," I say. "So if you wish to remain here, you'd best keep it to myself."

She reddens as if scalded by my Arctic tone, then huffs up like an affronted cat. "Geez. You give some people a little power and look what happens."

I give her the roomlet next to the Duprees. I figure they deserve each other.

I get a young, traveling salesman from Portland situated next, then a truck driver from Des Moines. In those few, 'free' moments in-between, I make more coffee, check for Clara's suitcase, and field a complaint about the latrines being too cold. Despite the headlong pace and unending demands, it's easy to see why this work means so much to Mom. The kind of satisfaction you get from helping people so obviously in need really sticks to your ribs. All of a sudden, I'm very proud of Robin Middlefield. I hope that, after today, she'll be just a little proud of me, too.

I'm scurrying down from the loft with another load of blankets when the next cluster of refugees comes shuffling in from the cold. Two look like college students in their faded jeans and Gor-Tex jackets; the third is a short, bedraggled man in a raincoat. Something about that one tickles a trip-wire in my brain. An instant later, I explode.

Fenton Davenport!

I go shooting across the barn like an armed torpedo, and catch up with the little weasel just as Mattie is handing him the guest book.

"Get any good pictures of the fire last night?" I ask. The haggard lines about his eyes and mouth harden. His shoulders lose their slouch. "Knowing you, you probably set it just so you could have the scoop."

"Raven!" Mattie says, her eyes wide with shock. "What a terrible thing to say!"

"That's all right, Mrs. Freeman," Davenport says. "We're old friends." Then he arches a mocking eyebrow at me. "I suppose you'll be showing me to the door now."

I'll admit, that's how the fantasy begins. Then, sometime in early April, a party of cross-country skiers discovers him in a half-melted snowbank, bluer than a Seven-Eleven Slurpie. Knowing my luck, though, it wouldn't end there. Some fool of a doctor would probably bring him back to life—or clone him!—and we'd all wind up on *Hard Copy*.

Thanks, but no thanks. As galling as his presence may be, Fenton Davenport stays.

"Sign in," I order him. He raises that mocking eyebrow at me again, but does as he is told. Then I sling a blanket into his unready arms and growl, "This way."

"I must say," he says, as I march him through the barn, "this is awfully sporting of you. When things finally settle down, maybe we could find an out-of-the-way corner and have a little chat."

I stop dead in my tracks, then turn and let him have it, both barrels at point-blank range. "There will be no little chats between you and me, Mr. Davenport. There will be no close encounters of any kind. You're only here because you had no other place to go, and because my mother believes in the goodness of all men. Accept that. Respect that. And stay out of my sight."

His eyes narrow. His thin, bloodless line of a mouth twitches like it's just been hooked. "You don't have to be shy around me," he says. "Just come right out and say what's on your mind."

An urge to wring his scrawny neck blows through me. I clench my fists against that wish and then grit my teeth as well because here come the Duprees, full steam ahead. *What, God? What did I do to deserve this?*

"Miss Middlefield," Willy says, as they approach. "I'd like a word with you."

"I'm sorry, Mr. Dupree," I reply, in a tone ringing with exasperation, "but your wife's suitcase hasn't turned up yet. As soon as it does, I'll get it to you. Until then—"

"That's not it." He's standing in front of me now. Clara hangs back a few steps, as if I'm radioactive. Her accusing silence rankles me into an outburst.

"Then what, pray tell, *is* it?" I ask. "The accommodations? The company? I know you're not exactly thrilled with this situation. I'm not, either. But until this storm blows over, we're stuck with each other, so let's put our grudge on hold. I'm too damn busy to—"

"I know," he interrupts. "That's what I wanted to talk to you about. Me and the missus want to help."

The offer is so surprising, it scrambles my circuits for a moment. Davenport takes the opportunity to insert himself into the conversation. "Hello, Willy. Hello, Clara. Nice to see you again."

"Oh, hello, Mr. Davenport," Willy says. "How very good to see you again. We wondered where you got to after they evacuated us. Covering the story, I suppose."

Davenport shrugs, trying to look modest. "You know how it is—a reporter's on call twenty-four seven."

Willy turns his attention back to me and says, "Mr. Davenport took us to dinner last night. Afterward, he wound up renting a room at the motel because of the weather."

"How convenient," I sneer, jabbing at Davenport with my eyes.

"Not really," he says flatly. "I have a family, too, you know."

"But anyway," Willy goes on to say, "if there's anything that Clara and I can do, I hope you'll let us do it. It goes against our grain to stand idly by when there's work to be done."

My first impulse is to refuse them. They're the enemy, they can't be trusted. And the fruit of their accursed loins held a gun to my head! But as much as I'd like to give in to my prejudices, I can't because it wouldn't be fair to anyone else.

"As soon as I'm finished here," I say, "I'm going back to the house to fix lunch. A couple of extra hands on deck would get everyone fed that much sooner."

"I'd like to help, too," Davenport says.

"Fine," I say. "Go outside and look around for a tall, good-looking kid with a snow-shovel. I'm sure he could use a break by now."

I can tell by the frown that flashes across his brow that heaving snow wasn't what he had in mind, but that's just too bad. I hope Dex gives him the job of shoveling around the latrines.

"You can stow any gear you might have in the last room to your right," I instruct him in parting. But if I could have, I would have stuck him in the freezer with the rest of the turkeys.

I whisk the Duprees off to the house. There, I bring out the fixings for lunch: four loaves of Wonder bread, a gigantic jar of peanut butter, a block of American cheese, and a squeeze-bottle of French's mustard. My helpers belly up to the counter and get to work.

"You don't like Mr. Davenport much, do you?" Willy asks, as he slaps a sandwich together.

"Nope," I say. "Not much."

"I'm sure that makes his job a whole lot easier."

Irritation sweeps through me like a desert wind. Like I really need his homespun insights! He wasn't the one who had his face splashed across the front page of a freakin' tabloid newspaper, courtesy of dear Mr. Davenport. He wasn't the one who was lionized against his will and then shot down. So who is he to talk? I set down the knife that I've been using to slice the cheese and step away from the counter. I need to get away for a moment. Somebody somewhere is asking way too much of me.

"I'm going to check on my mother," I say. "She's recovering from a stroke, you know."

Willy nods. Clara looks down at her hands. I break for Mom's bedroom only to find her parked in front of a window in the living room. She looks old and neglected, like an Easter Island statue. I hurry over to her like a good, guilt-ridden daughter.

"Mom!" I exclaim, as I sink into a crouch alongside of her wheelchair. "What are you doing out here?"

Her head swivels toward me. Her gaze follows an instant later.

"Bathroom," she says then, very distinctly.

"What? You have to go to the bathroom?"

My hands dart toward the handles of her chair. She bats them away with an impatient wave of her hand.

"No, no. Done." Although I hate myself for doing it, I secretly sniff the air for the tang of urine. It isn't there. Thank God. "Watch now. Eyes glad."

She points. At first, I think she wants me to look at the yard, which is a muddled patchwork of snowmobile ruts, heavy-duty tire tracks, and footprints. Then I notice the space just beyond her window. It's full of snow-angels. The two little angels who made them are now bounding toward their dad, trailing clots of compacted snow behind them. Once again, I wonder what it would be like to have a few of my own.

"They are special, aren't they?" I ask her.

My mother does not answer me.

There's a lopsided smile on her face now. That faraway gleam is back in her eyes. I've resented that look for as long as I can remember, because I thought it was designed to shut me out. But all at once, I recognize Mom's sleight-of-mind for what it really is—a coping mechanism. She's not trying to get away from me, she's just trying to get away, period. I don't know why it took me so long to pick up on this, it seems obvious enough in the rear-view mirror. I guess I was just feeling too sorry for myself to put two and two together. Now that I have done the math, though, I feel liberated, and strangely grateful. For while I still don't know anything about the pressures that drive Robin Middlefield to wink back and forth between realities, at least I can now dare to hope that those forces have nothing to do with me. And that leads me to hope that the old bird might love me a little after all. I kiss her brow, then nick off to fetch a sandwich for her. When I return, her eyes are closed. I set the plate on her lap like an offering. And in a way, I suppose it is.

Back in the kitchen, lunch is all made and ready to go. I give Willy and Clara first picks as a roundabout way of thanking them for their help. Almost shyly, they each select a cheese-and-mustard sandwich. I choose a peanut butter wedge for myself, but the first bite gripes my still-tender stomach, so I set the rest of it aside for later.

"I'll go ahead and take this out," I say then, reaching for the first of two heaping trays. "You can bring the other one when you're done eating."

I'm no more than four steps out of the house when I hear the gritty pop and crunch of snow-tires rolling up the driveway. I glance over my shoulder, and see a truck stuffed with faces heading my way. The driver is Kyle Hobson. My insides go warm and mushy at the sight only to freeze up again as I flash back to last night. Did I really throw myself at him like some horny fifteen-year-old?

Yep. 'Fraid so.

I want to dive into a snowbank and hide until he's gone. But that's not one of my smarter impulses, so I step up my pace instead.

"Raven!" Kyle calls then. "Wait up!"

Damn.

I put on a brave face, then half-turn to watch as he ushers a man, a woman, and two children toward me. I have a feeling that I know these people from somewhere, but Kyle's proximity has put me in such a dither, I can't quite place them.

"Hi," I say, as they all close in on me. "Lousy day to be out and about, hey?"

"Raven, meet the Fowler family," Kyle says, and presents each one of them to me. As he does so, that nagging sense of recognition grows stronger. Papa Tom with his dour mouth and missing fingers, hollow-eyed Lea and her ragamuffin kids: *where have I seen those people?* "They're the last of the lot."

"Welcome to Angelhaven," I say. "As it happens, you're just in time for lunch."

I hold out the tray. The kids look to their father for permission. He squints at me like a man who has forgotten how to trust, then grudgingly gives them the OK.

"You, too," I urge the grown-ups. "There's plenty more where this came from."

"Thanks," Kyle says, not the least bit shy about helping himself. "I've been so busy, I haven't had a chance to eat." He downs two sandwiches in quick succession— a man after my own heart. "There," he says afterward, "that should keep me for a few more hours. I've got to get to the barracks before the roads close completely. Before I go, though, I have some things in the back of the truck for you."

"OK," I say, and thrust my tray at Mrs. Fowler. "Will you do me a favor and take this into the barn? I'll join you just as soon as I see Officer Hobson on his way."

"But Daddy," the Fowler boy squeaks, before anyone can go anywhere. "What about our Christmas tree?"

Huh?

I follow the kid's gaze back to Kyle's truck. And sure enough, there's a pine tree sprawled in the flatbed. I can't believe they talked Kyle into stopping at a stand to pick it up.

"Not another word about that damn tree, Ken, do you hear me?" Mr. Fowler says. "These people have more important things on their minds."

His pointed tone harpoons the memory that's been lurking just beyond reach of recall. I happened into these folks in Fred's parking lot on the morning after the robbery. They were fussing with a tree then, too. Two and two come together at that, and my jaw falls open like a trapdoor.

"You dragged a tree from a burning building?"

Tom Fowler looks down at his scuffed up boots. He could be angry; he could be embarrassed. The two look the same on his kind of face. "It's all we had for Christmas," he says.

The bleakness of that confession sends big-hipped pangs of pity crashing through me. To risk so much for so little! The line between hard times and true misery must be O-ring-thin for them. Something in me wants to do more than just give these people shelter for the night. It wants to make them smile.

"Tell you what," I say, addressing Ken and his red-nosed little sister. "I'll haul the tree into the barn right after lunch. Then you and the other children can decorate it. You don't mind sharing your tree, do you?"

"Sharing is good," the girl solemnly informs me.

"You won't forget, will you?" her brother asks, begging me for a promise with his puppy-dog eyes.

"No, I won't forget. Now get going. You'll feel a lot better once you're out of the snow."

The kids go dashing toward the barn. Their parents follow at a more dejected pace. I watch them with a curious ache in my heart and wonder how they came to be so downcast.

"It looks like you have a knack for this kind of work," Kyle says.

"Excuse me?" I say, as I snap out of my thoughts.

"The tree," he says. "It was a good idea."

"Oh. Yeah. Thanks."

I wait for him to say something about last night, something gentle and half-joking that'll put my mind at ease. But all he does is mosey back toward his truck. I guess it's true, I think, as I follow on his heels. A leopard can't change his spots. And neither can Kyle Hobson. He's still Mr. Use-'Em-And-Lose-'Em. I'm so angry and disappointed, with myself as well as with Kyle, that I cannot bear to look at him as we unload the flat-bed. So I focus on the flotsam instead. In addition to the tree, there's an assortment of hastily packed suitcases; a plastic crate filled with shoes and toys; a small cooler complete with beer; and the latest *People* magazine. Funny what some people will grab in a crisis.

"Well," Kyle says, when we're done, "I guess it's time for me to hit the road. I'll catch up with you later, OK?"

"Sure," I say, and then kiss him off in turn. "See you around."

He climbs into the truck without a backward glance, then goes ram-jetting down the driveway and away. I scowl at the plumes of blue-gray exhaust that linger ghost-like in his wake, then grab a couple of suitcases and start marching toward the barn. Halfway there, I cross paths with Sal. Her hair is messy. Her cheeks are flushed. She's wearing a pair of Mom's shiny-kneed sweat-pants and one of Jay's old coats. I don't think I've ever seen her so casually dressed. Or so pleased with herself.

"Did you guys have a good time at the party last night?" I ask her.

"It was OK," she says, and then blows a wisp of hair away from her eyes. "If I'd known that I was going to have to keep eight kids quiet and dry the morning after, though, I might've passed on that last glass of eggnog."

"I know what you mean," I say, although it feels like the worst of my hangover is starting to pass. "The good news is, I think I have a project that'll keep the little rascals busy for the rest of the day."

"That's a great idea!" she declares, after I fill her in on my plans for the Fowler's Christmas tree. "The girls have a huge stash of paper and glitter and glue in the house, so we're all set there, and I can pop some corn for stringing, too."

"Sounds good," I tell her. "You round up the materials. I'll meet you in the barn with the tree as soon as I solve this little luggage problem."

I do that by dumping the job on Dex. He's not crazy about the idea at first, but when the pretty, red-headed girl with whom he's been sharing his coffee-break offers to help, he changes his tune real fast.

"I don't care how you do it so long as every piece gets to its rightful owner," I tell him, and then take off to fetch the tree. When I return to the barn a few minutes later, I'm met by a mob by laughing, jumping, squealing kids. That's the high point of my day.

The construction of decorations begins: paper-chains and silver bells; snowflakes, Santa Cwauses, and whatever else we jolly well please. It's not just me and Sally and the kids, either. Our Lady of The Bigots, otherwise known as Grace, is folding squares of old newspaper into origami cranes. Some of the other adults are stringing corn. Everybody is talking, mostly about last night's fire.

One of the college students says it started in the laundry room. Grace says it was probably one of the clothes dryers because she had one that burst into flames once, but the trucker from Des Moines reckons it was a cigarette in the trash. They all agree, however, that it spread fast. The salesman from Portland—Hank? Hal? God, I'm so terrible with names—says his room was already filling up with smoke when the alarms went off. Mrs. Fowler murmurs something about waking up to warm walls.

Crikes. I'm suddenly very grateful that all I had to deal with this morning was a champagne hang-over.

Eventually, the chatter turns to other things: *where are you from, where were you going, what sorts of plans did you have?* The college guys admit that they were on their way to Vermont for a week of nonstop drinking and skiing; Grace says she was taking her daughter to see her grandmother. At that, I think of *my* mom, marooned in her own home, and decide that it's time for her to join the party.

I find her in front of the living room window—exactly where I left her. But to my surprise and instant fury, she's not alone like I'd imagined her to be. Davenport is crouched beside her wheelchair. His expression is that of a man who's biding his time. I go storming into the room like an off-season typhoon, and then spin him around so I can get right in his face.

"What in hell do you think you're doing?" I hiss at him. "Have you no respect for anything?"

"I saw her sitting here while I was shoveling the walk," he says. "She looked like she could use the company, so I stopped in for a visit when I was finished with my work." He takes my mom's hand and gives it a gentle shake, then flashes her a patronizing smile. "We had a nice visit, didn't we, Mrs. Middlefield."

"Nice," she echoes, looking straight at me. "Heavenly hosts proclaim."

Oh, God! Don't tell me the angels are on this rat-bag's side. No way. I refuse to believe it. Those heavenly hosts must be out of their heavenly minds.

"I'm glad to hear it, Mom," I say, which has to be the biggest lie I've told since I listed one fifteen as my weight on my international driver's license application. "And now that you two are done talking—" Accent on *done*. "—perhaps you'd like to come out to the barn and meet some of your other guests."

A smile gives life to the seams in her face. She takes my hand and gives it an eager squeeze.

"I guess I'll be moseying along," Davenport says.

"Don't mosey too far," I tell him, in a stropped tone. "It looks like you and I are going to have that little chat after all."

To his credit, he looks unsettled by the prospect.

"Nice," Mom repeats, as he high-tails it from the house. "Only human once."

"Whatever you say," I reply.

I bundle her up, then wheel her into the kitchen only to balk at the door. I could probably lift her up and carry her down the steps that are waiting beyond that threshold. In an emergency, she could probably take them by herself. But while I've gambled on 'probably' in the past and won, I won't risk it today. If something went wrong and she got hurt, the guilt would probably kill me.

"I'm sorry, Mom, I wasn't thinking," I say. "I'll go and find Jay."

Just then, someone knocks at the door. I tug it open to find Mr. Fowler standing there. His cheeks are flushed beneath his five o'clock shadow. The wary edge in his eyes is submerged.

"Thought I'd come out and take my turn with that thing," he says, glancing at the shovel that someone left in a nearby snowbank. "Then I happened to see you two through the window and figured you might need some help. If you want, I'll lift the lady."

I study his face as he once studied mine. And now that it's my turn to tender trust or not, I understand what he was looking for. But Mom is not as guarded as I am. She reaches right out to this taciturn stranger like a baby who wants up. He picks her up with surprising ease and respect, then takes the stairs one sure step at a time. I follow with the wheelchair and blankets.

"My wife's dad had a stroke a few years back," he tells Mom, as he settles her back into her seat. "She took care of him right up until—" He narrows his eyes, as if to restrict himself or perhaps the memory. "Well, pneumonia got him. But anyway, Lea knows some physical therapy tricks that could help you build the strength back in your arms and legs. If you'd like, I could ask her to come and see you later."

"Good," Mom says, and favors him with a full-fledged smile. "Silver clouds."

"Sounds like a 'yes' to me," I say. "And I think it's a terrific idea. What with the holidays, this weather, and everything else that's been going on, we've only been able to get a PT out here once to see her. Any help that Lea might like to give would be greatly appreciated. Thank you very much, too. You've been very kind."

"It's the least me and mine can do to repay you for the roof over our heads," he tells me. "I'll do any other chores you might need doing, too. I may be shy a couple of fingers, but I'm still able enough."

The almost defiant note of pride in his tone prompts me to look him over again; and what I see beneath the anger and hard choices is a mongrel's fierce loyalties. I'll bet he'd break Fenton Davenport's legs if I asked him to. I'll bet he wouldn't even ask why I'd want such an awful thing done, he'd just nick off and do it. I'm awed by the power he would cede to me in exchange for food for his family. I'm very humbled, too.

"Thank you, Mr. Fowler," I say. "If anything comes up, you can bet that I'll come looking for you. In the meantime, though, why don't you join us in the barn? We're decorating your tree."

"I'll leave that to Lea and the kids," he says tersely. "There's work to do out here."

With that and a wave, he takes his leave of us.

"Good," Mom says, as I steer her toward the barn. "Mattie like."

"Yes," I say, "I'm sure Mattie likes him, too."

The Fowler's tree is almost all trimmed by the time we make our entrance. Most of the decorations are hanging from the first three-and-a-half feet of branches, but nobody seems to care—not even Sally, who likes everything just so. She's the first one who sees us when we come wheeling in. She nudges Jay, who then sends Lisa and Gail our way. Little Lisa brings a friend.

"Gwamma," she says, as they all pile to a stop in front of the wheelchair, "this is Mawgwet. She ain't got no home."

"Here now," Mom says, and offers her hand to Tom Fowler's daughter.

Margaret's gaze darts from that pale, crepe-skinned appendage to the wheelchair and back again. There's worry in her eyes, and a hint of fear, too, but Lisa urges her on. "Don't be afraid, Mawgwet. That's just Gwamma's chaih. She hadda stwoke and her legs ahwen't working wight yet."

By slow, wary degrees, Margaret reaches out and touches Mom's hand. Upon contact, the fear fades from her eyes, and a shy smile creeps across her freckled face.

"Hi," she says.

The next thing I know, Mom's surrounded by kids. They pet her hand and her iron-gray hair, and poke at the pieces of her wheelchair. They ask her what a stroke is, and if it hurts, and point to the things that they've hung on the tree. Then Mattie comes strolling into the room with the little transistor radio that we listen to while we're doing the laundry. The look of satisfaction on her face blossoms into pure joy as she realizes who it is that the children are thronging.

"Robin, hello!" she exclaims. "I was just on my way to get you." She flashes me a grateful smile, then assumes my place behind the wheelchair. As she guides my mother toward the tree, she says, "The children and I made an ornament just for you, Rob. Jay, would you be a dear and bring it here?"

He delivers a cone of white construction paper with fat, snowflake wings and a paper-clip halo unto them. Mom blesses it with a smile, then points to where she wants it. A moment later, there's an angel perched on top of the tree.

Mattie turns the radio on. The static-y strains of a Christmas carole come spilling into the barn. 'Angels We Have Heard On High', I think it's called. I hear Mom croak, "Glor-i-ah. An Alka-Seltzer A Day, Oh!"

I do not know if I should laugh or cry.

CHAPTER 11

"Well," Sally says, as she glances around the table. "I have to admit—this isn't the picture that comes to my mind when I think of Christmas Eve."

I know what she means.

There are five of us for dinner on this night of nights: Mom, Mattie, Jay, Sal, and me. The girls are out in the barn, slurping down shells and spaghetti sauce with their new friends. They wheedled and begged for the privilege, and when Dex volunteered to keep an eye on them—and that pretty redhead, too, I'll bet—nobody had the energy to insist otherwise. In the next generation's absence, we are a quiet, listless lot. Jay is resting his head in one hand as he eats; my appetite is still shattered from last night; and Mattie is so pooped, she's not even fussing over Mom.

"My mother is serving goose with all the trimmings tonight," Sally continues, in a more wistful tone. "And plum pudding for dessert."

"I've never tried that," I say. "Is it really made of plums?"

"Nah," Jay pipes up. "It's just an overgrown fruitcake that has to have the snot steamed out of it before anyone can put a fork to it." Prompted by his wife's offended bleat, he adds, "It's good, though."

Mom mumbles something. All heads at the table turn her way. There's a ring of spaghetti sauce around her mouth, and more on her chin. She looks childishly content, or maybe just extremely tired.

"What was that, Rob?" Mattie asks. "I didn't catch it."

Rob does not reply.

Mattie searches Mom's face for a long moment, a reading both tender and weary, then heaves a sigh that lifts her to her feet. "Come on, Rob," she says. "It's time for you to get washed up and ready for bed."

"I could say the same about you," I tell her, as she reaches for the wheelchair's handgrips. "You look like you're running on fumes."

"You're not all wrong," she replies. "But like the poet says—I still have miles to go before I sleep."

"What's so important that it can't wait until morning?"

"I heard on the news that half of Connecticut is without electricity because of this storm. I want to get a couple of birds in the oven before the power goes out around here, too. That way, we can at least serve turkey and stuffing sandwiches for Christmas dinner tomorrow."

"Oh. I never thought of that." Which just goes to show you what a beginner I am when it comes to thinking of others. Beginner or not, though, and hung-over or not, I am determined to take care of my own tonight. "I'll tell you what. If you get the birds ready, I'll sit with them while they roast."

Everybody raises an eyebrow at that—everybody but Mom, who has never pretended to be anything other than the world's worst cook. I dismiss this vote of no confidence with a tsk. "Come on, you guys, cut me some slack. I may not be the next Julia Childs, but I can certainly babysit a turkey."

Sally maintains her dubious expression, but Mattie seems prepared to give me the benefit of a doubt. Poor thing. She must be even more tired than I thought. "OK, Rave," she says, "you've got yourself a deal. I'll be back out to square my end of the deal just as soon as I get Rob settled."

She and Mom go rolling off toward the bathroom. As they do so, Jay shakes his head in a bad-news sort of way and mutters, "Just look at 'em, would you? They're both ready to fall on their faces. I'm telling you, Raven. This situation has to change."

"Please, Jay," I beg him, "not tonight."

"Then when?" he demands, suddenly all hot-eyed. "When are you going to open your eyes and face the fact that this place is too much for those women? One's a gimp; the other should be so lucky. They can barely help themselves, never mind a barn full of strangers."

"I think things went pretty well today," I say.

"Thanks, in no small part, to you and me," he fires back. "But what about next time, hey, Raven? Where are you going to be the next time Mom needs your help?"

I'll be right here, bro'. Right freakin' here.

A vision from that future taps my frontal lobe. In it, I'm running Angelhaven with just a little bit of help from Mattie. Mom's walking again, albeit with a cane; every other Monday, we drive into H-C to buy supplies and eat lunch. Tuesdays and Saturdays are studio days, me taking pictures of whatever finds its way to the back of the barn. Friday afternoons, Ab and I meet at a local watering hole and bitch about men as we knock back half-price glasses of wine. I'll take my darling nieces to Disney movies and the Agawam Roller-Rink in the winter. Come summer, we'll spend at least one weekend per month at the beach. My days will be hectic. I'll sleep clear through the nights. Sunday will be lap day at the YWCA. But while I can finally envision a life like this without breaking into a cold sweat, I still can't bring myself to tell others about it. It feels like the last secret I'll ever have.

"Ask me again after the holidays," I say. "You can wait that long, can't you?"

He can, but he doesn't want to—I can tell by the sour look on his face. Before he has a chance to press the issue, though, somebody knocks at the door. He shoots me an accusing look, as if I somehow pre-arranged this latest distraction, then reluctantly gentles his scowl and opens the door. Gail and Lisa come striding into the kitchen. In their fluffy snowsuits and mittens, they look like The Michelin Man's next of kin. Both of them are toting kid-sized loads of dirty dishes.

"Look at me, Daddy," Gail says. "I'm helping."

"So you are," he says, and then ushers her out of the doorway so Dex can get through. He's carrying a big, plastic tub full of dishes. His redheaded friend is right on his tail.

"Did we give you enough time to finish your supper?" he asks. "If not, we can bring the rest of the stuff in later."

"Don't worry, we're done," I assure him. "Just put what you have down by the sink. I'll take care of it from there."

"If you want," he says, "me and Sara can clean up. It's better than hanging out in the barn with a bunch of kids and old folks."

My gaze zips from him to the girl and back again. She's all rosy-cheeked and dewy-eyed. His stance is just a bit too offhand. It's all so deliciously cute, I'm tempted to tease. I refrain, however, because it's Christmas Eve, and because I was young once upon a time, too.

"Go for it," I tell them. "And thanks. Washing dishes has never been one of my favorite pastimes."

"I can attest to that," Sally says, as she pulls her children out of their wraps. Then she flashes me an impish grin. There may be hope for her—and us—after all.

Dex and Sara trudge back to the barn for the rest of the dirty dishes. Sal escorts my stripped-down nieces toward the bathroom. That leaves me and Jay all by ourselves, but to my relief, he makes no move to pick up where we left off.

"So, what's next on the agenda?" he asks me. "I haven't spent Christmas Eve at home since I got married."

"Beats me," I say. "The last time I was here, I spent the evening with Ab. What happens at the Harper house?"

"Sally's mom stuffs us all silly, then herds us into the family room for Christmas caroles and presents. I suppose we could do a scaled-down version of that once the girls are out of the tub."

Normally, I love the gift-giving scene, especially when kids are involved. But 'normal' isn't a word that I'd use to describe this particular Christmas, and I cannot bring myself to feel right about us exchanging mostly superfluous luxuries in the comfort of our home while people like the Fowlers lay awake in the barn on borrowed cots, wondering where on earth they're going to sleep tomorrow.

"Nah," I say. "Let's do that in the morning. Like we used to when we were kids."

He nods as if to say that was his thought, too, and then flops himself into the chair by the window. "Maybe we should follow Mom's lead and turn in early. It's been a long day."

"That's for sure."

Dexter and Sara return with the rest of the dishes. Moments later, the kitchen comes alive with sounds of stoneware being scrapped and stacked for the sink. Jay sticks around for a minute or two, then wanders off to help Sally with the girls—or so he says. I grab my coat and slip outside for a smoke so Dex and his sweetie-pie can have a moment alone.

Christ, it's cold out! Not only can I see my breath, I can feel it turning to frost in my nostrils. And yes, it's still snowing. Trees are beginning to sag beneath the weight of so much whiteness. Froghollow Lane has disappeared. I've never seen such a relentless fall, and it won't grieve me if I never see its like again. All I want for Christmas is a clear sky, Mom's return to health, and world peace.

But I'll probably just get clothes.

I fish a cigarette from the pack in my coat pocket, then stroll toward the foot of the drive. Despite the snow and the cold, I like being out here simply because there's no one else around. I never quite realized what a solitary creature I am, or how well that lifestyle suits my temperament. After a day like today, though, there's no denying it. People suck the psychic starch right out of me, even when they don't want anything. Their presence is a demand in and of itself.

And, I think, as I catch a shadowy flicker of movement out of the corner of one eye, *some presences are more toxic than others.*

I flick my cigarette into the snow, then swing around to blast the bogie on my tail. Davenport doesn't turn up in my sights, however. Tom Fowler does. He's standing on the far side of the driveway and back a few yards. His face is half-hidden by a scarf, but I recognize him by the way he holds himself—stiff like a soldier, yet uneasy to the bone. I hold my fire, then close the gap between us.

"Something I can do for you, Mr. Fowler?" I ask.

"No, ma'am. I just came out to clear the driveway," he says, and then glances at the shovel in his hand like someone who's used to being asked for an alibi. "When I saw you, I decided to hold off so you could smoke in peace."

"That was very kind of you," I say. "But you don't need to be out here. You've already done more than your fair share of shoveling. Let someone else have a turn."

"That's OK, I want to do it. Really," he insists, when I doubt him with a scowl. "It's nice to have something useful to do for a change."

The hint of bitterness in those last three words invites questions. I wonder where he's from, and why he left, and what those missing fingers of his have to do with where he is now. But I won't ask. Will not. Because he'd probably feel obliged to answer me whether he wanted to or not, and I have absolutely no desire rob a poor man of the last bit of privacy he still owns.

As it happens, though, he throws the doors to his house open of his own accord.

"I've been out of work for three years now—ever since I lost my fingers and then some to a boiler room explosion at my last job. I get disability, but that's not a lot when you have two kids and a wife to feed. We lived with Lea's father for a while, but then he died and the bank took his house and we didn't have enough money to buy it back, so we got kicked out. Now we're heading south because they say that's where all the good jobs are these days.

"All I want to do is give my family a decent life, Miz Middlefield. Is that so much for a not-so-terribly-crippled man to ask?"

"Not at all, Mr. Fowler," I reply, humbled once again by the simple urgency of his needs. "Not at all."

A silence comes between us. It is so quiet, I can actually hear the faint hiss of snow as it falls in the dark. He shifts his weight from one foot to the other. I stuff my hands into my pockets and count my many blessings.

"Well," he says, "I guess I'd better get shoveling. Merry Christmas, Miss Middlefield."

"Same to you, Mr. Fowler," I say, and then leave him to his work. It is the only gift, par-rum-pa-pa-pum, that I have to give him.

Back in the kitchen, things are hopping. Dexter is washing dishes; Sara's drying; and Mattie's stuffing the first of two birds. The room smells of soap, heat, and buttered herbs. I shed my shoes and jacket, then sidle over to Mattie just as she's pulling her hand out of the turkey's backside. Her fingers are caked with stuffing.

"Oh, yeah, that reminds me," I joke. "I need to make an appointment with my gynecologist."

"Lord, but you can be gross when the mood takes you," Mattie says. "I may never eat stuffing again."

"Good. More for me."

"Greedy creature."

Meanwhile, over by the sink, Dexter and Sara are having a lively, scatter-shot conversation. I hear Pearl Jam and a possible tour mentioned. A moment later, they're raving about inline skates. Then the topic of college comes up. Mattie's face goes very still and stays that way until she hears her son brag about being on the short-short-list for a U-Conn scholarship.

"Is that true?" I ask her.

"Yes, ma'am," she replies, all smiles and pride now.

I'd love to go over there and give Dex a hug for being such a brain—and maybe a sock in the arm, too, for keeping me in the dark—but before I can do so, a rap at the door pulls me the other way. Halfway there, a second rap urges me to hurry.

I open the door to find Grace standing on the step. Her hair is disheveled, a garish halo. Her jacket is misbuttoned. If it weren't for her eyes, which are wild with worry, I'd be tempted to think that she'd been drinking.

"I'm so sorry to bother you," she says, before I can get a word out, "but I can't find my daughter. I'm afraid she might've wandered off in this storm and gotten lost—"

"Relax, Momma," a voice from behind me says. "I'm right here."

Surprise flickers across Grace's road-worn face like TV static. Then she barges right past me and plants herself in the middle of the kitchen.

"Sara? What on earth are you doing?"

Her daughter is standing by the sink, dishrag in hand. The soap-bubble goatee that Dexter gave her a second ago is still glistening on her chin.

"What does it look like I'm doing?"

Grace's eyes flick from Sara to Dexter, who's up to his elbows in suds. As she jumps to obvious conclusions, I can't stop myself. I lean in close and whisper, "And you said they never washed."

She shoots me a look that could blister old paint, then turns back to her daughter. "I was worried sick, Sara. You had no business running off without telling me."

"Oh, Momma, you're such a spaz."

"Don't talk to your mother like that," Mattie scolds. "It's her job to worry after you."

"OK, Mattie," Sara replies, politely contrite.

Grace's disapproving mouth puckers at the edges. I can tell that she's pissed at Mattie for ordering the fruit of her superior white loins around. I'm sure Mattie can tell, too. "It was decent of you to help these good people out, Sara," she says, "but it's time we left them to their own lives. I'm sure they've had their fill of strangers for one day."

Now, I know it's Christmas Eve and all, but I just can't resist the chance to twist this woman's tit. "Oh, Sara's no stranger," I assure her, "leastwise not to anybody here. As far as we're concerned, she's part of the family already."

"Nevertheless," Grace insists. Her smile is so forced, it looks like molded plastic. "I'd feel better if she came back to the barn with me. Now."

Sara opens her mouth, presumably to voice the protest that's stamped on her face, but before she can get a word of it out, Mattie puts her foot down.

"You go ahead, Sara. We'll finish up here. Thanks very much for all your help."

Disappointment flashes across Dex's face, but he's quick to recover. When Sara looks to him for support or maybe just sympathy, he's all blank-faced and cool again.

"See you later," he says. "Watch out for snow trolls."

"Too late for that," Sara mutters, and then goes skulking off after her mother. An instant after the door bangs shut, Jay comes striding into the room.

"Who was that?" he asks.

"Just another satisfied customer," I say.

"What's this about a customer?" Sally asks, as she rounds the corner with Lisa and Gail in tow. The girls have that delicious, fresh-scrubbed glow about them. There's an excited light in their blue eyes. As soon as Lisa sees me, she breaks free of Sal's grip and throws herself at my knees.

"Auntie Waven," she says, "could you pwease call Santa and ask him to bwing my fwend Mawgwet a new house? She don't got one no more."

"I dunno, pumpkin," I say, touched by the size of her heart. "Santa might not be able to fit a house on his sleigh."

"Oh." Her baby-fat face slumps with disappointment only to rebound with her next thought. "Then how 'bout a Pwincess Baby? Can he bwing her one of those?"

"I guess we'll just have to wait and see," Jay says, and then takes her by the hand. "Now come on, it's time for bed. Santa Claus won't come if you're awake, you know."

"I know. 'Night, Auntie Waven. 'Night, Mattie and Dex."

"If you don't need us," Sally says, "we're going to turn in, too."

I waggle my eyebrows suggestively. She turns a fetching shade of red. *Pay-dirt*, I think. And: *lucky devils*. I wish I had someone to curl up with tonight.

"See you in the morning," I say.

The turkeys are all buttered up and ready to go now. As I commit the first of them to the oven, Mattie hovers in my shadow and frets.

"Are you sure you don't mind doing this?" she asks. "I could come back and check on them later if you—"

"I can handle this, Mattie," I say. "Cross my heart and hope to die. Now go upstairs and get some rest."

"All right then." She folds me into a hug. She smells of butter and good, clean sweat. "If you're going to be that way about it." She hobbles over to Dex and squeezes him, too. "Watch yourself," she tells him. "Those snow trolls don't care who they have for dinner, you know."

He laughs. "Whatever you say, Mom."

She squeezes him again, then leaves the room.

"Looks like it's just me and you, dude," I say, "and unless I miss my guess, you're bound for the barn. If you want, I can give you a list of official reasons for being there."

The corners of his mouth twitch—a charming betrayal of pleasure and teenaged pride. He gives the pot that he's been drying one last swipe, then lowers his defenses.

"I know I don't know her very well," he says, "but I want to give her something for Christmas. You know, so she won't feel like she's missing out. Problem is, I don't have anything a girl would like." He clears his throat, then says, "Would you maybe have something?"

"So that's how it is, is it?" I ask, only half-teasing. "You'll hit your friend Raven up for a favor, but you won't tell her about your up-and-coming, all-expenses-paid trip to UConn? I'm not sure I like my place in this pecking order."

He flushes. "I thought you already knew, Rave. I mean, jeez, Mom's been telling *every*body about it for months now."

"Oh, so it's Mattie's fault."

For a moment there, I think I've pushed him too far, for his downy upper lip goes suddenly stiff, but then he chokes his medicine down like a man and says, "Nah, it's not Mom's fault. I should've told you the other day when we were talking about it, but I was ticked at you for busting my chops. Sorry."

"Apology accepted," I say, and immediately get off his case. "Come on, let's go and see if there's any treasure fit for a pretty girl buried in my closet."

As we enter into my room, I tell him to sit anywhere and then begin to excavate. The first thing I dig out is the box of old pictures. The photograph that Francois took of me in that string bikini is sitting right on top. Dexter lets out an astonished gasp when he sees it.

"Whoa! Is this you?"

"'Fraid so," I reply, and then hold up a Ron-Jon's Surf Shop T-shirt that I bought several years back but never wore. "How's this?"

He looks up from the photo, then scrunches up his nose. "What else you got?"

I burrow past a collection of old bathing suits and into a layer of fish stuff: books, guides, a stack of photos that never made it to market. I riff through these, thinking that there might be one good enough to give away, but they're all hopelessly amateurish, an almost embarrassing reminder of how far I have come.

But I don't want to think about that.

"What about this?" I ask, dangling a red plastic lobster key-chain from my finger. "He squeaks when you squeeze him."

"Cute," he says, "but not quite what I had in mind. Got anything else?"

I continue digging, but the stuff at this level is dates back to my high school days. I find a cache of old swim-meet medals, my then-favorite pair of sandals, then a shoebox full of earrings and costume jewelry.

"Something in here maybe?" I ask, rattling the box.

He doesn't answer. He's staring at a picture—not that pin-up of me, but one I snapped of Mom and Mattie just before I left home for the first time. They're standing arm-in-arm in the backyard. Mom has that distant, Easter Island look about her; Matt's smiling for the both of them. They look young, younger than I remember them being at that time. It's hard to believe that fifteen years really makes that much difference.

"Raven?" Dex asks.

"Yeah?"

"Do you think—" His tone is choppy; his expression, conflicted. "Do you think your mother and my mother are—" He swallows hard, then blurts, "Do you think they're gay?"

Whoa! Talk about being blindsided! Part of me wants to shout: *no way*! Part of me wants to laugh. At the same time, another, more detached voice admits that this could explain a lot. So I proceed with caution.

"What makes you ask, Dex?"

"It's been floating around town for quite a while now," he says, with an offended scowl. "You know—a whisper here, a snicker there. Some of the kids at school have started making jokes about it, too. They call our moms dinosaur dykes, because they're old and always together."

"Yeah, well. That's some people for you," I tell him, thinking of the old DeeDee Harcourt and all the other bottom-feeders who live on other people's shit. "They make stuff up about oddballs like me and Mom so they can feel better about their own sad-ass lives. Pathetic, isn't it?"

"Yeah," he says, but then jumps right back to the heart of the matter. "But it's not like what they're saying isn't true. Your mom and my mom *are* together almost all of the time. And since Robin had her stroke, it's gotten even worse. Sometimes at night after I've gone to bed, I hear my mom get up and go downstairs. She doesn't always come back up, either. Do you—do you think they're—"

He can't bring himself to finish the question. Or maybe I don't let him.

"I think they're two friends who have grown to love each other very much over the years," I reply. "I think they want to live and grow old together. If you need to know more than that, well—you're just going to have to ask one of them."

"But it's not fair," he says. "I mean, what about me? What will people think?"

"You already know what some people are thinking," I say. "And the worst of them are going to continue thinking like that no matter what's fair or true, so there's no point in worrying about it. And as for you, well, you should be happy that our moms are so close. That way, when it comes time for you to go to U-Conn or wherever, you won't have to worry about Mattie being all heartbroken and alone. *Every*one will have a life. *Every*thing will have a place. Home will be an anchor, not a ball-and-chain."

A resistant scowl creases his handsome young brow. His mouth starts to open only to stall.

"Give yourself some time to think about it," I say. "Then, if you want, we can talk some more. Meanwhile—" I drop the shoebox into his unready hands. "—let's see if there's anything in here that Sara might like."

He shoots me a how-can-you-eat-at-a-time-like-this sort of look, then shakes his head and opens the box. A few moments later, he pulls out a pair of Egyptian-cross earrings.

"How 'bout these?" he asks.

"Good choice," I say. "If I remember rightly, the *ankh* is a symbol for enduring life."

"Cool." A smile curves across his mouth. It's got Sara written all over it. "How much do I owe you?"

"*Nada*, dude. They're going to a good home. You'll have to scrounge a box for them elsewhere, though."

"I guess I'd better get cracking then." He flows to his feet. An instant later, he's at the door. "Catch you later. And oh," he adds, as he lets himself out, "thanks a lot. For everything."

His parting smile is all for me.

I take a moment to savor the sense of pride and accomplishment that's coursing through me. This is, I think, what big sisters must enjoy on a regular basis. I start to get up. As I do so, a stiffness in my joints catches up with me. Damn! I didn't think it was possible to get so out of shape in such a short time. At this rate, I'm going to be as soft as Sally by the time the new year rolls around. The thought scares me into doing a round of calisthenics. That leaves me sweaty if no less sore, so I lumber off to the bathroom for a long, hot shower. I stay there until my muscles get so water-logged, they loosen up.

Afterward, as I'm toweling off in my room, the snapshot that Francois took of me catches my eye. Maybe I'm a masochist. Maybe I'm just bored. All I know is, I saw that bikini while I was rifling through my closet, and now some seriously curious part of me wants to see if it still fits. So I dig the thing out and put it on, then dare a peek at the mirror that's hanging on the back-side of the bedroom door. On the plus side, I'm more muscular in the chest and shoulders than I was when that snapshot was taken. In the minus column, there's my stomach, which isn't as flat as it used to be; and that clump of spider veins on my right thigh that looks like a permanent bruise. All in all, though, I have to say that I look OK for a woman of my age. Well, OK, maybe better than OK. OK, maybe a lot better. *Hey, Sal—has any of that fat gone to my hips yet?*

As I'm congratulating myself, a wonderful, buttery smell expands in my nostrils. At first, it doesn't register as anything more than an extension of my own pleasure, but then awareness strikes me like a thunderclap.

"Shit!"

Imagining turkeys flambé and then Fred's Motor Inn, I fast-break for the kitchen. The birds are doing just fine without me, though; their skins are just starting to turn gold. I give them a basting, then ease them back into the oven. As I'm shutting the oven door, the telephone rings. I hasten to grab it before it can wake the whole house up.

"Hello?"

"Hey, Rave! It's me, Ab. How's your X-Mas Eve going?" She actually says *X-Mas*, like there's no room for Christ in this holiday anymore. "It's bloody boring over here. My folks went to bed an hour ago. Bruce and Vince are watching 'Law & Order' reruns on TV in the den."

"It's pretty quiet here, too," I say, "though it's only gotten that way in the last few hours. You know that Fred's burned down last night, don't you?"

"Yeah, it got a passing mention on the morning news. I suppose you guys got all the DPs."

"But of course, darling. And you'll never guess who was among them."

"You're right, I never will. So just tell me."

"Well, for starters, there was Willy and Clara Dupree." She treats me to a scandalized gasp, which I greatly appreciate. "Then Fenton Davenport showed up."

"No way!"

"Yes way! And can you believe it? The bastard actually snuck into the house and tried to talk to Mom while everybody else was in the barn."

"That scumbag!"

We discuss Davenport's dubious parentage and other shortcomings for a while, then move on to other topics: the fire and its probable causes; this damn storm; and of course, last night's party.

"I have to admit, I was a little miffed when you turned your nose up at Vince like you did," she says. "But after being trapped in the same house with him all day, I'll never question your judgment again. All he does is piss and moan, mostly about how his head hurts and how upset his folks are that he's not there and how Kyle scratched his precious BMW's rear bumper with the tow-chain."

The memory of that ditch, or maybe the mention of Kyle, raises goosepimples on my arms. I give them a quick rub, then walk over to the coat-rack and slip on my bomber jacket. Meanwhile, Abby continues to complain.

"...and Bruce is even worse. All he's done today is sit on his ass and order me around. 'Fix us some sandwiches'. 'Turn up the heat.' 'Get us a brew.' Like I'm his goddam valet, right? I'm telling you, Rave, as soon as the holidays are over, he's history, and good riddance to the big, lazy lump."

Yeah, right. I would sooner believe that she was going to give birth to a litter of bug-eyed alien babies. But I don't say that because she's my best friend and I'd like to keep it that way.

"I dunno, Ab. January is an awfully long month to spend alone."

"You have a right to your doubts," she says, "but this time, I'm serious. I might even go somewhere after I kick him out just so he can't charm me into thinking that I miss him." She pauses for a moment, then slyly adds, "I hear the Caribbean is nice this time of year."

It just figures. I've been trying to talk Abby into visiting me on-site ever since I made underwater photography my trade, but she's always had something better, more important, to do. Now that I'm about to dip my toe in other waters, she finally gets the urge to travel.

"Where did you say you were going to be?" she asks. "Aruba? Do they have nice beaches there?"

"I don't know," I say, too curt, I know, because she's breaking my heart. "I'm not a freakin' travel agent—"

On the other end of the line, a masculine rumbling breaks out in the background.

"Excuse me a moment, Rave," Abby says. She cups a hand over her mouthpiece then, but I catch fragments of the conversation just the same. Something about 'brandy' and 'fire'. A moment later, she's back again. "Rave? I have to go. His royal lumpiness desires a nightcap. I'll call you tomorrow, OK?"

"Sure, Ab," I say, happy to let her go. "Merry X-Mas."

"Same to you, girl." Then, in the instant before she hangs up, I hear her snap, "Hold your damn horses, Bruce. I said I was coming."

I hang up, then shake my head. She'll probably wind up marrying the asshole.

I wander over to the oven and baste the turkeys again. They seem to be taking forever to cook. Damn. I'd love to hit the sack right now and hopefully sleep away the funk that's overtaken me, but—oh, well. That's what I get for being a nice guy. I shuffle over to the kitchen window, draw the inner and then the outer pane open, then flop myself down in the chair and light up a cigarette. Back in the olden days, Ab and I used to sneak smokes like this from my room when it was too cold to smoke outside. I wish she could be here now. No, scratch that. I wish the old Abby could be here, with the old Raven. They had all the answers. I don't have a clue.

I take a drag, then blow the smoke downwind. It weaves its way through the falling snow like a fleet-footed specter. I think of my dad, and Clifton Dupree.

Ghosts of Lifetimes Past.

In the driveway, my rental car is entombed by snow. The yard is so full and white, it hurts my eyes. *Spirit! Is that what my future is to be?*

A distant, mechanized whir intrudes on my thoughts. I glower, broadcasting a telepathic wish that it be gone—and quickly—but the noise grows louder and louder. A bobbing headlight snares my attention. No doubt about it, it's heading this way. *Merde.* Another stranded traveler. It has to be. Why else would anybody be out and about on a night like this? As I'm trying to figure out where I'm going to put the damn crazy fool, a snowmobile roars across the yard and up to my still-open window. Its driver kills the motor right away, then pulls off his snow-encrusted helmet.

"Hey, Raven," Kyle says. "Merry Christmas." When all I do is boggle at him, he cocks his blonde head at me and grins. "I told you I'd drop by later, didn't I?"

My thoughts are scrabbling like a dog caught on a patch of glare ice. I am, in turn, hopeful and humiliated; amazed and abashed. It embarrasses me to look at him, and yet I cannot seem to look away. I resent him for making me feel this way. I resent him for lots of things. But I cannot let him know that, I've shown too much weakness already. So I take a last leisurely drag from my cigarette, and then flick the butt into a distant snowbank like I'm made of pure cool.

"I guess it must've slipped my mind," I say. "As you know, we had our hands full today. Now that you're here, though, what can I do for you?"

"Well, for starters, there's this." He twists around in his seat to thump the lumpy, oversized garbage bag that I had mistaken for a second rider. "It's not very much—just the tail-end of this year's 'Toys For Tots' drive that got stuck in the barracks. But at least it'll give your younger guests something to open in the morning."

"How incredibly thoughtful of you!" I say, stunned all the way down to my toes by the extent of his goodness, a goodness I keep wanting to disbelieve even though it's been popping up everywhere lately. What is wrong with me? "The kids will be thrilled. I know I am."

"There's just one problem," he says. "The presents need to be wrapped. I meant to do it when I got home this afternoon, but I crashed as soon as I pulled my boots off and didn't wake up till an hour ago."

Which is, no doubt, his polite way of reminding me that he's had a long day, too. I'm ashamed of my churlishness now, and confounded by the number of emotional hoops he's managed to put me through in a very few minutes.

"I have paper," I tell him. "I could wrap them."

"OK." A moment later, he cocks his head at me again and asks, "So, are you going to let me in or what? I don't think this bag's going to fit through that window."

"Oh! Sure." I think about smacking myself upside the head, because the way I'm acting, something in my brain must surely be stuck. "Come around to the door."

He shuts off his light and starts to dismount. I bolt into action like I've been shot from a circus cannon. Hiss, boom, bang—the window's shut and locked. With a musical rattle, the Venetian blinds are down, too. I open the door then. Kyle's standing there with a sack of toys slung over his left shoulder. He doesn't come right in, though. His mouth is agape. His eyebrows are twin arches that have 'Oh my God, a string bikini!' stamped between them. I've spent the better part of my life in one bathing suit or another, usually in the company of men, so getting caught out in my togs now doesn't bother me in the least. But—joy of joys, and hardy-har-har—I've finally found a way to consternate Kyle Hobson.

"Come in already," I say. "You're letting the heat out."

He clears his throat, then steps inside. As I close the door after him, he asks, "Aren't you cold?"

I shrug, the very picture of nonchalance. "Not really. "This jacket is warmer than it looks. Besides, I've got a couple of turkeys in the oven at the moment, so the kitchen's nice and toasty."

"I see," he says. "And do you always dress like this on Christmas Eve?"

I twitch him what I hope is a blasé smile. "Not quite. I was just trying on some old work clothes."

"Oh. Yeah. You're into underwater photography. I forgot."

My smile runs suddenly aground. I turn toward the stove so he won't see. "You must be freezing after a ride in this weather. Would you like a cup of hot chocolate or coffee?"

"A hot chocolate would be nice," he says. "If you don't mind."

"Nothing to it." On goes the teapot. Up goes the heat. "Why don't you get out of that snowsuit while you're here? Otherwise, you'll catch a chill when you go back out."

"Good idea. While I'm doing that, why don't you go and put something warmer on? It *is* flu season, you know."

Flu-shmu. He just doesn't want to deal with me in a bathing suit.

If this were any other day, I'd be slinking off to my bedroom with my tail between my legs already. But not tonight. Tonight, I'm shipping out with all my flags unfurled. I shuck my jacket and hang it up on the coat-rack, flexing like a Venice Beach weightlifter as I go. Next, I pivot on my heel to show off my butt to best advantage and then saunter away without so much as a backward glance.

There, that'll teach him.

I only wish I knew what the lesson was.

I return to the kitchen just as the teapot's starting to scream. Kyle's snowsuit is hanging next to my jacket now; his ass is parked in my chair. He's dressed in those ultra-faded blue jeans and a red, cable-knit sweater. I'm wearing baggy gray sweats and bunny slippers. God knows what my hair looks like. I didn't bother to look.

"One hot chocolate coming right up," I say, forcing a cheerful tone. On a whim, I tear a packet open for myself as well. "I'd offer to spike it for you, but there's no alcohol in the house."

"Guess again." He gets up and frisks his snowsuit, then joins me at the stove with a silver flask in hand. "You never know when a drop of Christmas cheer is going to come in handy." He doctors his mug, then glances at me. "Want some? It's Bailey's."

"No, thanks," I say, meaning it in fifty different ways. "I'm still recovering from last night." Then, before he can start in on that subject, I raise my mug to him in a mock toast. "Merry Christmas."

We drink. The cocoa tastes sour in my mouth.

"Since I'm here," Kyle says, "why don't I help you wrap those presents? It'll go faster that way."

There's no way I can turn down the offer, not after all the trouble he went through to deliver the goods in the first place. So I scurry off to fetch my stash of wrapping paper, ribbon, bows, and tape. As soon as I return, we get to work.

"So," he says, as he removes the price tag from a box of Dominos. "Underwater photography, huh? What's that like?"

"It has everything a girl could want," I say, "action; adventure; romance." OK, so maybe 'romance' is stretching it a bit. He doesn't have to know that. "The pay's not bad, either, but I'd do it for free. Have done it, in fact. When I first started out in the business, the pay for stills was often just copies of the magazine in which they appeared."

"How'd you live?" he wonders.

I laugh—a short, nostalgic hoot. "Mostly, I went from one dive resort to the next, offering my services as a dive master in exchange for room, board, and pocket money. It wasn't what you'd call a posh lifestyle, but I met a lot of people, made a few connections, and eventually fell in with the folks at SeaDoc."

He reaches into the bag and pulls out a Tonka truck. As he tries to figure out a way to wrap it, he says, "I saw some of your pictures in *National Geographic*."

"Which piece: 'Wrecks Of The South Pacific' or 'Calling Mr. Octopus'?"

"Both," he says, surprising me. But that probably only means that he subscribes to *National Geographic*. "How'd you get that octopus to curl around that old phone like that?"

"I just happened to be in the right place at the right time. Although I must admit, I did stake out his hole in the hope that he'd come out and pose for me. I chowed through half a tank of air waiting for him."

He shudders. I'm not sure why. I decide it's time to let him do some talking.

"How do you like being a cop?" I ask.

"It has its ups and downs," he says. "Pass me the tape, would you?" I toss him the dispenser. He casually snatches it out of the air. "I'm not crazy about the hours," he goes on. "Or the pay, for that matter. But like you say, I like the action. And the chance to help people."

He doesn't seem inclined to say anything more about the job, so I switch tracks. "So what do state cops do in their spare time?"

"Mostly, we try to catch up on our sleep and/or stay in shape. I run when it's not too cold out, and play basketball with my nephews. I'm big on snowmobiling, too."

"Ever do any swimming?"

"Nah. I was never much good at it. In fact, I flunked that section of Phys-Ed back in tenth grade. That was Pallin's fault, though. Remember that pathetic excuse for a gym teacher? He said I'd have to wear a bathing cap in the pool because of my long hair. I told him to go screw and took an 'F.'" His eyes narrow into vindictive slits. "Man, what I wouldn't give to find that chicken-choker behind the wheel of a car that I've just pulled over for speeding."

I beat a hasty retreat for the oven, because Mr. Pallin was my swimming coach and we got along just fine.

The turkeys are starting to look like the real McCoy now, but their juices are still pinkish so I give them another basting and then close them back up in the oven.

"Shall I freshen up your hot chocolate while I'm up?" I ask.

"No thanks," Kyle says. "I'll take another splash of Bailey's, though."

I bring him the flask. He pours a dollop into his empty mug, then tries me again. "Are you sure you don't want any?"

"I'm sure," I say firmly, and then reach into the bag again. There's only one toy left now; and to my high-flying delight, it turns out to be a Princess Baby. I wrap it up in bright red paper and address it to Mawgwet.

All of a sudden, it feels like Christmas.

"This is wonderful," I gush, as I look upon the pile of nattily wrapped gifts. "We can tell the kids that Santa left these under our tree by mistake."

"In that case, we'd better put them there so your nieces can find them when they wake up," Kyle says. "Kids make pretty good detectives, you know."

"And state cops make pretty good Santas," I say.

The transfer takes almost no time at all; and when it's complete, I go around and turn off all of the lights except for those on the tree. Their muzzy white glow makes Kyle appear younger, and somehow less substantial.

"It's beautiful," he murmurs, as we stand there admiring our handiwork. Then he turns to me with and says, "So are you."

He moves in for a kiss, and for one wistful moment, I'm tempted. What the hell, it's Christmas, right? Then I catch a whiff of alcohol beneath the chocolate on his breath, and flash back to last night's fiasco. At the last moment, I shy away.

"Sorry," I say, mocking his look of surprise with a wry half-smile, "but I'm not drunk tonight."

"Yeah? So?" he says, with the half-amused, half-leery poise of a man who is waiting for a punchline. When I give it to him in the form of silence, he steps back like he's trying to get a better fix on me. "Do you honestly believe that makes any difference to me?"

"The thought crossed my mind," I say bluntly, forcing myself to look him right in the eyes. "It *was* you who used to take girls behind the tobacco barns and liquor them up in the hopes of getting lucky, wasn't it?"

His jaw falls open. For one long moment afterward, all he can do is gape at me. I'd bet dollars to donuts that he didn't expect me to remember *that* little anecdote.

"But that was kid-stuff!" he says. "Things are different now."

"Are they?" I remember how it was back then—me in heat for Hobson Corner's hottest bad-boy, and him barely aware of my existence--and have to look away. "You were known in both locker rooms as Mr. Use-'Em-and-Lose-'Em. "What do they call you at the gym these days?"

He strangles on a sound—I think it might have been my name. Then he takes me by the chin and gently compels me to face him. His gaze is state-trooper tough.

"How long are you going to hold who I was twenty years ago against me?" he asks. When I don't answer, he makes the jump from bad cop to good cop. "OK, I'll admit it—I was a king-sized heel in those days. Rules were made to be broken; getting girls was a sport. But you were different back then, too: distant and aloof, like you were too good to breathe the same air as everybody else. Come to think of it, you haven't really changed that much in that regard."

"That's not—" True, I want to say, but he cuts me off before I can spit it out.

"No, Raven, let me finish. You accused me of trying to pull a hit-and-run on you tonight, and you need to know that that's not right.

I'm here because I can't help myself. Ever since I saw you in Green's lot that first night, calmly smoking a cigarette in front of a shot-out window, I haven't been able to get you out of my mind."

I loose a derisive snort. It's like putting a match to gasoline.

"Damn it, Raven, I'm serious! Didn't you get the flowers I sent? What about the candy?"

The question is as shocking as a pail of ice-water down the back. I didn't tell *anyone* about that box of chocolates, not even Abby. So how on earth could he know unless—

"That was you?"

"Of course!" he says, passionately emphatic. "Who'd you think?"

I'm in a daze now, and can't think straight. The name slips past my lips on the back of a breath.

"Junior?" he echoes incredulously. "Junior Mayhew?"

"I must've read him right the first time," I murmur, remembering how ill at ease he had been at the Big Y yesterday. "He really *is* afraid of me now."

"I don't blame him. Sometimes, I'm afraid of you, too." That gets my attention in a hurry. "You're smart and strong-willed and independent. You've been places and seen things that most of us stick-at-homes can't even imagine. And—it seems like you don't need anyone else in your life to make it good. I don't know about Junior, but that scares the hell out of me."

The direction in which this conversation seems to be heading makes me nervous. I don't know why, exactly. Maybe it's the idea of him making himself vulnerable to me that's giving me palpitations. Maybe it's because I'm afraid he's going to expect me to do the same. I feel like I'm down deep, on the verge of nitrogen narcosis. That blood-gas imbalance can disengage a diver's common sense, and muddle her ability to tell right from wrong. While under its influence, you think and do things that might not be all that good for you.

"Look, Kyle," I say. "I might give off the impression that I can handle just about anything that rocks my boat, but more often than not, I'm just tied to the mast. What you perceive as aloofness is only me trying to play it safe. If I don't get involved, I won't get hurt. Right?"

"I suppose," he says.

On any other night, I'd stop right there and congratulate myself later for daring to open up that much. But I'm feeling brave all of a sudden, or maybe just reckless. Either way, orders have already been issued: *dam the torpedoes, full-speed ahead.*

"And since we're being so upfront and personal here," I hear myself say, "I guess you should know that you have the power to hurt me in a big way."

I square my shoulders, wordlessly daring him to do his worst. He stares at me for a long moment, his trooper's eyes sifting through my defiant expression for evidence that can be used against me later in a court of law. Then he jams his hands in his pockets and sighs.

"Christ, Raven. The last thing I want to do is hurt you. I only wish I knew what I could do to make you believe that."

The ache in his eyes and voice tips a scale in my head. The next thing I know, I'm pulling him close.

"I believe it," I say, just before I press my lips to his. "All you have to do is be patient."

The kiss is exquisite: a sensuous pressure that goes on and on like the sweetest of summertime dreams. As it unfolds, his hands slip out of his pockets. One curves around my waist, the other strokes my hair. A Christmas glow begins to build within me. It feels like a fire in the hearth. It smells of Bailey's, pine trees, and roasted fowl.

Oh, shit!

I bolt for the kitchen. Kyle follows on my heels. As I whisk the dark-brown turkeys out of the oven, one after the other, he starts to climb into his snowmobile suit.

"What are you doing?" I ask, then immediately berate myself for being such a jerk. Two minutes into this would-be relationship and I'm already asking him to file a flight-plan.

"It's getting late," he says. "And I've got a long ride back."

A moment's panic races through me. *There, I think, I've gone and scared him off.* Or, worse, he's not interested after all. But as much as I want to dive behind the sandbags of my pride, I stand my ground. I know I won't get hurt if I don't get involved. But I'll never get much of anything else, either.

"You don't have to go, you know," I tell him, trying not to blush like a precocious schoolgirl. "You could stay here, there's plenty of room." Then, because I cannot bear being so far out on this limb all by myself, I add, "I think it would nice if you were here in the morning when the kids open their gifts."

He arches an eyebrow as if to say that he's seen through me, but then a sly smile curves across his mouth and he stops fiddling with his suit.

"I think it would be nice if I were here in the morning, too," he says. "But what makes you think I won't try to take advantage of you in the interim?"

"Actually," I reply, matching him grin for grin, "I was kind of hoping you might."

I saunter toward him. On the way, I turn off the kitchen light. I am amazed at how liberating a little trust can be.

CHAPTER 12

Christmas morning dawns cold and gray. The sky is still full of snow. Yesterday, that weather report would've bummed me out big-time. Today, I couldn't care less.

Kyle and I are in the kitchen at the moment. Yes, we've been up all night. No, we didn't do *it*. I wanted to, no doubt about that. As soon as I dropped the electrified fences of my guard and let him into my life, I wanted him in all the way. Moderation, it seems, is *not* my middle name.

But Kyle had other ideas. "Not here," he said, the first time our clinch got too feverish. "Not with your family in the house." The second time, he chased my hands out from under his sweater and groaned, "I didn't bring any protection." We backed off and tried to stick to talking, but then he said something about enjoying undercover work. I came back with something clever like, "Oh, yeah?" and—blam! We were at each other again. And just when I thought he was going to give in and go for broke, he rolled off the couch without a word and went outside to stand in the snow. That's where he was right up until a minute ago.

Maybe he knows more about starting a relationship than I do. Maybe this is his way of paying me back for accusing him of being interested in only one thing. All I can say for sure is, I haven't been this hot to trot since Francois taught me how to dance.

"So," he says, as he warms his hands on the mug of hot chocolate that I whipped up for him, "what shall we do now?"

A number of replies come to mind. All but one of them are lascivious. I leer, just so he knows what I'm thinking, then follow through with the respectable option.

"How 'bout giving me a hand here in the kitchen?" I ask. "Twenty or so people are going to be up and wanting breakfast soon. And there's Christmas dinner to worry about, too."

"I thought you already took care of that," he says, and glances toward the pantry where the two birds from last night are now roosting.

"Those were Plan B," I tell him, "just in case the power went out. We'll carve those up later for sandwiches. But since the power's still on, and please Lord, let it stay on, we here at Angelhaven going to have *hot* turkey and *hot* stuffing for Christmas dinner. *Hot* mashed potatoes and *hot* gravy, too."

"Oh," he says, looking semi-amused at my vehemence. "OK."

"You don't have to help," I hasten to add. "You can camp out in my room and catch a few zees instead. If you shut the door, you might not hear my nieces when they go into holiday overdrive."

"Thanks," he says, "but I think I'd rather stay here and help you out. For some strange reason, I'm not tired." He plants a soft, lingering kiss on my lips, and then withdraws again before something more can come of it. "Besides, I want to be on hand when the kids hit the tree. It's the best part of Christmas."

My legs go rubbery on me. My thoughts spiral. If this were any other day, I'd blame this feeling on low blood sugar and maybe lack of sleep. Today, though, I'm sure it's his fault. He's doing and saying all the right things. I feel as giddy as a schoolgirl on Cold Duck.

"So what's for breakfast?" he asks.

"Cinnamon buns," I say. "They were my dad's specialty, and Christmas was the only day of the year he ever made them. Jay and I begged for them all the time, but Dad never gave in. He said men didn't belong in the kitchen."

Kyle snorts. "He would've starved in our house. It was every man for himself there, even before my mom left us." He pauses for a moment, and then adds, "Do you miss him?"

"On occasion," I admit. "Mostly when I'm here at home." I smile, remembering his flour-spattered apron and wingtip shoes. I recall the uncharacteristic flair with which he frosted his oven-fresh rolls, too.

Merry Christmas, Daddy. Wherever you are.

"If we're going to do this," I say, "we'd better get cracking. We use ready-made dough instead of homemade these days, but there's still some prep-time involved."

"I'm yours to command," he tells me.

"So you say."

We're busy filling cookie sheets with doughy swirls when Mattie comes shuffling into the kitchen. She freezes in mid-step as she lays her still sleep-swollen eyes on Kyle and me, then looses a surprised little gasp as she realizes what we're doing.

"I knew someone was down here," she stammers, in lieu of a greeting. "But I had no idea—"

"Merry Christmas, Mattie," I say. "If you want, you can crawl back into bed for another hour or so. Everything's under control here."

"Raven Middlefield, you are the sweetest thing this side of chocolate," she says, and hobbles over to give me a big holiday hug. "Merry Christmas, girl. And to you, too, Officer Hobson," she adds, swinging her smile his way. "What brings you here so early? Nothing bad, I hope."

"Kyle stopped by with some presents for the displaced kids last night," I hasten to explain. "By the time we were done wrapping them, it was too late for him to be out and about in a storm, so I invited him to stay here."

She presses her hands to my cheeks. They're chapped as well as callused, but all I feel is love. "She's a thoughtful one," she tells Kyle. "Just like her mother." To me, she says, "Thank you for so much the offer, but I can't go back to bed. I'm wide awake and ready to work. So why don't you let me finish up here? That'll give you a chance to get cleaned up before the little ones wake up and turn the day on its ear. Unless, of course—" A sly half-smile crimps her mouth. "—you *want* to spend Christmas looking like *that*."

I turn instantly self-conscious. After a whole night of slap-and-tickle, I can just imagine what *that* looks like.

"Well, um," I say, trying not to blush and thereby blow my cover, "now that you mention it, I am sort of grubby." Kyle won't look me now. He's too busy grinning down at his cookie sheet. Bastard. "Maybe I will take a quick time-out to put something more festive on."

Then I'm out of there like a rifle-shot.

By the time I return to the kitchen, the rolls are in the oven, Mattie is mixing up a fresh batch of stuffing, and Kyle is parked in the chair by the window. I'm getting used to seeing him there. He springs to his feet as I approach, and grins like I'm wearing a prom gown instead of black stretch jeans and a fuzzy red sweater.

"Wow," he says, "You look great."

The next thing I know, I'm in his arms and he's kissing me. On the mouth. My cheeks blaze, hot and astonished. My insides go all fluttery inside.

"Kyle!" I say, a *sotto voce* protest. When he arches a wondering eyebrow at me, I cock my head in Mattie's direction. She's staring at the contents of her mixing bowl with the unswerving intentness of one who's seen or heard too much.

"Oh," he says, a loud, circular sound of comprehension. "I'm sorry. Were we going to keep this affair a secret?"

This *affair*? The unmitigated tabloid splashiness of the word leaves me even more flustered than I was a moment ago. I feel the way I did the first time I found myself in the water with a shark: exposed; cornered; more than a little light-headed. My first impulse is to dive for cover, but Kyle's blocking my way with his deceptively amused eyes.

"Well?" he prompts.

"Um." I lick my lips and try again. "I guess not."

"Good."

He kisses me again, then returns to his chair. Still in a daze, I wander over to the stove and put on the kettle. As it heats up, I roll that word around in my mouth like a piece of rock candy. Affair. Uh-fair. Is that really what's going on between us? On the one hand, it sounds too advanced, like we're already doing our laundry together. On the other, it implies impermanence; a use-by date. Both prospects leave me scared. But as tempted as I am to pull up anchor and go speeding off to safer waters, all it takes to stay my hand is one peek at Kyle. It's not his looks, though there's nothing to complain about there. It has more to do with who he is: a kind man, a decent man; a man who goes out of his way to help homeless kids and holiday drunks, and who kisses like the devil himself. I want him. I know that. I'm just not sure about anything else.

Jay comes shuffling into the kitchen, bleary-eyed but nicely dressed. Either he keeps a stash of clothes here at the house or he's wearing the outfit he wore to the party the other night. Either way, he looks sharp—like the man of the house.

"'Morning, Rave; 'morning, Mattie," he says. "Which one of you is responsible for that pile of presents in the living room?" As he homes in on the now-steaming kettle, he notices Kyle in the seat by the window and adds, "Hey, Hobson. Merry Christmas. Did you bring us more storm victims? Or is Raven in trouble again?"

On the surface, my brother's tone is facetious, a mild joke, but there's a nervous undercurrent running through it, too. His willingness to expect the worst from my corner pisses me off. So even though I know I'll probably regret it later, I decide to give him a Christmas jolt.

"Kyle's the one in trouble this time," I say. "He and I are having an affair."

Jay glances from me to Kyle and back again. As he does so, an incredulous smile works its way across his face like a crack in thin ice and then breaks wide open.

"Quick, call Ripley's!" he says. "Raven's got a boyfriend. Wait till Sal hears!"

"Wait till Sal hears what?" his wife asks, as she comes strolling in. She's dressed in forest green leggings and a matching sweater. Every hair on her head is in place. "The girls are up and ready, by the way, so brace yourselves."

As if on cue, a delighted squeal peals forth from the living room. It's followed by a sister squeal, and then the happy crackling of wrapping paper being groped.

"Nothing gets opened until I say so," Sally calls out. When the rustling goes on unabated, she pokes her head around the corner and tries a different tack. "Why don't you go and see if Dex is up yet? We can't open presents without him."

The groping comes to an abrupt halt. An instant later, four tiny feet go galloping out of the living room and up the hallway stairs. Mattie grins, approving Sal's strategy. She knows, as do we all, that her big, strapping son doesn't stand a chance of sleeping through an onslaught spearheaded by those two little girls.

"While they're doing that," she says, "I'll go and check on Rob."

"Mattie," Jay says testily, "Mom needs her sleep."

"Don't worry, love," Sally tells him, "she's up. I heard her moving around while I was getting the girls ready."

Mattie nods, vindicated, then goes over to the sink and washes the stuffing mix from her hands. Over her shoulder, she says, "Those buns should be just about ready to come out now, Rave. You'll want to frost them while they're hot."

"Gotcha, Matt," I reply, and then immediately pass the buck to Sally. "You don't mind, do you, Sal?" I ask. "I have to dig my camera equipment out."

"No prob," she says, and then swings her curious, eight-by-ten smile in Kyle's direction. "Especially since I seem to have *two* big, strong men here to help me."

I flash Kyle a wink, and then leave him to fend for himself. On the way to my room, I catch up with Matt. She's moving extra slow today.

"I want you to take it easy today," I say. "Keep Mom company and leave the rest to younger legs."

The look she lobs me then is half-amused, half-scornful, like I'm some raw recruit trying to tell the drill sergeant how to run the platoon. "Any other advice you'd care to dispense?"

"Yeah—don't mind Jay. He doesn't mean to be rude. He's just overprotective."

"It runs in the family," Mattie says, in the same stropped tone, and then smiles to leach the sting from her reproach. "Me and Rob will manage one way or another, girl—just like we always have. You worry about something else." Her smile broadens into a teasing grin. "Like that nice man back there in the kitchen, for instance."

"Oh, Mattie." I can't help myself. I fold her into an embrace. "He is nice, isn't he."

She laughs, then smacks me on the rump and continues on her way. I waltz into my room and dig my trusty Nikon out of the camera case. Out of habit, I put it through its paces to make sure it's still in good working order. As I'm doing so, a bright red blur chances into my sights. It's the key-chain that I dug out for Dex last night. I find myself thinking of Kyle. It doesn't seem right that he should be without a present to open after everything he's done to transform this would-be bust of a Christmas into a joyous event. So I wrap Señor Lobster up in a handy scrap of Santa Claus paper. It squeaks once as I press a bow on it. I imagine Kyle making a similar sound when he opens it.

"C'mon, Auntie Waven! We'ah waitin'!"

In my absence, the party has moved into the living room. Dex is cat-napping on the couch; Jay, Kyle, and Sal are chatting; and my nieces are champing at the Christmas bit. As of yet, there is no sign of Mattie or Mom.

"OK," I say, stalling for time, "it's time for pictures. Lisa, Gail—come and sit for me in front of the tree."

The girls whine and complain, but Sal wheedles them into grudging compliance. I shoot a series of Christmas portraits: nieces solo, nieces together, nieces with Sal, nieces with Jay, and the whole lot of them together.

"Kyle," I ask then, "would you mind taking one of all of us? All you have to do is stand here and push this button."

"No problem," he says. "Just say when."

I position myself behind my brother's family, then give Kyle the go-ahead with a nod. An instant before he takes the shot, though, Mom appears in the hallway. And by God, she's walking! Granted, she's using a walker. And granted, her grip on the handle-bar is so tight, her knuckles are white. But still! She's walking! As the camera flash goes off, I'm singing her name. So is everyone else.

"Sweet," she replies. "Happiness all." She half-turns to Mattie, who is standing behind her like a bridesmaid, and adds, "Angels bless."

Jay rushes off to the kitchen. When he returns, he has two hard-backed chairs with him. "Here, Mom," he says. "Sit down. You, too, Mattie."

It is an apology of sorts. Mattie accepts it with grace and dignity. Then, as she settles down beside Mom, an impish grin dances across her face. She turns it on my nieces.

"Well?" she says. "What are you waiting for? Let's open presents!"

Jay dons the Santa's hat that he always wears for this part of the program, then begins to pass out packages. An instant later, wrapping paper and bows begin to fly.

I spend the first few minutes taking pictures at random: Jay in that silly hat; Sally holding up the plaster-of-Paris handprint that Lisa made for her in school; Dex crinkling his nose at the kangaroo-leather vest that I brought him from Adelaide. Then, as the pace of the exchange shifts into a less frenzied gear, I train my camera on Kyle. He's standing by the fireplace with an elbow resting on the mantle. He looks mildly off-balance but not out of place. There's a wistful glint in his eyes. I take the shot, then saunter over with his gift.

"But I don't have anything for you," he says.

"Don't sweat it," I say. "It's just a souvenir I picked up somewhere. You don't even have to like it."

"I'm sure I'll love it."

He pops the package open with a flick of his thumb. His expression becomes a handsome blank. He could be looking at power tools or a shrunken head. I get the sense that I've just made a huge mistake, but before I can start babbling apologies, the corners of his mouth curve upward. An instant later, he chuckles.

"Thank you," he says. "It's just what I needed."

"It squeaks, too," I point out, sounding like a used-car salesman who's desperately trying to unload a clunker on some hard-sell. "Check it out."

He squeezes Señor Lobster, then chuckles again. "You're a very strange woman, you know."

"You have no idea," I say.

The next thing I know, we're wrapped up in one of those lovely, lingering kisses that I can't seem to get enough of; and when we finally come up for air again, my whole family is grinning at us. Even Gail and baby Lisa have taken time out to watch their aunt make a fool of herself. My cheeks blaze, a blend of embarrassment and defiant pride.

"What can I say?" I quip. "It had to happen sooner or later." Meaning that I'd find someone insane enough to want me eventually. But judging by the peculiar look that Kyle's sporting now, I think he thinks I was talking about us—him and me—in particular. Ha! I never saw us together, not even in my dreams—leastwise not the post-adolescent ones. But I don't tell him that.

The rending and tearing resumes. Fifteen minutes later, there's nothing left for the Middlefield clan to unwrap. I'm now the proud owner of a hideous pink sweater from Sally and Jay, a diary from my nieces, a sturdy cribbage board from Dex, and—a dry suit from Mom and Mattie.

"We special-ordered from it a magazine," Mattie says, as I gape at it. "The guy I talked to said you can exchange it if the fit isn't right. Do you like it?"

I hold the suit up to myself as if it were a debutante's gown instead of a knife in my heart. "It's perfect," I tell her, the most complicated lie I've ever told. "Just perfect. Thank you both very much." Then, because I desperately need to change the subject, I ask, "So what do you think of my present to you?"

Mattie strokes the lamb's wool sweater that she's draped across her shoulders like she might stroke a cat. Her smile is gently radiant. "It's the most luxurious thing I've ever felt," she says. "I haven't decided if I'm going wear it every day or save it for special occasions."

"Every day special," Mom says.

My gift to her is sitting on the floor next to her chair. It's a lead-crystal figurine of—what else—an angel. It has sweeping juts of opaque glass for wings; a rich swirl for skirts; and a head with long, flowing hair but no face. This is how I think real angels must be: beautiful, mysterious, and vague.

"Do you like it, Mom?" I ask. "The angel, that is?"

"Nice," she says.

Her tone is like her smile: half-flat and disengaged. I know then that this year's offering will end up in Jay's room with the fat-lipped donkey and all of the other rejects. *Oh, well,* I think, *it's just a chunk of glass.* And it's not the only thing I'm giving her this year.

Jay joins our little group. He's got a Christmas afterglow about him. "Are you guys ready for cinnamon buns?"

"Absolutely," I say. "You bring 'em in. I'll start picking up."

"Deal."

As he hustles off toward the kitchen, I grab a cardboard box and begin filling it up with wads of discarded paper and ribbon. A moment later, Kyle pitches in.

"So," he says, "a dry-suit, huh? It looks like something an astronaut would wear."

I laugh. "I'll admit, they aren't very appealing to the eye. But when it comes to diving in butt-cold water, looks take a back seat to staying warm and dry."

"Why would anybody want to go diving in butt-cold water in the first place?" he asks.

"Because it's there? Because they want to see what's down there?"

He snorts—a half-disbelieving, half-disdainful sound. "Would you really go that far out of your way just to see a few half-frozen fish?"

"Why, yes, yes, I would—if the conditions were right. But God, Kyle, there's so much more to see than fish. Take the Baltic Sea, for example. The fish-life there isn't all that exciting, but the shipwrecks are out of this world. I'm not talking about your ho-hum steel-hulled tankers, either, but *bona fide* wooden galleys. They're usually in great shape, because the water is too cold for worms, and the currents are very mild. In fact, the Swedish government recently salvaged an imperial warship from the sixteenth century that was still completely intact and provisioned. It's in a museum now. I would've loved to have seen it when it was still on the bottom."

"Why?" His tone is pointed now, sharpened by a need to understand. "What's so wrong about seeing it in a museum?"

Restless undercurrents surge within me—my blood yearning for buoyancy and compressed air and a return to Earth's blue womb. You can't put a feeling like that into words. You either have it, or you don't. Nevertheless, I make an effort to answer him. Because something about him has found its way into my blood, too.

"A wreck sprawled on its side on an ocean floor is a compelling sight," I tell him. "It speaks of pride and presumption and power. It speaks of men who dared too much. In the water, it's a grave; a monument; and a warning. In a museum, it's just an exhibit." Then, because I've ventured too far into perilous waters, I add, "Besides, anybody with the price of a ticket can see it in a museum. Where's the adventure in that?"

My brother strides into the room with a plate of frosted rolls. His girls abandon their newfound loot and go clamoring toward him, but he curbs their headlong rush with an upraised hand.

"Company first," he reminds them, and offers the tray to Kyle.

"Many thanks," Kyle says, as he helps himself. "I'm starving."

"I would be, too," my brother remarks, "if I'd stayed up all night." He's fishing for a reaction here, something that he can tease me about later, but I've already adjusted to the idea of me and Kyle together, and don't even flinch. When he sees that, he sneaks me a wink and says, "Merry Christmas, Rave. It's good to see you happy."

"Interesting," Kyle says, as Jay moves on. "I would've pegged you for the type who's always happy."

"And for the most part, you would've been right," I say, eyeing him over the rim of my sticky roll. "But these last few weeks have put a big dent in my sunny disposition. Funny how killing a man will do that to you."

His frown slumps into a look of contrition. "Oh. Yeah. I almost forgot about that."

"I wish I could," I say.

But while I'll probably never forget Mr. Clifton Dupree, I have to admit that his shabby ghost has kept pretty much to itself these past few days. Maybe it's hiding from Willy and Clara. Maybe it's waiting with a specter's infinite patience for a chance to take me hostage again. Whatever. All I know is, he's not bothering me at the moment, and I sure as hell don't miss him.

Kyle's roll is gone already. Mine is still in my hand. It's odd, but I still have no appetite. Everything looks and smells a half-shade off. Hungry or not, though, I force myself to eat so I won't go hypoglycemic later. As I'm doing so, Lisa toddles up to Jay and tugs at his sleeve.

"Let's bwing those pwesents out to the bawn now, Daddy," she says, pointing to the presents in question with a sugary finger. "Mawgwet's gonna think Santa forgot her."

Jay glances at the Rolex that was Mom's gift to him this year, and then breaks into a Grinch's grin. "Eight-twenty-six. If it's late enough for us to be up, it's late enough for everyone else. Go and wash your hands, girls, then get your coats. We've got a delivery to make!" As they go bounding off, he sidles up to Kyle. "Since you're the secret Santa here, you get to wear this stupid hat!"

With that, he doffs his cotton-tipped cap and sets it on my would-be lover's head. It looks just as ridiculous on him as it does on Jay. I snicker and snap his picture. He casts me a dirty look, but says nothing.

"Do you feel up to visiting your guests, Robin?" Matt asks. "Or would you rather save it for another time?"

"We go," Mom says firmly.

A few minutes later, we issue forth from the house—a rag-tag procession of big hearts and good intentions. It's still snowing out, but the path to the barn is clear. So is most of the driveway, thanks to Tom Fowler. He's down by the road now, shoveling away. Scrape, sling; scrape, sling. The snowbanks are almost as tall as he is. I hail the man with a wave and a shout, then motion him to join us. He waves back, but keeps on shoveling.

"He's a good egg," Mattie tells Mom. "A bit rough around the edges maybe, but who isn't at that age?"

The smells of brewing coffee and electric heat greet us as we come shambling into the barn. A moment later, we're treated to a round of holiday hellos. Almost everyone is awake already. Mrs. Fowler is telling her kids to mind their manners; Grace is scowling at an ankh-eared Sara; and Willy Dupree is trying to head me off at the pass.

"I hope you don't mind," he says, as I set my platter of cinnamon buns on the picnic table, "but the missus went ahead and started the coffee."

"That's why the urn is out here," I say.

At the same time, Lisa shouts, "Mawgwet! Come and see! Santa left some stuff undah the wong twee last night."

Kids start to migrate toward Kyle like iron filings toward a magnet. Their faces are aglow with renewed beliefs. I think I might be glowing, too. Before I can melt into the background to watch the show, though, Kyle catches me by the hand.

"Santa needs a helper," he says, "and you're his first and only choice."

My knees go all buttery. I can't believe he's flirting with me in front of a whole freakin' crowd. It makes me feel naughty; sexually self-conscious. I'm not sure if I want to kiss him or kill him for that. He grins at me like he knows what I'm thinking. Jay and Sally are smirking, too. I look at them, standing hand-in-hand, happy exactly where they are, and think: *that wouldn't be so bad.*

It only takes Kyle and me a few minutes to distribute the gifts; and when we're done, the kids retreat to an adult-free corner to ogle their booty and play. The rest of us converge around the coffee and rolls. The atmosphere is festive. You'd never guess that we're all strangers here.

"Nice earrings, Sara," I say, as she and Dex weave their way through the crowd.

"Thanks," she says, and gives her head a saucy little toss. I'm glad Grace isn't here to see that, because there's a big hickey just below her hairline. "Dex gave them to me," she goes on to say. "He says they're a symbol of eternal love."

I cock an eyebrow at Dexter. He flashes me a sheepish grin and shrugs. Then Fenton Davenport intrudes on our fun.

"Good morning," he says, in a sprightly tone, "and Merry Christmas." He trains his weasel's smile on me. "The gifts were a nice touch, Raven. I'm impressed."

"It wasn't done to impress you—or anyone else," I say.

"Nevertheless," he insists, "it was nicely done. Did you have the toys on hand? Or did you have heavenly help in procuring them?"

"You'd best ask Officer Hobson about that," I say, with a smirk that has 'heavenly indeed' stamped all over it. "I have to go and check on dinner."

I do an abrupt about-face, then exit stage left. On my way to the door, I happen to catch a glimpse of Clara Dupree. She's staring at my mom instead of me for a change, and once again, I see tears in those shipwrecked eyes. I wonder what she's thinking. I wonder if she's seen Clifton's ghost.

Back in the kitchen, dinner seems to be shaping up just fine without me. Mattie's pulling a platoon of pumpkin pies out of the oven; Lea Fowler is peeling potatoes; and Sally's disemboweling butternut squashes. I ask if there's anything I can do, but Mattie shakes her head and shoos me out from underfoot, so I go over to the telephone and call Abby.

"Merry Christmas," she wishes me. "You'll have to wait till the snow stops to get your present, though."

"Likewise," I say. "I just hope Bruce doesn't drive you stark raving mad before then."

"Oh, Raven," she says, in a chiding, sing-song tone that I've heard before, "don't be so hard on the poor guy. We had a long talk after I got off the phone with you, and he promised to change his bratty ways. And you'll never guess what he got us for Christmas this year!" Possibilities tickertape through my brain: soap on a rope, dime-store perfume, maybe a sweater if it was on sale. Before I can spit any of these out, though, she bubbles on. "Cruise tickets! He's taking me to the Caribbean in January! Is that freaky or what? We were just talking about that."

I'm tempted to point out that there was no 'he' in last night's conversation, that the whole idea behind her going to the Caribbean was to get away from that bonehead, but what's the use? She'd only laugh it off, ha-ha-ha. Like she can't take me or maybe herself seriously.

"Yeah, it's freaky all right," I say, trying to keep the irritation from my tone. Then I lob a cherry-bomb of my own. "You want to know something even freakier?"

"Tell," she says.

"Kyle Hobson and I are an item."

"No way."

"Yes way. He came by last night with a load of toys for the kids and wound up spending the night."

The line falls silent, but only long enough for her to digest that morsel. Then she oh-so-casually asks, "So how was he?"

"Abby!" I squawk, appalled by her bluntness even though that's Abby all the way. "We didn't get that far. Mostly we just talked."

"Mostly." She sniggers—a sly, raunchy, sound—and then laughs outright as I damn myself with silence. "Oh, well, I guess we all have to start somewhere. Keep me posted on late-breaking developments, OK?"

"Assuming there are any developments worth posting," I say.

"Raven Middlefield, you've been lusting after that man for almost twenty years," she says. "So what in hell are you waiting for? Go for him! Use both hands! You could do a whole lot worse, you know."

An image of Bruce comes to my mind. As I curl my upper lip at it, Kyle comes walking into the house. He has an empty platter in his hands, but I can tell that's just an excuse.

"I'll call you back later," I say, then hastily hang up the phone and saunter back into the kitchen. Mattie winks at me in passing. I crinkle my nose at her, then cozy up to Kyle.

"Looking for me?" I ask.

"You betcha," he says, and then gives me a peck on the lips. Sal titters. I pretend not to hear. "I was wondering if you'd care to go for a little ride with me."

I turn to Mattie. "How long till the big feed?"

"I'm shooting for one o'clock," she says, "but two's a better bet."

"Do you need me?"

"Girl, I have a barn-load of bored people all looking for something to do. Go for a ride. Have a good time. And just in case nobody's said so yet," she says to Kyle, "you're more than welcome to join us for dinner."

"Thanks, Mattie," he says, and flashes her one of his killer smiles. "I'll be here." Then he turns back to me and says, "You'd better go and get bundled up. It's bound to get a bit brisk on the Cat."

I do as I'm told; and when I return a few minutes later, I'm better layered than a four cheese lasagna. My arms feel like overstuffed sausages. I can barely bend my knees. I'm so hot, I feel queasy. I say as much to Kyle, but he just laughs.

"You'll thank me later."

'Later' turns out to be a mere fifteen minutes. We're cruising along an unplowed road, seemingly the only people in the world on this gray, snowbound morning. My face is pressed against the insulated span of Kyle's back. My arms are wrapped around his waist.

"Howya doing?" he asks, shouting to make himself heard over the snowmobile's roar.

"Fine," I shout back. But to tell the truth, I've been better. The tip of my nose is freezing. My guts feel slick. And all the sweat I generated back at the house has turned into slush against my skin. As I huddle closer to Kyle, hoping to leach his body heat, I remember why I've never liked winter.

We veer off-road, then begin to zig-zag through a stretch of woods. It's a wild, stomach-cramping ride, full of fast turns and cold speed. In spite of myself, I yelp as he cuts one corner way too close.

"Still with me?" he shouts.

"Where are we going?" I shout back.

"What?"

I scoot forward, trying to thwart the wind, and then repeat myself. He nods, signaling his comprehension. "Don't worry, we're almost there."

We continue our high-speed weave through the trees, like we're trying to dodge individual snowflakes as they fall from the sky. I despise the noise we're making, and the tracks we're leaving in the clean, white snow, and the cloying stink of exhaust. I long for the warmth of a sunwashed beach, and the silver-bubbled silence of a dive. Splash, you're in; splash, you're out; and if you do it properly, you leave no trace of your coming and going behind.

Kyle shifts the Cat into a lower gear, and begins to follow the haphazard curves of what can only be the Scantic River. The overgrown mounds of snow on its banks make it look small and clean, more like the sort of stream you'd see in a Colorado beer commercial than a local dumping grounds for old tires and trash. As we round a bend, a massive water oak spans into view. There's a rope dangling from one of its muscular, snow-packed limbs; I know it well. The memories that it calls up are all warm.

The snowmobile comes to a stop. I wonder why, but don't want to ravage the sudden, glorious silence with the sound of my own voice. Kyle removes his helmet, then swivels around to face me. His grin is broad. His eyes are exhilarated. "What did you think of the ride?" he asks.

"It was something," I say, hedging because I can see how much he wants me to like it, and how disappointed he'll be if I tell him the outright truth.

"I could spend the whole day on the back of this thing," he tells me, and pats the machine like he might pat a living creature. "It's like sledding, only better."

"I went sledding maybe once a year in the old days. The only time I really liked it was when we greased our skids with blackberry brandy beforehand."

He chuckles. "That'll certainly take the sting out of a wind."

Flakes of snow are starting to collect in his hair and eyelashes. I don't like the effect—it looks too much like dandruff. The impression leaves me feeling green around the gills.

"So," I say, trying to sound offhand, "did we come here for a particular reason? Or are we just resting the horses?"

"This is the place I remember noticing you for the first time," he says.

As cold as I am, I can't resist this chance to compare notes. So I hunker deeper into my jacket and say, "Do tell."

"You were with Abby," he recalls. "The two of you were riding that rope out over the water and dropping in, again and again and again. Me and a couple of the guys were sitting on the other shore, skimming through comic books and drinking warm sodas. I wanted to go someplace else, because your laughing and splashing was getting on my nerves, but Dan Jackson thought it would be fun to join you. As soon as he jumped in the river and started swimming toward you, though, you two went running off."

"Sounds like me, all right," I say. "Always looking for attention, but never knowing what to do with it once it comes my way."

He smiles like a missionary who's just found his life's work. I try not to shiver.

"Anyway," he says, "Dan came slogging back to shore in a royal snit and vowed that he'd never have anything to do with girls again.

The rest of us thought that sounded like a good idea, so we sliced our thumbs with Mark Richard's pocketknife and swore a blood-oath to that effect.

"I still have the scar." He slips off his Gor-Tex glove and presents his thumb to me. "See?"

I don't, but that's OK. It's enough just knowing that I left some kind of a mark on him after all.

"It's kind of funny," I say, "but I don't remember that day. I don't remember the first time I saw you, either. You've just always been there."

"A tradition I hope to continue," he tells me, and then folds me into his arms.

His breath smells of cinnamon and coffee, a surprisingly sexy combination that makes me want to swoon. We kiss for a long, spiraling moment; and when we finally separate again, I'm shaking inside and out. That confuses me. I thought I was getting warm.

Kyle presses his bare hand to my forehead. His palm is like ice. I try to tell him to put his glove back on before he catches something, but all that comes out is a croak.

"Christ!" he swears, in a tone full of consternation and awe. "You're burning up. We've got to get you out of those wet clothes and into a warm bed right away."

"Now you're talking," I say, feeling punch-drunk.

In reply, he starts up the snowmobile. Then he points to something beyond the white-limbed trees and hollers, "My house is just over that ridge. We'll go there, OK?"

Before I can say yea or nay, we're off, tearing straight through the woods like an angry cyber-hornet. The wind from our headlong race strips me of the illusion of warmth that being in Kyle's arms had conjured, and I begin to tremble in earnest. I shut my eyes and try to transport my thoughts to the warmest part of my body. *Think warm, be warm*, I tell myself. This is the mantra I use after a long day of diving in cool water. Sometimes, it works. Today, it does not.

By the time we get to his place, all I can see is a dark brown blur. I open my mouth to tell him that, but as soon as I unclench my jaws, I throw up all over his back.

CHAPTER 13

I'm diving in a tropical sea. It's nighttime and everything's dark, but even so, I can see clear to the bottom without a light. I have no tank on my back and no reg in my mouth, but even so, I'm breathing. A distant part of me is aware that something's wrong with this; the rest of me doesn't care. As I'm swimming aimlessly along, I spot a lobster emerging from its hole. It's the biggest one I've ever seen: dinner for two and then some. I make a grab for its antennae. With a muscular thrust of its tail, it escapes me.

"*Go after it,*" a damselfish with bright red lips advises me in passing. "*You could definitely do worse.*"

A dish-sized yellowfin starts nipping at my toes: a beggar demanding a hand-out. I shoo the sharp-toothed pest away again and again, but it won't leave me alone, so I pull a spear-gun out of a fold in space and shoot it through the eye. As its piscine brains cloud the water, a pair of thick-necked moray eels ribbon their way out of the reef and toward me. I offer them the spitted fish.

"*Thank you,*" the male says. "*You're much nicer than we thought you'd be.*" But the smaller female swims away without a word.

The current tows me into deeper, darker waters. There's a shipwreck down here; I can sense its tragic mass. As I set off in search of it, the giant lobster reappears.

"*I wouldn't if I were you,*" it says. "*Disneyland's a better value.*"

Annoyance swells like a rogue wave within me. An instant later, my spear-gun is back in my hand. Before I can shoot the meddlesome crustacean, though, a blunt-nosed shadow in the darkened distance grabs my attention. Instinct tells me that it's heading my way. Instinct tells me to be afraid. I fast-break for the shipwreck, which suddenly reveals itself to me, and then duck into its bowels. But the darkness there is crusted with razor-lipped oysters; every time I brush into one, it slashes me to the bone. Excited by the smell of my blood, the shadow pursues me through the wreck, out a hatch, and back into open water.

"*You should've listened to me*," the lobster says, as I go racing past its hole.

Overhead, I see a shiny, distant meniscus that can only be the surface. I know I'll be safe if I can get there. I know I'll be free and clear. But I'm tired now as well as hurt; and the shadow is relentless. I can sense it gaining on me, catching up, overtaking. It has no breath. No pity. I close my eyes and give one last desperate kick. My feet get fouled in strands of seaweed that hold me fast. As the shadow engulfs me, all I can do is shout.

"No!"

The shadow vanishes, leaving me upright on a beach that stinks of sweat. I blink back a wave of dizziness, then run trembling fingers over my scalp. My hair feels tacky, like it would if I'd been swimming in salty water for a very long time. But I'm sitting up in a bed, not on a beach; and the seaweed wrapped around my ankles is nothing more than a clammy sheet. I have no idea how I got here. The last thing I remember, I was—well, I can't remember that, either, but I'm reasonably sure that it wasn't bed-related.

I free myself from the sheet's grip. As minor as it is, the effort leaves me wasted. *Good Lord*, I think, as I lapse back into a boneless heap on the mattress. *What in hell has happened to me?* I remember snow, a television show, and talking eels. All seem equally unreal to me.

As I'm trying to winnow real memories from dream chaff, Mattie comes strolling into the room. There's no stealth about her, no reluctance to intrude, only an inured sort of weariness that disappears as soon as she realizes that I'm sitting up.

"Well," she says, "look who's finally back. How you feeling, girl?"

Before I have a chance to reply, she breezes over and presses a warm, dry hand to my forehead. "Ah," she says, "much better. Are you hungry?"

"Hungry?" I echo, an incredulous warble. "Hell, Mattie, I'm not even sure I'm alive. What in hell happened to me?"

"Flu," she says. "Jay and the girls had it at Thanksgiving, but none of them got as sick as you did. You've been out since Christmas."

"And when was that? Yesterday? The day before?"

"Try five days ago, girl. Today's the twenty-ninth."

"Shit."

The shock of losing all that time jars a swirl of memory loose: a sack of presents, the smell of cinnamon buns, a break-neck ride through a snow-cloaked thicket. Then I remember something else and a feeling like fever flares anew in my cheeks.

"Oh, God!"

"What's the matter?" Mattie asks, instantly concerned.

"I threw up all over Kyle."

Her worried frown melts into an unspoken oh-is-that-all. "I wouldn't have known if you hadn't told me," she says. "He sure didn't mention it when he finally brought you home. Or any of the other times he's been here since then."

Finally?

Since?

Obviously, there's more to this saga than meets the memory. A full debriefing will have to wait, though, because the dream-time has me by the heel again and I lack the strength to resist its downward spiraling. All I can do before it whisks me away is slide bonelessly back into bed.

🍁   🍁   🍁

The next time I return to consciousness, I find my mom sitting in the chair next to my bed. There's no telling how long she's been there. Her expression is as patient and remote as ever, and she's left no impression on her surroundings.

"Mom!" I say, and then suffer a sudden pang of guilt for forgetting all about her and her problems until this very moment. "How are you feeling?"

"Better," she says, and then holds out her left hand. It's not quite steady yet, but it's not all over the map like it used to be, either. "Spitch still messy, but s'OK. I got not to say much."

"You always were a woman of few words," I say, joking because I don't know how to tell her how happy I am with her progress. She nods, a simple acknowledgment of the truth. I push myself into a sitting position and glance around the room. There's no clock in here, though, and the curtains are drawn, so I have no way of telling if it's day, night, or somewhere in between. "How long have I been out this time?"

Mom does a very good job of shrugging. "Two owas, maybe three. I lots sleep too after stroke at first. Scary waking up so different."

Now, I've waited my whole adult life for her to admit to having mundane human emotions like fear, anger, or worry. And I've resented her like crazy in the meantime for being so far removed from the like. But this milestone doesn't satisfy me like I thought it would. In fact, it actually bothers me. It occurs to me that I want a mother without fears or doubts. I want an imperturbable Easter Island stone. I suppose that's funny in a sad sort of way. Or maybe it's called perverse.

We stare at each other for a long moment—the woman of few words versus the woman of few certainties. I wish I knew how to be a proper daughter. I wish I knew what to say. But the sad fact is, I'm as clueless as ever. All I can do is hope that I'll suss out at least some of the basics in the years to come.

Mattie comes padding into the room with a breakfast tray. "Ah-ha," she says, as she strides toward me. "I thought I heard two voices. You hungry yet, girl?"

Come to think of it, I do feel sort of hollow. I'm not sure if that's my stomach or what, but I'm willing to give it a shot. Mattie sets the tray over my lap, and then pulls a chair up next to Mom so they can both watch me eat.

Lunch is turkey soup, a stack of Saltines, some vitamins, and a glass of orange juice. The pills hurt going down because my swallowing muscles are sore from disuse, but the juice feels wonderful, so cool and wet, I almost weep when it's gone. I give the soup a try. It tastes great, like a kiss after diving. Just like that, my appetite is back.

"So," I say, between one bite and the next, "when did it finally stop snowing? It *did* stop, didn't it?"

"It sure did," Mattie says. "Right after dinner on Christmas Day. It took the plows another day and a half to clear all the roads, though. According to Laura Lacey, that storm cost the state over forty million dollars."

An image of the woman tries to take shape in my head. I stop its formation with a frown, then banish the would-be memory to that dark and dreary place in my back-brain where talking morays and assorted other nightmares dwell. The eels aren't happy about the new addition. I can relate.

"So the barn must be mostly vacant by now," I say.

Mattie nods. "Emptier and emptier by the day. Sara and that no-account mother of hers were the first to go. They left in such a rush, you would've thought that we'd we were a family of cannibals." She chuckles—a wicked, infectious sound that no one in her right mind would want to be on the wrong end of. "That woman is going to have a royal fit when Dexter shows up at her door next weekend. They only live in New Britain, you know."

"He and Sara are going to keep in touch?"

"He says so. But we'll see." Her knowing half-smile is seasoned with a pinch of bitterness. There's no way that I'll ever know that taste like she does, and of that, I'm both glad and abashed. "Stranger things have happened."

Mom makes a gurgling noise. I turn toward her, instantly alarmed, only to see her reach into the fanny-pack that Mattie got her for Christmas and pull out a small scroll of white construction paper. It's bound with a scrap of red holiday ribbon.

"Almost forget," she says. "Claree gone now. Give this me for you."

I scowl, trying to place this Claree, then realize that she's talking about Clara Dupree. An image of the woman pops into my head: it's all glaring eyes and unspoken accusations. I have no doubt that this scroll is more of the same. I take it from Mom's hand, then set it on the nightstand. She cocks her head at me, obviously wondering what's up.

"I'll look at it later," I say. "When I'm feeling a little stronger."

My soup's gone now. So is the juice. But part of me still feels hollow. I comb my fingers through my hair, then frown at the tackiness I feel.

"God," I say. "I need a shower."

I don't get up to take one, though, because the soup in my stomach is a fast-acting sedative. I feel drowsy and warm; deliciously lethargic. I push the breakfast tray away, then go horizontal. That feels very nice indeed.

"Tomorrow," I say, just before I close my eyes. I think Mom might know what I'm trying to say.

🍁 🍁 🍁

Sometime later, the tidal-like tuggings of a full bladder rouse me from a dreamless sleep. I roll out of bed on groggy auto-pilot only to have my legs buckle as soon as I hit the floor. Fortunately, the bedpost is right there. Otherwise, I would've gone down.

Man, I'm in miserable shape. My head feels like a two-day-old helium balloon, and my knees are so stiff, it hurts to stand. Nevertheless, I still have to pee, so I resume my trek to the bathroom. Along the way, I use doors and walls and anything else in easy reach to steady myself. The house is dark and pin-drop quiet. I feel like a cross between an invalid and an intruder. Then I see myself in the bathroom mirror and feel even worse. My tan is gone, faded to a sallow shade of beige; and the underlying flesh is slack. There are dark half-moons beneath my eyes, and darker roots in my sun-bleached hair.

Shit! This friggin' winter is killing me!

I plop down on the toilet, all gloom and wounded vanity. When I'm done there, I strip down to take a shower. The sweatshirt I peel off says 'Property of Connecticut State Police' on the front. The sweatpants bear the state seal on the left hip. It's obvious that these clothes belong to Kyle, but I have no clue how I came to be wearing them. I'm not sure if I want to remember, either. The fever has burned out a lot of circuits.

I climb into the shower and turn the tap to full-bore. *Oh, yeah.* The water's hot, just like I like it, and the shower-head delivers a spray that feels better than a deep-muscle massage. Five days of fever-sweat go down the drain. My outlook gets a much-needed steam-cleaning. By the time I splash my way out of the bathtub, I'm ready to go another round with life.

But my body insists on another nap first.

The first thing I do when I get up the next morning is strip the old sheets from my sickbed. It's like a declaration of independence, or perhaps a good riddance. I'm going forward, getting on, doing what needs to be done.

As I'm stretching a fresh fitted sheet over the mattress, I bump into a corner of my nightstand. The impact sends the scroll that

Clara Dupree wanted me to have rolling onto the floor. Now seems as good a time as any to see what she had to say, so I pick it up and slip the ribbon off. The scrap of paper bears a single line of black, spidery script.

I forgive you

BFD, I think. And: *Get bent*. It's me who ought to forgiving her for turning such a twisted bastard loose on the world. Then I toss the note back onto the nightstand and get on with my work.

I'm in the midst of sorting my dirty laundry into heaps of whites and colors when Mattie comes barging into the room. She strikes a drill sergeant's hands-on-hips pose in front of me. Her expression is foreboding.

"What do you think you're doing?" she asks.

"What does it look like I'm doing?" I ask.

"It looks like you're trying to give yourself a relapse," she says. "And if you think I'm going to nurse you through another five days of fever and vomit, girl, you're out of your pea-picking skull. Now get away from there. And put some slippers on. These floors are cold."

I do as I'm told, but not gracefully. I'm resentful, almost shamed. I hate being treated like a baby. Afterward, I watch on in churlish silence as a sixty-year-old woman does my work for me.

Over the round of her shoulder, Mattie says, "There's no need for you to stand there and supervise. I've been doing laundry longer than you've been alive. Go and get yourself something to eat. You're looking thin as a razor-blade these days."

As much as I want to, I can't argue that point with her, either. My tightest pair of jeans are loose around the butt and thighs now; and if I were to lift up my sweater, you'd be able to count my ribs. I'm almost glad that no one will be seeing me in a bathing suit any time soon.

Almost.

"Are you sure I can't help in some little way?" I ask.

"Get out," she says.

The kitchen is spotless, as tidy as Santa's workshop. For some reason, I'd been expecting heaps of Christmas dishes on the counter, and half-frozen turkeys in the sink. I snort at my pathetic, deluded self. As if they haven't had five days to clean up. As if they couldn't have managed without my help.

As if. As if. As if.

There's nothing immediately edible in the fridge, so I decide to cook myself some eggs. Poached, I think, because that's tough to screw up. As I'm waiting for my frying pan full of water to come to a boil, I sit in the chair by the window and check out the yard. The snow has lost its fresh-fall brightness and taken on the dreariness of dirty underwear. There are fallen tree branches and twigs everywhere. And, of course, the sun is nowhere in sight.

Bleah.

The water is boiling now. I get up and break a couple of eggs into it, then toss two slices of bread into the toaster. A few minutes later, they pop back up—smoking just like old times. As I'm scraping margarine over their blackened faces, the kitchen door creaks open and a woman steps in. She sheds her old army coat and hangs it up on the rack, then slips off her boots. I have no idea who she is.

"May I help you?" I ask, half-curious, half-amazed.

She stiffens like a deer that's been caught out in the open, then folds her arms across her meager chest and turns to face me. Her gaze is shy, almost submissive.

"I'm sorry," she says, in a voice as mousy as her looks. "I didn't mean to disturb you. I was just on my way to help Mrs. Middlefield with her exercises."

"And you are?" I prompt, still groping for a connection.

"Lea," she replies, "Lea Fowler. You took me and my family in when the motel burned down. Remember?"

The memory comes back to me with the flattened clang of ringside bell: scruffy kids, a Charley Brown Christmas tree, a man with seven fingers shoveling the driveway. I knew I'd seen that being-eaten-alive-from-the-inside look somewhere.

"Yes, of course, Mrs. Fowler," I say, and then hasten to apologize. "Please excuse me. I've had the flu for the last few days and I'm still a little muzzy."

"I understand," she says, and then glances toward my mom's room. "May I go? Mrs. Middlefield is expecting me."

"Yes, of course." As she turns to leave, I add, "You're doing a great job with her, by the way. Thank you."

The ghost of a smile flits across her careworn face; and for a brief moment, she loses that hunted, haunted aspect. I want to tell her that she should smile more often, but that's not my place, and besides, she's already heading for the back of the house. So I finish fixing my breakfast and then carry it over to the table. There's a folded newspaper waiting for me there. Curious as to what's going on in the world, I open it up. And just like that, Lea Fowler becomes the last thing on my mind again.

Christmas With The Heroine of Hobson's Corner.

the bold-faced tabloid headline declares. The byline is Fenton Davenport's. Annoyance bristles to life within me. I can just imagine what that rat-bag had to say about his stay at Angelhaven.

To my slow-spreading wonder, though, the piece isn't at all what I expected it to be. There are no references to me as a cash-hungry killer, and no mocking mentions of Mom's angels. And while, as usual, vague half-truths abound, they are of a most unusual flavor. In one paragraph, Davenport describes me as *protective*. In another, he has me down as *selfless*. The way he tells it, I collapsed from exhaustion while ministering to the poor and homeless. He weaves Willy and Clara Dupree into the piece, too, but refrains from OK-Corral analogies. They are, in his words, 'a tragic couple searching for an end to grief.' Last but not least, he honors Kyle for his contributions, likening him to a white knight on a snowmobile. 'Officer Hobson is a brave, giving man,' Davenport writes. 'A man who exemplifies the ideals of a state trooper. The people of Connecticut are lucky to have him.'

Ha! Put that in your pipe and smoke it, McNalley!

Now, if I were as considerate and caring in real life as I am in print, I'd probably be thinking that Fenton Davenport wasn't such a shit-heel after all. But I'm not Mother Teresa or Joan of Arc; and I'd still wish the little weasel all the way to Siberia if wishing could make it so. I would, however, wish him there with a slightly warmer raincoat now.

Although I don't remember eating any of it, my breakfast is almost gone now. I sop up the last smears of yolk with a last corner of toast, then wonder if it's too early for lunch. My belly says no, my brain says yes. A knock at the door cancels the debate. I drag a sleeve across my mouth, then go to find out who's there.

"Kyle!" I blurt, an instant after I swing the door open. He's dressed in his uniform and trooper's cap. My immediate impulse is to run and hide. "Hey, there. Come on in. I was just reading about you."

"Shouldn't you be in bed?" he asks, as he steps inside.

"Shouldn't you be at work?" I say.

He chuckles, a sound both amused and relieved. "Welcome back, Raven. It's good to see you on your feet again."

"It's good to see you, too," I say, but it's also weird, distorted somehow. It's like I'm seeing him on dry land for the first time. Underwater, everything appears twenty-five percent larger.

He hugs me, gingerly, as if he's afraid that I'll break apart if he applies too much pressure. I hug him back, but there's a subtle distortion to this, too—an awkwardness I don't remember feeling before I got sick. I suppose I just need to get used to the idea of him and me being affair-fodder again.

"So what brings you here today, Officer Hobson?" I ask. "If you came for those sweatclothes you loaned me, you're out of luck. They're in the wash."

"Keep them," he says. "I just stopped by to see how you were doing."

"Oh." My right hand gets away from me and goes racing through my hair. It feels pretty tousled. "I'm feeling OK. A little beat-up, but I guess that's to be expected."

"Good. I was starting to kick myself for not taking you to the hospital when I had the chance."

I crinkle my nose, a reflexive reaction. "I'm glad you brought me home instead. I hate hospitals." Then, prompted by fuzzy memories and an after-surge of guilt, I say, "I'm sorry I ruined your Christmas."

"No apologies necessary," he says. "In some ways, this was the best Christmas I've ever had." He reaches into a pocket, and pulls out Señor Lobster. As he dangles it in the space between us, he adds, "It was certainly one of the most memorable."

Something twangs within me. I'm not certain, but I think it might have been a heartstring. The possibility encourages me to be bold.

"I'm glad one of us remembers it," I say. "The last thing I recall with any clarity is me spewing all over your snowsuit."

"Yeah, well." His mouth twitches. "These things happen from time to time."

"I'll pay the dry-cleaner's bill."

"Forget it." He draws me into another gentle embrace. He smells good, like Ivory soap and aftershave. And there's nothing awkward about the way we fit together. "Have dinner with me tomorrow instead. It won't be anything fancy," he adds, "just you and me at my house for a quiet New Year's Eve."

My sense of time fishtails, leaving me shaken. "Tomorrow is New Year's Eve?"

"Yep."

Christ.

I feel like I've come to the bottom of a winding staircase two steps too soon. I'm not ready for the new year yet. I'm not ready to make the switch. I sneak a peek at Kyle, who's patiently waiting for my answer. He looks like he would wait forever if he had to. Another twang shivers through me. My panic subsides. Ready or not, I tell myself, the time has come. And, God willing, there will be compensations.

"You're cooking?" I ask. He nods. "Mashed squash isn't on the menu, is it?" He shakes his head. "All right then, you have yourself a date. I can't guarantee that I'll make it all the way to midnight, though."

"We'll ring in the new year early." His smile is dazzling, like sunlight on a stretch of calm water. "I'll pick you up around seven."

"You don't have to do that," I say. "I have a car."

"Not anymore," he tells me. I glance out the window, searching for the mound of snow that used to be my rental. As I do so, he says, "Your brother didn't see any point in you paying for a car when you weren't in any shape to drive it, so as soon as the roads were clear, we shoveled it out and brought it back to the lot."

Resentment flares within me. How dare they make a decision like that for me? I was sick, for Polly's sake, not comatose. They should have let the damn car sit there. Despite my irritation, though, I try to keep a civil tongue in my head because part of me realizes that they had my best interests at heart.

"All right then," I say, "I'll take Mom's car. Unless, of course, you and Jay took that back to the dealership."

Oops. So much for good intentions. I am not sorry for the slip.

Kyle has the good grace to look abashed. Likewise, he keeps quiet about Jay, who undoubtedly deserves most of the blame. In spite of my mood, I'm impressed. So much so that I let him off my deep-sea hook.

"How does one get to your place anyway?" I ask. "Something to the tune of over the river and through the woods comes to mind, but I think I'm going to need more than that."

"No problem." He reaches into his breast pocket and pulls out a notepad and pencil, then begins to jot down directions. His handwriting is pretty, almost girlish. It's funny, but I never noticed that he was a southpaw until now. "There." He tears the page free and hands it to me like a traffic ticket. "Let me know if you change your mind about driving," he adds. "I'll be glad to come and pick you up."

"Is there anything I can bring?"

"Just yourself. And dress is strictly casual."

"OK."

An awkward silence wells up between us. Kyle stuffs a hand into his pocket and starts to jingle his keys. I stand there like a dummy, thinking, *OK, now what?* We might have been stuck like that forever if Mattie hadn't come walking into the room with a basket full of laundry.

"Don't keep Raven by the door, Kyle," she says, like I'm somebody's dear but demented auntie. "She'll catch a chill."

"I was just leaving, Mattie," he tells her, and then taps the tip of my nose with his forefinger. "You should go back to bed and rest. Drink plenty of fluids, too."

"Yeah, yeah," I say. But what I'm thinking is: *I don't need you or anyone else to tell me what to do.*

Kyle zips up his coat, then plants a chaste little kiss on the tight little seam of my mouth. I'm both relieved and disappointed that it's nothing more.

"I'll see you tomorrow," he says, as he reaches for the door-knob. "OK?"

"Sure," I say. But that feels like a mixed bag, too.

The rest of the day goes by in a slow-mo funk. I take a nap, then get up and have a snack, then take another nap only to wake up and eat again. Abby calls somewhere around six to invite me to a client's New Year's Eve party, but she's still singing Bruce's praises, so I'm quick to inform her that I've already made plans with Kyle.

"You don't sound too thrilled about that," she says.

"I've been sick for the last freakin' week," I reply, a passive-aggressive dodge. "I'm not thrilled about anything."

She hmmms like my gynecologist does when he's going over my charts, then offers a prescription. "Sounds like you need to get laid."

"That won't solve anything," I say.

"Maybe not," she cheerfully concedes, "but it might make you feel better. And honestly, Rave—what in your life needs solving anyway? You've done it all, girl."

Although I'm sure she's just being glib, she has a point. I've made my choice. The path is clear. All I have to do is accept that. The realization knocks the wind right out of my self-righteous sails.

"You're right, Ab," I say, in a less stringent tone. "I have no problems worth speaking of. I guess I'm just sick of being sick. Everybody around here is a medical expert all of a sudden. Know what I mean?"

"Take your vitamins," she says, in a high-pitched nasal voice that is much like her mother's. "Blow your nose. Stay away from dairy products and open flames.

"Any of that sound familiar?"

"Too," I say, and then laugh. Abby's always been able to jolly me out of a bad mood. It will be good to live close to her again.

"Anyway, Rave," she says, "I have to run. Bruce is taking me to the movies tonight. Have a grand time tomorrow. And don't do anything that I wouldn't do."

"Like that's possible," I say.

An instant after I hang up, Jay and family come spilling into the house. Lisa squeals when she sees me, then charges across the kitchen and throws herself at my knees. I stagger upon impact, but do not fall down.

"Auntie Waven!" she exclaims. "I thought you was never gonna wake up!"

"Likewise, kiddo," I say. "Likewise."

"Lisa," Jay scolds, "you're tracking slush all over Gramma's clean floor. Come back here and let Mommy take your boots off." As his daughter dutifully complies, he moves in to pay his respects.

"So," he says, giving me a speculative once-over, "how are you feeling?"

"Picture a Mack truck," I tell him. "Then picture me plastered to its grill."

"You didn't get hit by a truck, Aunt Raven," Gail says, as sober-faced as a judge, "you had Peeking Flu. Daddy said so."

"Oh. Well." I try hard not to grin. "That just shows you how much I know. C'mere and give your dumb-bunny aunt a hug anyway."

Sally is mopping up Lisa's muddy tracks with a kitchen rag now. She's wearing a jogging suit instead of her usual soccer mom duds, and there's room to spare in the seat of her pants.

"Looks like you've lost weight, Sal," I say.

Hope and gratitude bloom pink like roses on her cheeks. "Do you really think so?"

"Absolutely."

She erases the last of her daughter's mess with a little flourish, then draws herself upright. She groans as she does so, but her smile is one of satisfaction and pride.

"I joined a health club last week," she says. "I've been to the aerobics class three times." She casts Jay a sly look, and then adds, "Your brother joined, too."

Jay stands suddenly straighter, with his gut sucked in. "They have a good weight room," he says. "I used to lift back in school, you know."

My affection for these silly people swells to ridiculous proportions. It'll be nice to spend more time with them.

"How's Mom today?" he asks.

"Downright spry," I say, as we stroll into the living room. "She came to the table without her walker tonight, and ate with a hand as steady as mine. That Mrs. Fowler has really worked miracles with her."

"Her husband's not such a bad sort, either," Sally says, "once you get used to that perpetually sour puss of his. The day after Christmas, he went up on your mom's rooftop and swept off all of the snow so it wouldn't leak into the attic when it melted.

"Did he ever mention how he lost those fingers?"

I seem to recall someone mentioning something about an accident. But the memory's still locked in Fever-Land, and going in after it would consume time and energy that I have no wish to spare. So I just shrug and shake my head. Sally shrugs back.

"Oh, well," she says, "I was just wondering. Are you doing anything for New Year's?"

"I'm having dinner with Kyle."

Jay's in the process of mediating a minor fracas between Lisa and Gail now, but that doesn't stop him from tossing his two cents into the pot. "You could do worse, you know."

"So I've been told," I say, and then return to my conversation with Sal. "What's up with you guys?"

"We're going over to my parent's house," she says. "It's sort of a raincheck on Christmas Eve."

Jay heaves a long-suffering, son-in-law's sigh. At the same time, his daughters ask for Gramma.

"I think she's in her room watching television," I tell them. "Shall I go and get her?"

"Nah," Jay says in their stead. "She's had more than enough exercise for one day. Let's just pile in on her."

The girls welcome the chance to visit Gramma—or perhaps her TV—with a shrill cheer, and then go scampering off. By the time we adults catch up with them, they're already snuggling up to Mom and Mattie, who are stretched out next to each other on Mom's bed.

"Make the bed sit up, Gwamma," Lisa begs. "Pwease?"

Mom obligingly fingers the controls to her special-order bed. As the head of it begins to tip forward, the girls howl like excited monkeys.

"Make the other end go up, too, Gwamma!"

"Lisa! Gail!" Jay barks. "Behave yourselves." His face is puckered. His spine is ramrod stiff. "Your grandmother's bed is not a plaything."

"It's OK, Jay," Mattie assures him. "We do this all the time."

Suddenly, his glare is all for her. "No, it's not OK," he says. "It's definitely not OK."

Then he turns on his heel and storms out of the room.

Sal and I exchange a look, like we're flipping a coin between us. She wins. I go after Jay. He's in the kitchen now, shoving himself into his parka. I cut him off before he can make good his escape.

"Hey, bro," I say, keeping my voice low. "What's going on?"

"What are you asking me for?" he growls in reply. His face is mottled, like he's coming down with a rash. There's a murky turbulence in his eyes. "They—" He flicks a wrist toward the back of the house, a furious gesture. "—they're the ones who're in bed together."

"Yeah, so?" I feel like a rookie firewalker here. One misstep and it's blister city. Yet there's no way to go with this except forward. "It's not like they were naked."

"Oh please, Raven," he says, in a bilious tone, "spare me the wide-eyed innocent act, OK? I've heard the rumors. Everybody has. I never wanted to believe them, but Christ!" He points again. "You saw them. Worse, the kids saw them. They don't need that kind of influence in their lives."

"I can't believe you just said that," I say. "You're talking about Mom and Mattie here. They're the best influences a kid could have."

"Yeah, right. Like teaching little girls that it's OK to go to bed with other girls is a good thing."

My patience starts to fray at both ends. "Careful, Jay. Your ugly little prejudices are starting to show."

Jay's face isn't mottled anymore—it's a full-on, livid red. "I am not prejudiced," he says, in a low, sulfurous tone. "Mattie could be orange with purple polka dots for all I care. The only thing I object to is the way she's carrying on with Mom."

"They're *friends*," I say, sharpening my tone yet again in the hope that it'll punch through that thick skull of his this time. "Best friends. Soulmates, maybe. Yes, Mattie's lavish with her affections. And yes, Mom takes that from her like she doesn't take it from anybody else. But the only one who's carrying on here is you. You're acting like a big, spoiled baby."

He sputters, strangling on a denial. I don't give him a chance to spit it out because I'm pissed off now, too, and on a roll. "This is why you're so keen to get Mom out of here, isn't it? The issue isn't the farm being too much work. The issue is Mattie."

"That's not true," he says. "You're just saying that so you won't have to face the facts. If you don't face them, you won't have to take responsibility for them. Right?"

I'm savagely tempted to salt and pepper that accusation with a few choice 'facts' that he doesn't know about yet and then cram the whole kielbasa down his self-righteous throat. But knowing Jay, he'd probably think that he had finally guilted me into doing my duty, and taste victory rather than crow. So I sandbag my ace of trumps for a later date, and play the spiteful queen of clubs instead.

"Grow up, Jay," I say. "Grow up and let Mommy have a life of her own."

His hand clenches into a fist, and for one mesmerizing moment, it looks like he's going to haul back and sock me. I stand my ground, ready to take the blow just so I can hold it against him, but it never comes. Instead, he shoulders me aside and goes storming out the door. When he returns, some twenty minutes later, he tersely rounds up his family and takes off. Mom and Mattie look to me for an explanation, but I just say, "Go figure," and retreat to my own room for the rest of the night. My feet are definitely blistered.

🍁   🍁   🍁

The next morning, Mom and Mattie corner me in the kitchen while I'm scarfing breakfast. Mom's expression is as reserved as ever, but Matt's eyes and mouth are hard around the edges.

"We want to know why Jay was in such a snit last night," she says. "It's not like him to go barreling out of here without so much as a see-you-later."

The spoonful of cottage cheese in my mouth goes suddenly sour. I choke it down like a starving man might choke down a grub, and then try to redirect. "Don't you think it would be better to ask him what was up?"

"We're asking you," she says.

Deep in my heart, in a place where I alone have ears, I curse Jay for landing me in this jam. He's the one with the problem, dammit! He's the one who should be squirming in the hot seat. Still, there's no point in arguing when Mattie has her jaw cocked like that. There's no point in beating around the bush, either. So I give them the truth, straight-up.

"He thinks you two are lovers."

I don't know what kind of reaction I was expecting from them—a flush maybe, or maybe a guilty little flinch. But I never, ever would've guessed that Mattie would tip her head back and laugh. It's a high, arcing laugh, too: the kind you hear at a bar toward the end of happy hour. And Mom suddenly looks like she has a mouthful of feathers.

"What say him you?" she asks.

"I told him to get over it," I say.

"Good Lord," Mattie says. "You think so, too."

"To be honest," I say, "I've tried not to think about it either way. If you are, you are. If you aren't, you aren't. Either way, it's absolutely none of my business. But just so you know," I add, since cats seem to be jumping out of bags all over the place, "Dex was wondering the same thing about a week ago."

"What?" Mattie's smile falls flat. An instant later, she turns that frown on Mom for loosing a rusty chuckle. "What's so damn funny, Rob?"

"S'OK my kids confuse, but not yours, hey?" Mom says.

Mattie's high forehead crinkles into a that's-different scowl. "Smarty-pants," she says, but it's friendly fire. A moment later, she adds, "You always see more than I do."

Mom shrugs, a no-big-deal. Mattie goes to give her a hug only to pull back at the last moment. "Oops," she says, looking both sheepish and sly. "I guess I'll have to stop doing stuff like that, huh? We don't want people getting the wrong idea."

"No," Mom tells her, in a voice that's clear as crystal. "Not change nothing. We be who we be."

And nuts to the rest of the world, right? That's my mother for you. And at this particular moment, I have to say that I admire her style.

"I talk Jay," she goes on. "You talk Dex. And Raven," she adds, turning to me, "you be who you be, too."

I don't know why she said that or what it's supposed to mean, but before I can ask her to explain, she and her walker go clunking out of the room at a vigorous clip. Matt takes off, too, and now the flinty set to her eyes and mouth is all for Dex. I have no doubt that he'll soon be cursing my name.

Oh, well.

I think about having a cigarette, but the pack in my jacket is empty and I'm not motivated enough to go out and buy more, so I go back to my room instead. I feel OK now—a little windblown maybe, but surprisingly relieved as well. I mean, I was OK with the idea of Mattie and Mom as lovers, but deep down inside, I'm just as glad that they're not. I don't know why exactly. I guess it's some deep-rooted heterosexual hang-up. Or maybe it has more to do with the idea of my own mother getting more action than me.

The thought of sex brings Kyle to mind; and just like that, I'm nervous about tonight. I go through my drawers and closets in search of the right thing to wear only to remember that nothing fits anymore. Oh, well. It's about time I went out and bought some new stuff anyway. I wonder how I'll look in flannel.

As I'm putting my closet back in order, the phone rings. I pick up it immediately, hoping it's Abby wanting to talk. "Hello?"

"I can't believe you told Mom about our conversation," Jay grumbles, in lieu of a greeting.

"What can I say?" I reply, taken too much by surprise to pick and choose my words. "She asked."

"You could've warned me," he says.

"Yes, I suppose I could have," I say. "It just didn't occur to me. Besides," I add, because I simply can't resist, "I got the impression that we weren't speaking."

He grunts like a man who's just been kicked in the butt. "Yeah, well. You said some pretty mean things. I forgive you, though."

On some other cold and windy day, I might have come back with something like: *la-dee-fucking-dah*. But not today. Jay has reached beyond the ramparts of his pride to heal the breach between us. For my sake as well as his, I must do the same. "Thank you, brother," I say. "I forgive you, too."

"Good."

He starts to say something more, but a voice in the background interrupts him. "Oh, OK," I hear him say, and then he's back on the line with me. "I have to go now, Rave. Sal wants to get going. See you next year, OK?"

"OK. Have a good time at the Harper house tonight."

I hear a long-suffering groan, then a click, then a dial tone. I cling to my receiver for a moment, loath to let go. Suddenly, I'm restless and bored. I want something. Don't ask me what, though, because I don't know.

At a loss for a better distraction, I drag my camera out and use up the roll of film that I started back at Christmas. I get a shot of the faint depression that my butt made in the bedspread; one of the snow-scape beyond my window; and then an artsy close-up of the accumulated junk on my nightstand. Clara Dupree's tiny scroll is a part of that still-life. Almost in spite of myself, I pick it up and unfurl it. Her forgiveness is still there for all to see. For some reason, that doesn't seem as arrogant of her as it did before. I think of Jay. I think of me. I think of who we are and what we need. Clara, I decide, cannot be that different. So I jot five words down on the yellow Post-It pad that I keep by the phone, then peel the page off and tuck it into an empty film canister. Then I cap the container and stuff it into one of the manila mailers that I keep in my camera case. The Duprees' address trips me up—for one molar-grinding moment, I think I'll have to call Davenport for it. But then I recall those legal papers with which I was served and get it from there.

Although it's not much to look at, the finished package fills me with a sense of satisfaction and closure. As I pad off to pop it in the mail, I remember the message within over and over again.

Clara, I forgive you, too.

CHAPTER 14

Kyle's house is perched like a crown on the top a heavily wooded hill. He has no neighbors that I can see. I drive Mom's car up the winding driveway, then park behind a familiar-looking pick-up truck. As I start up the rock-salted walkway, I suffer a pang of disorientation. I've been told that I've been here before now. I've been told that I spent thirty-three hours on the premises. I don't remember any of it: not the house, which looks like a Lincoln Log chalet with its A-shaped roof and extravagant, full-length windows; or the sloping front yard, with its cross-hatchery of snowmobile tracks; or the tree-buffered silence. I have to admit, I'm impressed. I was expecting something smaller and much less modern, something with a junked car or two up on blocks in the back. I guess I must've been thinking of the place he lived in as a kid. Funny how some images stick with you. I wonder if he associates me with angels, the lottery, or gangrene.

I'm standing at the front door now. The porchlight seems exceedingly bright. An instant after I ring the bell, the door swings open and there Kyle is, smiling at me like I'm the best thing he's ever seen.

"Glad you could make it," he says, as he ushers me inside.

"Me, too," I say, and then hand him the bottle of red wine that I picked up at a package store along the way. "My contribution to the feast."

"Excellent."

He sets the bottle on the floor, and then helps me off with my jacket. As he's hanging it up on the coat-rack by the door, I take a surreptitious look around. The living room is in front of me. It's a spacious area with a large stone fireplace and hardwood floors, but aside from a beat-up old couch, a big-screen TV, and some dusty stereo equipment, there is nothing in it. The dining area to my right and the adjoining kitchen are equally Spartan in their decor. I don't remember any of it.

"Nice sweater," Kyle says.

"Thanks," I say, just to be polite, because it's that ugly pink thing from Sal and Jay. "Are you sure I've been here before?"

His smile goes lopsided with amusement. "I'm positive. C'mon, I'll show you around. Maybe you'll see something that'll jiggle your memory."

Like my mind is a wonky toilet handle.

Off we go, up the staircase to the second floor. One room here contains a weight bench and various bar-bells. The other is empty except for a twin bed, an ironing board, and a laundry basket full of wrinkled shirts.

"You do your own ironing?" I say, tickled by the notion of such a big, strong guy riding an iron. "Really?"

"No one's beating down my door to do it for me," he says. "Besides, it relaxes me."

"You're a strange man," I tell him.

"It only seems that way," he says.

He leads me out of that room, and up another flight of stairs. There's only one room here, and it's fabulous—a bedroom suite with a gigantic fireplace and cathedral ceilings. The wall at the top of the landing is all window.

"Wow," I say, dazzled by the view. "You can see all of H-C from here. Look, there's Main Street. The lights look like a double strand of fuzzy pearls."

He comes up behind me and slips his arms around my waist. His breath teases the tiny hairs on my nape. The pit of my stomach starts to flutter.

"I'm glad you like it here," he says. "It's my favorite place in the whole house." Then he turns me toward the huge, four-poster bed. The fluttering in my stomach spreads to my knees. I'm not ready for this. It's much too soon. But all he says is, "Remember yet? That's where you spent the better part of two days."

I try to envision myself beneath that comforter, tossing and turning; febrile; *sick*. But the images that take shape in my mind are flat-out erotic. Peeking flu, indeed. I'm so confused. I don't know what I want anymore.

"Well, that's it for the tour," Kyle says then. "And as luck would have it, dinner's just about ready. I thought we'd eat in the living room, in front of the fireplace. If you're feeling up to it, that is."

"Don't worry about me," I say, as we head downstairs. "I'm up for almost anything."

I think.

So he spreads an old-fashioned picnic blanket on the floor and sets it with all the accouterments necessary for civilized eating: forks, knives, spoons, wine glasses, napkins, candlesticks, a dish of butter, and a bottle of catsup. I offer to help, but he sits me down on the moth-eaten couch with a command to save my strength and then goes hustling off to the kitchen. In his absence, I have a more leisurely look at my surrounds. It wouldn't take much to spruce the place up: some photography on the walls, an area rug for color, houseplants for depth and texture. This mangy couch would have to be banished to the spare room or better yet, destroyed, but the coffee table could probably stay.

"Dinner is served," Kyle announces, and rounds the corner with two plates. The fare is what you might expect from a long-term bachelor: roast beef and baked potatoes with canned peas on the side. Everything is slightly overdone, but there's plenty of it. "I wanted to make you something fancy," he says, as he pours the wine, "but cooking isn't exactly a strong point of mine, so I went with what I know instead."

"It looks great," I assure him. "If I'd been the one in the kitchen, we'd be having rubberized eggs and burnt toast."

We discuss our lack of culinary skills for a while, and then move on to other subjects. He asks how my mother is doing. I tell him what great progress she is making with Mrs. Fowler's help. He says physical therapy is the best idea to come along since sliced bread. I ask him about the guys he used to hang with in the olden days.

"The only one I've seen since the last class reunion is Mark Richards," he says, "and that's only because he happened to be working for the guy who black-topped my driveway." He takes a bite of roast beef and chews reflectively, then adds, "I think about looking some of the others guys up every once in a while, but I never get around to doing it. The job just eats up too much of my time."

"What's the weirdest case you ever worked on?" I ask.

"That would be the Stafford Boa Incident." Relieved to hear that it wasn't the Hobson's Corner Hold-Up, I encourage him to elaborate. "It started out as a domestic disturbance call: somebody had phoned in to complain about the screaming and shouting that was coming from their neighbor's place. An instant after I pulled up in front of the house in question, a wild-eyed midget came running out, demanding that I arrest his wife for attempted murder. According to him, the love of his life had tried to feed him to her boa constrictor while he was passed out on the living room floor. To hear her tell it—and she was full-sized, by the way—the snake had gotten loose and gone hunting for supper of its own accord."

"So what'd you do?"

He shrugs. "I told the guy that he might want to think about seeing a lawyer if he was that afraid of his wife. Then I called Fish and Game in to come and get the snake. It was a big sucker, too, at least fifteen feet long. Swallowing that guy would have been as easy for it as swallowing oysters is for us. Lucky for him he woke up when he did."

A chill skates up the length of my spine. I may never eat oysters again. "Stuff like that makes you wonder about people, doesn't it?"

"Sometimes," he says. "Mostly, though, it just pisses me off. If the average Joe spent as much time and brain-power trying to help his neighbor as he does trying to screw him, we'd have colonies on the moon by now.

"But enough about my fellow man already," he says, and wrests his mouth into a gentler bend. "Tonight, there's no one in the world except you and me. Are you ready for dessert?"

"What did you have in mind?" I ask. Maybe it's the glass of wine that came with dinner, but suddenly, *all* of my appetites are back in good form.

"Chocolate cream pie," he says, like there's nothing better in the cupboard. "I ordered it special at the bakery for you."

Oh, well. At least it's chocolate. "Sounds great. Can I help with anything?"

"Not a chance," he tells me, as he gathers up our dirty dishes. "You stay right here and enjoy the fire. Would you like more wine?"

"Half a glass maybe. I have to drive tonight."

His mouth twinges at one corner. It could be amusement. It could be relief. I try not to think about it either way. Meanwhile, he pours me another dollop of wine and then bustles off to the kitchen. When he returns a few minutes later, he has a heaping dish of pie in each hand.

"Here we go," he says, as he strides toward me. "I hope you—Whoa!"

His foot catches on the edge of the blanket. He flails to regain his balance. As he does so, both pieces of pie go flying. One splashes down smack-dab between my breasts. The other splatters all over on my face. For one dumbstruck moment thereafter, all Kyle and I can do is gape at each other. Then he lurches to his knees in front of me and starts wiping whipped cream away from my eyes. His expression is so crestfallen, it's comical.

"Oh my God, Raven," he says, "I'm so sorry. I've ruined your sweater."

I glance down at my chest. It looks like I've been shat upon by a giant pie-bird. I'm not the least bit upset, though. In fact, I'm suddenly giddy. I scoop up a handful of the sweet-smelling mess, then reach out and mash it in his face. As he gasps his surprise, I hook him by the collar and pull him close for a whipped cream kiss.

"But—" He draws back an inch to look me in the eyes. "Your sweater—"

"I never liked it anyway."

The tension flows out of his face and into his arms. *At last*, I think, and then dive into my dessert.

Chocolate has never tasted so good.

🍁　　　🍁　　　🍁

I'm in the shower, cleaning up after round one, when I hear the telephone in the bedroom ring. The next thing I know, Kyle's knocking at the bathroom door.

"Come on in," I shout.

He does so. The shower stall's Plexiglas walls are all steamed up, so all I can see is a fair-haired blur. I wonder what I look like to him.

"There's been a big accident at Devil's Bend," he says. "Three cars, maybe four. One of the vehicles is on fire."

I turn the water off, then poke my head out of the stall for a clear look at him. He's in the process of stuffing his shirttails into a pair of starched gray pants. His blue eyes are snapping like backyard bug zappers on a hot summer night.

"That's terrible," I say. "Was anyone hurt?"

"I don't know," he says. "But it looks like I'm going to find out. They want me on the scene."

"Oh, shit."

"I'm sorry, Raven," he says. Like it's his fault. "I'll be back as soon as I can, but this could take hours." He combs his fingers through my water-saturated hair, then rubs my chin with his wet knuckles. "Will you stick around anyway?"

His gaze is hopeful; ferocious; intense. I can't refuse it.

"Absolutely," I say, and then push him toward the door. "My keys are in my jacket. Leave them in the car after you move it. I'll see you when you get back."

He shoots me a grateful look, then disappears. A moment later, I hear a door bang shut. I towel off in the ensuing silence, then raid the bedroom closet for a button-down shirt just like the freshly fucked girls in the movies do.

OK, so now what?

I go downstairs, meaning to zone out by the fire for a while. But the log's nothing but cinders now and the floor's flecked with pie and what-not, so I wind up cleaning up instead. As I do so, I think about Mr. Kyle Hobson. I believe I could love him. I believe I could live here in this house with him and be his wife and bear his children, too. We'd have two, a girl and a boy. I'd bring them to Mom's house every day, and they'd play in the yard with their doting older cousins while I worked. I'd look after the farm, and take care of Angelhaven, and keep an eye on Mom and Mattie. I'd have a studio, too, at least part-time. Photography By Raven Middlefield-Hobson, I'd call it, or maybe Angelhaven, Inc..

I'm standing in front of that window at the top of the landing now. The glass is radiating cold. I huddle deeper into my borrowed shirt, then dare another peek at the future. I have a husband and kids, a house in the hills, a half-page advertisement in the Yellow Pages. I have everything there is to be had in this neck of the woods, and yet—

There it is again, that old, familiar stumbling-block. It's just a reflex, I tell myself, a bad habit that's begging to be broken once and for all. So I force myself to gaze into that crystal ball again. I see my hero of a husband, a man who comes home to me every night, although sometimes not until very late. He gives our children lots of good advice. He gives me his paycheck, and his undying love. We have everything we had ever hoped for when we were in high school, and yet—

I push forward, determined to see this vision through to its end. I push so hard, the stumbling-block bursts like a rotten dam, and the truth comes surging forth.

—it isn't enough. It will never be enough. For I am truly my mother's daughter; and like her, I hear voices. I've tried to ignore them, to deny and disavow them, but it's no use. They call to me like gulls. They tug at me like surf. They're louder than the roar of responsibilities, and more insistent than guilt. My children would grow up like I did, resentful and confused—hurt because their father didn't have enough time for them, and angry because their mother was always off day-dreaming about the things that she could neither quite have nor give up. I will not impose such a life on my would-be nearest and dearest, not for the noblest of intentions, not even to keep my word. Instead, I'll practice a higher form of love. And if, in some distant future, those voices lead me to a sorry end, then at least I'll be the only one who has to pay.

Tomorrow or the next day, I'll call Marcos—just to let him know that I'm still on my way. Jay won't understand, but I think Mom will. I'll urge her to hire the Fowlers on as caretakers. I'm sure they'll want to stay.

I shuck off Kyle's shirt and stand naked before the town where I was born. It glimmers in the clear dark night like a passing ship. I hope Kyle thinks of me in the months to come. I hope he remembers me fondly, as the one who got away.

About the Author

Kathleen H. Nelson lives in the San Francisco Bay Area with her husband and their dog. She has had three novels published to date: *Daughter Of Dragons*, *The Human Thing*, and *The Dragon Reborn*. Her short stories have appeared in a number of small-press magazines, including *The Baybury Review*, *Byline*, and *Space & Time*. Her writing has won awards in the 1995 Florida State Writing Competition and at the 1997 Jack London Writer's Conference. She is an avid scuba diver and has explored many of the sites mentioned in *Fish Stories*. She is currently working on a new science fiction novel and a short story collection.

0-595-23145-4

Made in the USA
Middletown, DE
25 October 2025